"All who wander are kin, no matter the star beneath their feet."

— The Celestial Proverbs

LUNIBELLE

LUNIBELLE

H.J. Damaris

To my dear wife

Prologue

At the heart of the night, when the moon pours down a gentle, liquid silver and the stars blink with curious, knowing eyes... something truly extraordinary happens.

You must lie quietly beneath the dining table—just as brave Jack does—perhaps with your faithful, fuzzy companion, Willy the dog, both of you staring with unwavering patience at the sturdy old refrigerator. Wait one night, two nights, maybe even three (for magic is never in a hurry) ... and then, a creature of pure wonder might just wriggle out. She is a tiny alien, barely two inches high, with a body like a whisper of moonlight—translucent, shimmering silver, possessing two dark, deep-set eyes and a mouth that is always curved into a delighted smile.

Her name is Lunibelle. Lunibelle will become terribly fond of you. She will beg you to take her to the sprawling blue sea (her first breathtaking glimpse of Earth!), and on your birthday, she will present a surprise gift, because by then, you are her very best friend.

Soon, you will gather more whimsical companions: Parcel the cat and her four fuzzy kittens, and a fast-talking, brilliant-gold canary named Canary.

Lunibelle, wishing dearly to celebrate Christmas, will invent a real one right in the middle of April!

She'll whisk you billions of years back in time to rescue a tiny, shimmering fish from a fiery volcano. And if mathematics makes your brain spin, she'll bring you to a wonderful world where numbers simply do not exist.

Together, you will dive into the heart of a movie, helping children find two identical, perfect

snowflakes. You'll visit Grandma and accidentally, but quite delightfully, stumble into a world entirely woven of enormous, bouncing magical bubbles! (The best adventures are always the accidents.)

You and Lunibelle will embark on marvelous journeys, forging the truest sort of friendship—one

braver than any knight, stickier than marshmallows, and stronger than the mightiest dragon.

This book? Why, it is only the very first, delicate flake of snow. The real, beautiful blizzard of adventure is just beginning.

Contents

Chapter I
The Mystery of the Missing Chocolate Buttons

Part I: The Math Problems That Become Spaghetti

Jack, freshly unburdened from school, burst through the front door—Willy, his loyal German Shepherd, trotted behind with the leash clamped in his mouth.

Jack dropped his backpack with a THUD that echoed like the last school bell of the day. "Let's ride!" he shouted, grinning.

Today Jack had a new idea—and he loved new ideas, especially the risky kind. He grabbed his skateboard, clipped Willy's leash to his wrist, and off they went: Jack pushing and gliding, Willy bounding ahead.

At the corner, they halted. "Stay!" Jack commanded. Willy, as noble as a soldier, plopped into a perfect sit.

"Now, remember," Jack said solemnly, "at intersections we stop. We watch the lights. And never, ever cross on red. Only green—green like grass. Then we go!"

The light blinked green, and off they zipped—past the playground with its squealing swings and the lake that winked as if a giant eye in the sun. Jack waved to the ducks bobbing near the reeds and to the old man who fed them every afternoon. Willy barked once—politely, Jack hoped.

They spun around the park, wheels buzzing on smooth ground. The breeze tugged at Jack's sleeves and filled his chest with something fizzy and bright.

Back at the red light, Willy sat without being told. "Good boy!" Jack cheered.

Once across the street, Jack planted both feet firmly on the skateboard, and Willy dashed ahead like a locomotive, pulling him so fast that Jack screamed with delight.

Back home, Jack unhooked the leash. "Willy, we flew like rockets!" he said, brushing leaves from his hair. "Go drink some water."

Willy trotted to his bowl, tail wagging.

Jack made a beeline for the refrigerator. Fluttering there was the day's challenge: a white sticky note with one of Dad's math puzzles—and, beneath it, Mom's trademark doodle: a pink heart with eyelashes and a goofy smile.

Jack plucked the note and dropped into his seat at the dining table. He pulled a clean sheet of paper from his backpack and stared down the puzzle.

"Okay... focus," he whispered, imitating his father's voice.

First try: one. Second try: two. Third try: two again.

"That's two!" Jack announced triumphantly. He scribbled the answer as if signing his name, then pressed a kiss to the heart on the note.

"Willy, guess what?" Jack called.

Willy looked up mid-sip, water dripping from his chin.

"Dad put ninety chocolate buttons in a jar—three for each of the thirty days this month! If I solve the puzzle correctly, I earn three buttons!"

"It's nice!" Willy blinked.

Jack grinned. "You know, Dad says math is everywhere—from the stars in the sky to the grass underfoot. Even you, Willy, are made of math!"

"Really?" Willy angled his head.

"Think about it!" Jack said, warming to the idea. "How many hairs are on your body? Hundreds of thousands? Millions? If you barked once for every hair, you'd be barking for centuries!"

Willy gave a single bark. Jack took that as agreement.

Jack reached for the chocolate jar and shook it—CLINK-CLINK-CLATTER! For a moment, he frowned. Was it lighter than yesterday? Nah. Impossible. He shrugged and twisted the lid.

He plucked out three chocolate buttons and lined them up on the table like treasure.

"Even to eat chocolate," Jack muttered, "I have to solve a math problem first."

He popped one into his mouth. Sweet. Smooth. Perfect.

Then he leaned back in his chair and sighed. "But math still hates me," Jack murmured. He was sure math hated him more than he could ever hate it.

Willy padded over and laid his head in Jack's lap.

Jack scratched between his ears. "Every time there's a test, I mess something up. My brain goes scrambled—like someone stirring my thoughts with a big wooden spoon."

He looked up at the ceiling. "I try. I really do. That's why Dad gives me puzzles—so I can get better. But it always feels like math is a giant gate between me... and the good stuff. Like chocolate. Or fun."

He glanced at the jar—still mostly full.

Jack wrinkled his nose. "What if there were a place with no math at all? No numbers. No quizzes. No problems—except the fun kind, like where to find the nearest chocolate-button bush."

He stood and patted Willy. "One day we'll find that world—a place with no math. Just chocolate. And maybe a few dancing goats."

Willy gave him a puzzled look.

"Okay, fine," Jack laughed, "maybe not goats. But definitely chocolate."

He scooped up the remaining two buttons and looked out the window.

The sky was soft and purple now, the clouds the color of cinnamon ice cream.

"I must find that land!" Jack said dramatically, holding up the last chocolate button as a magic token. "Then I could gobble all the chocolate I wanted—no equations, no puzzles, just... chomp-chomp-chomp!"

He tossed the last button into the air and caught it in his mouth. (Jack was the best on the basketball team at catching chocolate buttons in his mouth—even the coach said so.)

Part II: Who Eats the Chocolate Buttons?

One afternoon near the end of the month, Jack tumbled home after playing with Willy in the woods. His sneakers were caked with mud, his hair tousled by the wind, and his clothes speckled with fallen leaves.

He peeled a blue sticky note from the refrigerator—today's math challenge—and beneath it was his mother's neat reminder in slender handwriting: *Sweetheart, remember to take the steak out of the freezer.*

Jack sat down. First try: three. Second try: one. Third try: two. He scratched his head. "Ugh. Brain, don't fail me now."

Then a spark. "Willy! Come here, boy!"

Willy hopped off the couch and trotted over.

Jack held up the note like a detective presenting evidence. "Here's the deal. I'll read the problem aloud. You think carefully—no rushing. Then bark the answer: one bark for one, two barks for two, three barks for three. Got it?"

Willy wagged his tail, ears pricked, eyes bright.

Jack cleared his throat and read the problem grandly, as if proclaiming a royal decree before an imagined courtroom.

When he finished, he leaned close and whispered, "Now... what's the answer?"

Willy barked—once. Pause. Twice.

"Two it is!" Jack grinned. "You're brilliant, boy!"

From the treat jar he pulled two green Dental Chews, which Willy accepted with delighted chomps.

Then Jack spun toward the chocolate jar.

He tipped it upside down, spilling the buttons onto a plate. "One, two, three, four..." he counted—all the way to nine.

Jack frowned. "That's it?"

He leaned in, squinting. "Three red, two blue, two orange, two green..." He tapped the plate. "This is worse than math class—the buttons are lying to me! There should be fifteen left."

He turned to Willy. "Right?"

Willy only blinked.

"That's six missing!" Jack declared, pointing at the plate as though it were a crime scene.

He flopped into the chair with a theatrical sigh. "Another mystery?"

The jar's lid sat on—but not quite tight. Had it always been that way?

Dad's voice echoed: *Every puzzle is a math problem.*

Mom's words: *Fashion is a mystery too—fashion shows reveal the hidden riddles!*

Jack groaned. "Math is driving me bananas."

He poured the buttons back into the jar and shook it. They clinked as though tiny marbles muttering riddles.

That night at dinner, Dad smiled. "Jack, you solved many problems this month. Well done!"

"Keep it up!" Mom added, passing the salad.

Jack hesitated. "But... the chocolate buttons. There should be fifteen left, but only nine."

Dad raised an eyebrow. "Are you sure you didn't miss a row?"

"I lined them up in threes. I triple-checked," Jack said.

Mom leaned forward, eyes twinkling. "Maybe a chocolate fairy stole them."

Jack half-grinned, but his shoulders slumped. "I don't know. Maybe."

That night he lay in bed, moonlight scattering across the floor, drawing countless question marks.

Mom and Dad trusted him—he knew that. They trusted he wouldn't sneak extra chocolate buttons. "But do I trust myself?" he whispered into the dark.

He wriggled under the covers and began a whispered trial:

"Are you Jack?"

"Yes, I am Jack."

"Do you believe in yourself?"

"I believe."

"You didn't sneak any chocolate buttons, did you?"

"Not a single one!"

He rolled over and hugged the pillow tightly. "Yeah, Jack would never do that," he murmured.

Mostly comforted, he closed his eyes—but a minute later they popped open again. The bedside clock blinked 9:30.

Willy, curled at the foot of the bed, snored softly.

Jack turned toward him.

Willy wasn't just any dog; he was a proper, noble beast, like something straight out of a knight's tale. He was a big, brown German Shepherd, with a coat the color of a toasted marshmallow. He was brave, of course, but also super smart and loyal. When the sun was high in the sky and everyone was out on their quests, Willy would stand guard as if a stone statue. Anyone who even thought about sneaking a peek inside was met with his fierce, "Not today, villain!" bark. But at night, when all were snuggled up in their beds, Willy would patrol the house, keeping every shadow monster and goblin far, far away.

Jack sighed. "First math... now a chocolate-button mystery. My brain feels like spaghetti."

His thoughts began to slosh together.

Jack squinted sleepily. If only Willy was a cat, he thought—a big brown cat with rabbit-long ears and a crocodile's tail, snoozing beside the jar with one paw on the lid and another pinning down a naughty mouse...

And with that picture wobbling in his mind, Jack drifted into slumber.

Part III: Hiding under the Table at Midnight

The next afternoon, Jack and Willy wandered through the woods and then rushed home.

Pinned to the refrigerator door was a yellow sticky note—today's math puzzle. At the top, Dad had scribbled in blue ink: *New month, 30 days = 90 chocolate buttons.* Then came a math puzzle. At the bottom, Mom had drawn a little sketch—a big head, a small body, curly hair, stick arms—holding a balloon with the words *Go Jack!* inside.

Jack sat down and began solving. Every time the answer came out the same: one!

He shot out of his chair and whooped, "I WON! I WON!"

He scooped up Willy in a bear hug and spun in a circle. "Today's a holiday for you, buddy—no math quiz!"

Willy yawned, as if he had planned to take the day off anyway.

Jack reached for the chocolate jar. He was about to pluck three precious ones—then froze mid-reach.

"No," he said, wagging a finger. "I must count first!"

He grabbed a giant salad bowl from the cupboard, tipped the jar upside down, and out tumbled a clatter of buttons. They rolled and bounced, singing a song of PLINK-PLINK-PLONK.

Too jumbled!

"How am I supposed to count if you're all crowded together?" Jack frowned.

His eyes scanned the kitchen. "Plates!" he cried. "Yes, yes!"

He lined up nine small plates in a perfect row and began sorting—ten buttons per plate.

But when he reached the last plate—it held only eight.

He counted again. Slowly. Carefully. Still only eight!

"Unless mice had graduated from the Lid-Twisting Academy, this was no mouse job," Jack muttered.

He dumped the buttons back into the jar, his mind spinning faster than a merry-go-round.

"At this rate, there might be no buttons left before the end of the month," he whispered, horrified.

He clenched his fists. "I must solve this. Before it's too late. Before... before the buttons are ALL GONE!"

That evening, Jack told his parents "Good night!" in his brightest, nothing-suspicious-here voice.

Then he tiptoed back into his room and waited.

Tick-tock. Tick-tock. The wall clock ticked the time away.

He listened. Then—the soft thud of Mom and Dad's door closing.

DONG... DONG... DONG...

From the church down the street, the bell tolled ten slow chimes.

Jack crept out of bed like a ninja. He opened his door slowly—very slowly—so it wouldn't squeak.

The hallway was silver with moonlight. He padded down the stairs, his heart thudding like a drum in his chest.

The kitchen was bathed in sleepy, pale blue light. The chairs stood like giraffes in a dream. The curtains danced like footless ghosts.

There it was—the jar of chocolate buttons, sitting quietly on the counter next to the coffee machine, gleaming with mysterious light.

Jack crossed the dining room, tiptoeing as a shadow in socks, and he ducked under the table.

He nestled between two chairs, stretched out on his stomach, and propped his chin on his hands.

Now he would wait.

And wait...

The refrigerator hummed like a sleepy polar bear.

Jack's nose began to prickle, a furious, building itch that demanded immediate release. He clenched his jaw and pinched the bridge of his nose, trying to choke the sneeze back.

He curled tighter under the table.

What if he didn't see it? What if he blinked? What if it was a ghost—a ghost that loved chocolate?

His thoughts raced. "Stop it, brain," Jack whispered.

Then—nudge!

Jack jumped, stifling a yelp.

It was Willy, his loyal, silent-footed friend.

Willy pressed his nose against Jack's arm and gave a soft snuffle.

Jack pressed a finger to his lips. "Shhh," he breathed.

Willy lay down beside him, curling into a warm, furry beanbag.

Jack rested a hand gently on his back. "Willy," he whispered, "we're about to solve the Mystery of the Vanishing Chocolate Buttons!"

Willy didn't bark, but his ears twitched like antennas.

"I know it's late," Jack murmured, "but this is important. If I don't figure this out, we'll wake up one day and find zero buttons. And then what? No math rewards. No chocolate. Just... broccoli."

Willy let out a soft, scandalized puff.

Jack giggled.

The air seemed dusted with sleeping powder, and the whole house sank into slumber.

Jack's eyelids drooped, and he blinked hard.

"Stay awake," he whispered. "You have to—"

Then, just before his thoughts slid into dreams, a wild idea tiptoed through his mind:

What if the jar wasn't a jar at all... but a tiny portal? A secret door to somewhere else? A candy world where chocolate buttons rolled away like marbles on holiday?

He smiled sleepily. "That'd be weird."

Jack hugged Willy closer. If the jar really was a portal, maybe tonight the thief would tumble out of it—a chocolate thief in striped pajamas.

His head dropped gently onto Willy's back.

Part IV: The Silver Dancer under the Moonlight

Time slid past like a sleepy snail until—nudge! Jack opened his eyes.

Willy's ears twitched. His big, wet nose sifted the air for secrets. His tail—usually a happy windshield wiper—held perfectly still. He was all string and tension, a rubber band about to spring.

Jack held his breath. His heart did a drumroll—BA-BUM, BA-BUM, BA-BOOM.

Then he saw her.

A visitor. A very small, very impossible visitor.

Out of the freezer door—without it even opening—peeked the tiniest, most delicate creature Jack had ever seen. First came her head, with eyes like dark, polished marble. She looked left, then right.

WHOOSH—two slender arms. Her body shimmered: see-through, but not like glass—more like mist braided with starlight. Two wispy legs slipped out, and with a delighted wiggle, she was free.

The freezer door wobbled like jelly, then smoothed back into place as if nothing had happened.

Jack's mouth fell open. Was this real?

She was a dancer the size of a thumb. When she moved, the

counter caught glitter-footprints that faded like melting frost. She floated like mist, walked like flowing water, and stood—somehow—like a flower.

TIP-TIP-TIP, she crossed the counter.

Jack's brain shouted: *She's real!*

He liked her immediately.

The Little One stopped at the chocolate-button jar, hands on hips, as though a pirate inspecting treasure.

She pressed her palms to the glass—and her hands slipped straight through, as if the jar had decided to stop being a jar and start being a puddle.

Jack almost squeaked. *What?!*

She grabbed a red chocolate button, wobbled beneath its weight, legs trembling. For a second she teetered... then steadied herself and marched toward the refrigerator with her prize.

She stepped into the door without opening it; ripples shivered across the door's surface and stilled.

Under Jack's hand, Willy's muscles bunched. A low growl rumbled in his chest.

"Shhh," Jack breathed, steadying him. "Let's see if she comes back."

A few moments later, the freezer door rippled again, and out she popped, tiptoeing back to the jar. This time, she picked a yellow one. But—OH NO!—she bumped into a spoon left on the counter.

CLATTER!

A yellow button rolled off the counter.

Jack gasped. His hand slipped from Willy's collar.

Willy shot forward like an arrow and unleashed his loudest "WOOF-WOOF!"

The Little One squeaked—"Ah!"—and sprang up the side of the refrigerator, then vanished through the freezer in a silver POOF, as if the refrigerator itself had gulped her down.

"Jack? Are you down there?" Mom's voice floated from upstairs.

Jack's heart flipped. "I just wanted a glass of water!" he called, trying to sound normal. He gulped, hoping the sound would drown out the pounding of his heart.

"Next time, keep water in your room before bed," Mom mumbled.

"Got it, Mom!"

Willy sat statue-still by the refrigerator, eyes locked on the refrigerator as if it might sprout wings.

Jack picked up the yellow button from the floor. He stared at the door, wonder widening his eyes.

"You must never, ever chase her," he whispered to Willy. "Promise me."

Jack gently tapped twice on the door.

"Sorry," he whispered, holding out the button. "I'm Jack. I just wanted to give this back to you."

Silence.

He knocked again, softer.

"I want to help you," he said. "If you need anything... just tell me, okay?"

Still nothing.

"I'm your friend. Willy is too."

He opened the freezer just a crack, placed the yellow button inside, and closed it quietly.

The next evening, Jack waited a very long time in the kitchen—but the Little One never appeared.

Still, Jack carefully placed two chocolate buttons into the freezer.

From that day on, Jack put out two buttons every night.

He missed seeing her terribly.

Yet the small comfort was—every morning, the chocolate buttons were gone.

"She's still there, Willy!" Jack said, full of hope. "She took the buttons! That proves it!"

Willy tipped his head. "She's in there... but why won't she come out?"

"I don't know," Jack sighed deeply. "Maybe we scared her."

Part V: The Girl Who Whispers the Secret of the Cosmos

For several nights, the Little One didn't show up.

Not seeing her left Jack limp. At school he doodled snowflakes in his math book; at dinner he stirred his soup in circles, waiting for nothing to appear.

Mom noticed.

"What's the matter, honey?" she asked one morning, packing his lunch.

"Nothing," Jack muttered.

"You've been quiet. Did something happen at school? Did you

finish your painting for the exhibition?"

"I did, Mom. Don't worry—everything's fine."

She dusted an unseen crumb from his shirt. "You can tell us anything."

"I know." He hesitated, then blurted, "Oh! When you open the refrigerator... could you maybe knock twice first?"

Mom blinked. "Knock on the refrigerator?"

"Sorry. I mean... just open it gently."

One warm evening, Jack's parents went out to a movie—one of their small date nights. Jack and Willy stayed on guard.

Jack sat at the dining table, resting his chin in his hand. Willy lay nearby, eyes wide, watchful.

"Willy, do you want to watch TV?" Jack asked. "There's a new episode of that forest adventure show!"

Willy thumped his tail once—yes!

"Okay, but one rule," Jack said, wagging a finger. "If I don't call you, you mustn't come into the dining room. Promise?"

Willy blinked solemnly.

Jack turned on the TV, flipped to the right channel, and watched as Willy curled up on the couch.

"Enjoy," Jack whispered, smiling.

He returned to the table and grabbed a book at random—his old *Children's Encyclopedia.*

He glanced at the refrigerator. At the chocolate-button jar. Then back at the refrigerator.

The kitchen felt extra still. The refrigerator hummed softly. The shadows leaned a little longer.

Jack casually opened the book and turned to a page he had read many times: the Big Bang.

He traced the words with his finger.

The Big Bang was the huge cosmic BOOM that started our entire universe! Before it, there was nothing—no stars, no space, not even time! Then, suddenly... KA-POW! It exploded and stretched faster than light, creating space, time, the stars and the Earth and everything we know!

"Before the Big Bang—no stars, no planets, not even chocolate—BOOM! Everything began," he murmured.

"How can nothing suddenly poof into something?" He frowned.

But then he grinned faintly. "Well... once there wasn't a Jack. And now—there is."

Still, the thought itched.

"Zero plus zero should always equal zero," he said to himself. "So how does it suddenly become one?"

So many mysteries in the world. And yet, only one that truly mattered right now.

The refrigerator mystery, Jack thought fiercely, *is the most important of all!*

He looked up—and froze.

Perched atop the refrigerator, legs dangling over the door, sat the Little One.

His heart somersaulted. He didn't move. Didn't blink. Even a breath might scare her back to the unknown.

Her voice chimed. "Sorry—what are you reading?"

Jack's thoughts scattered like startled birds.

"What are you reading?" she repeated.

He held up the book. "*Children's Encyclopedia.*"

"The Big Bang?"

"Yes."

She brightened. "My parents saw the Big Bang," she said softly, as if confessing she had peeked at the answers on the first page of the universe's math book. "They watched stars take shape."

Jack opened his mouth to ask how—but her look silenced him, as if some answers weren't meant for Earth ears.

Jack stared.

"They saw a planet," she went on, "with creatures made of water and earth and story. So, they sent me to visit."

"Welcome," Jack breathed, the word finally finding him.

Suddenly she wavered, voice quick with alarm. "Oh no—I'm getting soft. I have to go back. Bye!"

Jack noticed the edges of her glow drooping—a clue to the rule she would later explain.

POOF—she vanished into the refrigerator.

Jack didn't even have time to wave.

Part VI: The Three Rules of Lunibelle

On the second night, Jack set down his notebook on the dining table early, pretending to work.

The Little One appeared atop the refrigerator again.

"What should I call you?" she asked sweetly.

"I'm Jack."

"I'm Lunibelle," she said with a tiny bow. "I've only been on Earth a few days."

"Lu-ni-bel-le?" Jack tried the name.

"Of course," she laughed, glanced down, then back at him. "Could you help me get to the table?"

Jack's heart thudded. "Of course."

"Hand, please," Lunibelle said.

He offered his palm. She leaped—cool and light as mist—and he carried her down.

Willy had crept in without a sound and now stared, saucer-eyed.

"This is my best friend, Willy," Jack said.

"Hello, Willy!" Lunibelle tapped his nose with her tiny hand.

"Woof!" went Willy's whole tail.

Lunibelle bounded onto the encyclopedia. She was barefoot; her flowing hair and graceful dress were the same silver color as her body. "My dad told me a friendly family was waiting for me." Her face lit up. "He promised they'd be my new friends, and then he let me in on the best secret of all: my new home would be inside the refrigerator, in a little kingdom of frost and glowing butter."

"Do you miss your mom and dad?" Jack asked.

"Hmmm..." Lunibelle's eyes darted. "Not yet."

"I promise—here will be your warm family," Jack said softly. "I mean... your cold family."

Lunibelle smiled. "I think so," she continued. "Now that we're friends, I must tell you the three rules my parents gave me."

Jack nodded, solemn as a referee.

"First: never use Doo to do mischief that would make the stars frown."

"Do?" Jack asked.

"D-O-O," she spelled. "It's a kind of power. It grows stronger as I grow." A tiny spark FIZZED on her fingertip, as if to prove it, then winked out.

"Second: never reveal important information about me."

Jack's face fell a millimeter, but he nodded.

"Third: never stay outside the refrigerator for more than thirty minutes. My world is very cold. If I stay too long here, I get... soft."

Lunibelle leaned closer, whispering: "Thirty minutes... that's all."

Jack pictured ice cream left out on the counter. "I wouldn't let it happen, no matter what," he secretly resolved.

"That's what happened yesterday," Lunibelle said, her voice fragile as a snowflake. "To visit Earth, I must become tiny—about two inches—the right size to live in the icy caves of your freezer."

She smiled, suddenly mischievous. "But I can change my size. I can be dewdrop-small... or as tall as you."

Jack's eyes were wide open. A thousand questions spun like tops.

"Do you always listen to your parents?" she asked, curious.

"It depends on whether what they say makes sense," Jack said, grinning.

"My parents say I'm too playful," she admitted. "When I play, I forget the rules."

"How do you forget?"

"We once visited a sweet planet. Mountains sweet, rivers sweet, trees delicious."

"Wow."

"Dad said, 'Only three bites.' But it was so good... I sneaked a cheeky fourth."

"And then?" Jack leaned forward.

"And then I turned SWEET—like MARSHMALLOW!" she laughed. "I got stuck to the ground and couldn't move an inch!"

Jack and Willy gaped.

"Dad used Doo to unstick me," she finished, tapping her forehead. "So—three rules!"

"I'll help you remember," Jack promised, feeling very big-brotherly.

Her glow dimmed a little. "I already broke one. I told you about the sweet planet."

Jack placed a hand over his heart. "I'll keep your secrets. Cross my heart—and hope to fly." He even puffed his cheeks solemnly, as if ready to inflate like a balloon and float off if he broke his promise.

"I'll keep one of yours," Lunibelle said. "Do you have one?"

Jack thought. Then, conspiratorially: "Once, my dad let me stay with Grandma if I followed three rules—bedtime, fold blanket, don't go near the woods. But, I went picking mushrooms... and got lost."

"Ah!" Lunibelle covered her mouth.

"A hunter found me and brought me back. Grandma said, 'From now on, pick mushrooms with me. And I won't tell your dad.'"

Jack laughed. Secrets, it seemed, were as delicious as chocolate buttons.

"I promise too," Lunibelle said softly, her whole glittering self-solemn.

"Will I see you every day?" Jack asked.

"I'm not sure," she said. "Sometimes I must talk to my parents. If you need me, write a note and leave it in the freezer."

"I will."

"It's time to go back," Lunibelle said gently.

"I'll carry you," Jack offered.

She hopped to his palm. At the refrigerator she smiled. "Don't open the door—I like going in myself. Thank you, Jack. Goodbye. Have a magical, button-sweet night."

Jack stood, smiling at the quiet door.

Then Lunibelle's head peeked out one last time. "Good night, Willy. Sleep tight." And with a hiccup of snow-light, she was gone.

That night, the refrigerator didn't hum; it TICKED—like a clock winding backward. A silvery whisper, thin as frost, curled through the kitchen: "Thirty minutes... that's all."

Jack stirred in his sleep, his dreams twisting into a race against an endless clock, the chalkboard of his old classroom dripping chocolate numbers he couldn't catch.

On the counter, a snowflake-shaped stopwatch winked into being, its face a vortex of ice pulsing with a wild, dancing glow. Each tick was a tiny, crystalline hammer against the silence, counting down to a mystery Jack didn't know he had to solve.

Chapter II
Chasing Time – The Crucial Thirty Minutes

Part I: Lunibelle Who Refuses to Be Left Behind

Jack was bubbling with joy—the grand opening of the school's art exhibition was today, and his painting was part of it! He had spent weeks perfecting it, mixing colors until Willy's golden fur looked just right—even adding tiny flecks of brown to his nose so it matched the real thing.

The moment he burst through the front door, his backpack thudding to the floor, he turned to Willy and exclaimed, "Guess what! The art exhibition opened today! And your painting—well, not your painting, but the painting of you that I painted—is on display! Shall we go have a peek?"

Willy, who had been snoozing on his favorite sunlit patch of carpet, lifted his head with a slow, dignified blink. Then, as if struck by inspiration, his tail began to wag—thump-thump-thump against the floorboards—and he scrambled to his feet. But instead of bolting for the door as usual, he trotted purposefully to the refrigerator and sat in front of it, his fluffy tail sweeping.

Jack raised an eyebrow. "You want Lunibelle to come too, don't you?"

"Yes!" Willy wagged harder.

Jack groaned, throwing his hands in the air. "But she can only be outside for thirty minutes! That might not be enough!"

Willy let out two sharp barks—WOOF! WOOF!—and planted his paws firmly, as if to say he would not budge without Lunibelle.

Just as Jack opened his mouth to argue, a silvery voice rang out from the refrigerator door.

"Good day to you both!"

There was Lunibelle, peeking from the freezer. Her tiny, translucent hands gripped the edge, and her frosty breath curled in the warm kitchen air.

"Hello to you!" Jack replied with a grin. "Lunibelle, today is the grand opening of the school's art exhibition. One of my paintings is in it. I wanted to take Willy to see it—but it seems he won't go unless you come too."

"Wonderful! Congratulations!" Lunibelle clapped her hands, sending little sparkles of frost into the air. "Your painting made it into an exhibition? And you didn't tell me this splendid news? Of course I want to go!" Her voice trembled with both thrill and a pinch of fear—it was no small thing for her to leave the safety of the refrigerator.

Willy looked at Jack with the smug satisfaction of someone who had been right all along.

Jack sighed dramatically, though his eyes twinkled. In truth, he wanted Lunibelle there more than anyone else. "All right, all right. But we'll have to be quick—you know, melting and all."

"How long does it take to walk to school?" Lunibelle asked, tilting her head.

"Just one block—about five minutes."

"And if you run?"

Jack grinned. "Two minutes flat."

"In that case," said Lunibelle, a mischievous glimmer in her eyes, "why not make it a race? You and Willy run!"

"Brilliant idea!" Jack agreed, secretly delighted she wanted to come.

"I haven't seen much of Earth since I arrived," Lunibelle said, her voice tinged with longing. "Now that I have a chance, would you be my tour guide, Jack?"

"Of course! Whatever you want to see, I'll take you," Jack promised. "Here's the plan—I'll put on a shirt with a pocket, and you can sit inside and peek out."

With that, he thumped up the stairs like a galloping goat.

"I'll wait in the refrigerator!" Lunibelle called after him, her voice buzzing with excitement.

A moment later—THUMP-THUMP-THUMP—Jack came bounding back down, wearing a white T-shirt (because, as Mom always said, "White keeps you cool"). On the front was a tidy pocket stitched right over his heart.

He gently knocked on the refrigerator door. "Ready?"

Out popped Lunibelle, her silver form glinting. With a swoosh of care, Jack slipped her inside the pocket. She nestled in, peering over the edge.

Then, with Willy on his leash and Lunibelle safely nestled above his heart, they stepped out into the wide, wild world.

Part II: The Art Exhibit's First Step

Jack and Willy jogged briskly down the sunny street, the breeze ruffling Jack's hair while Willy's ears perked straight up. Lunibelle clutched the edge of the pocket, her eyes wide as she took in the dizzying sights.

"What's that?" she asked, pointing at a bright red truck rumbling past.

"A fire truck!" Jack said. "They put out fires and rescue people."

"And that?" She gestured to a woman pushing a stroller with a giggling baby.

"That's a baby in a stroller. Humans start out very small, you know."

"Fascinating!" Lunibelle breathed.

Willy, thrilled to be part of the adventure, kept pace beside Jack, occasionally glancing up to make sure Lunibelle was enjoying herself.

They passed a bakery, and the warm scent of fresh bread made Willy's nose twitch.

"Oh! That smell is delicious!" Lunibelle said.

"That's bread," Jack explained. "You bake dough until it's fluffy and golden."

"Do I eat that?" Lunibelle asked curiously.

"Uh... I don't think so. You're made of frost."

"Ah. Pity."

Willy WOOFED in agreement.

Soon, Jack's school came into view—a red-brick building with colorful banners fluttering above the entrance: *WELCOME TO THE SPRING ART SHOW!*

They entered through a long corridor lined with student projects—clay sculptures, papier-mâché planets, and a giant cardboard castle—before stepping into the grand auditorium.

The room buzzed with chattering kids and proud parents, while the walls were covered with paintings: animals, trees, cartoon characters, cars, rockets, flowers, and even a very lopsided portrait of the principal. Jack, now in full tour-guide mode, pointed out his favorites.

"That one's a dinosaur!" Lunibelle said, spotting a T-rex with rainbow spikes.

"Yep! That's by my friend Mateo. He loves dinosaurs."

"And that?" She gestured to a swirling blue-and-green painting.

"That's the ocean. See the little fish hiding in the corner? There's a big turtle too!"

Lunibelle clapped in delight.

Then Jack stopped in front of his own masterpiece. "And this one's mine."

The painting showed Willy sitting proudly, his brown fur textured with thick brushstrokes, wearing a blue basketball cap. His tongue lolled out in a happy pant, and his eyes sparkled with mischief.

"Isn't that Willy?" Lunibelle asked, though of course she already knew.

"Yes indeed," Jack said, puffing out his chest.

"It's awesome!" she declared, peeking down at the real Willy. "Isn't it wonderful, Willy?"

Willy wagged so hard that his entire body wiggled.

"What's that on his head?" Lunibelle asked, pointing at the cap.

"A basketball cap. We're both big basketball fans."

"Jack is the captain of the school basketball team!" Willy barked proudly.

"I've never seen a basketball game," Lunibelle said dreamily.

"I'll take you one day," Jack promised. "Though games run a bit long. Speaking of time..." He checked his watch, his smile faltering. "We'd better head back."

They hurried outside, as Lunibelle now watched the world with the urgency of someone who knew her outside time was limited.

"Jack! What's that?" She pointed to a squirrel darting up a tree.

"That's a squirrel. They eat nuts and drive dogs crazy."

Willy growled playfully.

They passed a mailbox, a bicycle rack, and a group of kids playing hopscotch—each one a new marvel to Lunibelle. But as they turned the corner toward home, Jack noticed Lunibelle's usual shimmer was looking... dimmer.

"Lunibelle? You okay?"

"Just... a little... tired," she murmured, her voice faint.

Jack's heart leapt into his throat—she was melting!

"Willy, run!"

They sprinted the last stretch, Jack clutching his pocket protectively, Willy's paws skidding on the pavement. They burst through the front door, and Jack yanked open the freezer.

"In you go!"

Lunibelle tumbled into the frosty air with a relieved sigh. "Ahhh... that's better."

Jack exhaled. "Too close."

Willy licked Jack's hand as if to say, *We did it.*

"Thank you, Jack," Lunibelle said, her voice regaining its musical lilt. "That was my first adventure on the Earth!"

Jack smiled. "And next time we'll bring an umbrella."

"For shade?"

"Nope. For rain. You'll love it."

Lunibelle laughed as Jack and Willy high-fived—well, high-pawed—their successful mission

Part III: The Star Girl Who Wishes to See the Sea

One lazy afternoon, when the sun hung drowsily in the sky, Jack and Lunibelle sat at the grand wooden table in the dining room, chatting like old friends.

"Jack," she began, "do you remember the painting of the sea at your school's art exhibition? I liked it very much! Can you tell me—what is the sea?"

Jack, nibbling a biscuit, paused mid-crunch. "Have you ever seen the sea?"

"The sea?" Lunibelle blinked her icy eyes, wide as two full moons. "Is that a kind of... square-shaped water?"

Jack burst into laughter, nearly choking on his biscuit. "Oh no—that sea was only square because it was painted on square paper! The real sea is like an enormous mirror that never ends! It's blue—bluer than my schoolbag, bluer than the sky on the clearest day. And when the sunlight dances on it, the waves sparkle like a thousand fairy lights strung across the horizon. They tumble onto the shore going WHOOSH-WHISH-WHOOSH! like they're singing just for you!"

Lunibelle's tiny hands clasped together. "But why is it blue?" Her eyes shimmered with curiosity.

"Because it just is," Jack declared, as if that settled everything. "Like how my hair is yellow and not, say, broccoli green."

He leapt from his chair, arms flapping like a windmill. "And above the sea, there are seagulls! Big, white-winged birds who fly in loopy loops. They dive down—SPLASH!—and snatch up teeny fishies, then soar back up, squawking 'KAAW-KAAW.'"

"What's a fishie?" Lunibelle asked.

"Oh, Lunibelle, the sea is full of them! Fish in reds and blues, with stripes like mismatched socks (not actual socks, of course, but you get the idea). There are whales as big as houses, and little nibble-fish no bigger than chocolate buttons!"

"Do they play tag? Or hopscotch?" Her questions bubbled up like soda pop fizzing over the rim of a glass.

Jack shook his head. "Fish don't have legs, but they dart very fast! They leap, they splash, they chase—it's a grand, watery game down there. And the sand!" He sighed dreamily. "The sand's so shiny it looks like it has gold in it. It's so soft, too. When you walk on it, your feet just sink right in."

Lunibelle's mind whirled. Golden ground, dancing fish, birds that shouted—it sounded like the most splendid nonsense she'd ever not seen.

"And there are ships," Jack added, eyes alight, "great floating buildings with smokestacks puffing clouds, carrying people off to who-knows-where!"

"But houses can't walk!" Lunibelle cried, scandalized.

"They don't!" Jack grinned. "They sail—with great propellers churning the water!"

Lunibelle's heart fluttered. It didn't all make sense, but it sounded like magic.

"I must see the sea!" she cried suddenly, her voice trembling with urgency. "Will you take me? Please, oh please, dear Jack?"

Jack hesitated. His fingers drummed the table. "I can... but you can't be outside longer than 30 minutes, or—"

"Please! We went to the exhibition together, and everything was fine!" Lunibelle pleaded. "The sea may be the most beautiful thing in all the world—and I must see it before—" She stopped, biting her lip.

Jack's chest tightened. He knew what she meant. Before time runs out.

He tapped his fingers faster, calculating. "Ten minutes to get there... ten back... That only leaves us ten minutes at the sea."

"Can we run?" Lunibelle suggested, brightening. "Like we did last time, when we raced to the exhibition?"

"WOOF!" barked Willy, tail thumping the floor. "Willy agrees!" Lunibelle clapped.

Jack's eyes lit up. "If we run there in five and run back in five... that gives us twenty whole minutes!"

"Hooray!" Lunibelle spun in a delighted pirouette, her tiny dress fluttering. "Which day shall we go?"

"Tomorrow," Jack said firmly. "Tomorrow, I get out of school at lunchtime!"

"Tomorrow, tomorrow!" Willy barked, circling them like a furry tornado.

Lunibelle nodded, her voice suddenly calm and determined. "It must be tomorrow."

The next day, just before lunch, Jack zoomed home, gobbled down a sandwich in three bites, and glanced at the clock—half past eleven! His heart hammered. No time to waste.

He gently tucked Lunibelle into his shirt pocket, where she could peek out.

"Willy, come on!" he shouted as he flung open the door.

The sun beamed, the breeze tickled their cheeks, and they ran—faster than a melting ice-cream cone.

Jack's legs burned, his breath came in gasps, but he pushed harder. Thirty minutes. Thirty minutes was all they had.

At last, panting and sweaty, they skidded to a stop at the edge of the world.

Part IV: The Conch Who Sings a Song of Encouragement

"We're here!" Jack wheezed, doubling over. "Look, Lunibelle—look!"

Lunibelle peeked out, and her breath caught.

Before her stretched an endless ocean of blue, sparkling and alive. Waves rolled in from the horizon as if gentle mountains on the move, cresting in foamy white before crashing softly onto the shore. The sea breathed—in and out, in and out—never pausing, never tiring.

"It's amazing!" she exclaimed. "It's more beautiful than I ever imagined!"

Far away, white sails dotted the water like clouds. Seagulls swooped and called, their cries carried by the salty wind.

Jack strolled, leaving trails of footprints in the sand. Lunibelle was enchanted

"Even the word beach sounds beautiful," she sighed. "May I... touch it? Just once?"

Jack, seeing the longing in her eyes, nodded. "Just once."

He lifted her gently, and she pressed a tiny toe into the golden sand.

"Ohhh..." she whispered, eyes fluttering shut. "It's like a warm, fizzy cloud."

"What is this?" Lunibelle pointed, her finger trembling, to a brown spiral peeking shyly from the sand.

Jack, his eyes gleaming with adventure, knelt beside her. He dug eagerly, the warm grains sifting through his fingers until he unearthed a gleaming, spiraled shell the size of a soup bowl. "Wow!" Jack held up the conch. "Charonia tritonis!" he added proudly.

Lunibelle leaned in. "It looks like it's been sleeping here for centuries," she whispered.

"It's the pirate king's horn!" Jack said, cradling it reverently. "Look at this: chocolate lightning zigzags all over its rough surface. But inside, it's pink."

Lunibelle giggled and gently traced a swirl. "I think it's a sea-snail castle," she said. "With bubble chandeliers."

Willy barked once, as if to vote for the pirate theory.

Jack held the conch up to Lunibelle's ear. "SHH... listen. Maybe you can hear the sea's secret."

She closed her eyes. The wind stilled. A soft, pulsing hum filled her ear.

Her eyes flew open. "It's talking to me!"

Jack pressed it to his own ear. "Maybe it's whispering to a deep-sea whale."

"Mr. Conch?" Lunibelle said politely, bending her knees and bowing her head. "Hello?"

There was a pause.

And then—

"Hello...," said the conch.

Its voice was hoarse and wind-worn. "Lunibelle."

Lunibelle's eyes widened. "How did you know my name?"

Jack stumbled backward in astonishment. Even Willy sat, ears up, mouth open.

"I've been waiting for you," the conch continued, "for quite some time."

"For me?" Lunibelle tilted her head. "But how did you know I'd come to this beach?"

The conch hummed. "Because by knowing nothing, I may know everything."

"That sounds like something a philosopher would say," Jack whispered.

The conch chuckled. "You'll learn soon that answers aren't always straight. Sometimes they're curled like shells, with music tucked inside."

Lunibelle pressed it closer. "But you were really waiting for me?"

"Yes," said the conch, his voice softening. "Because you need help."

The tone shifted—no longer a stranger's whisper, but something warmer, with the hush of a lullaby. "You are very far from home, Lunibelle."

"Yes, Mr. Conch," she said. "I just arrived on this planet. Jack and Willy brought me here. They're my best friends."

"Hello, Jack. Hello, Willy," the conch said kindly. "You've done well."

Jack scratched his head. "Well... thanks. But we didn't plan this."

"Not all journeys are planned. Some are drifted to—like messages in bottles."

Willy gave a gentle WHUFF, perhaps in agreement.

"Mr. Conch..." Lunibelle asked, "Can you help me understand time?"

There was a long pause.

"Time," said the conch slowly, "is slippery. It hides in tea kettles and socks and the spaces between questions. But 30 minutes—ah, that's different. That is when everything may change."

Jack leaned in. "What happens in 30 minutes?"

The conch exhaled, as though a tired wave.

"That," it said, "is up to her."

"Up to me?" Lunibelle repeated. "But I don't even know what I'm looking for!"

"You don't need to know," said the conch gently. "You only need to look."

The inside of the shell began to glow faintly—blush pink to sunset gold to candlelight red.

"Your kindness will open doors," the conch murmured. "Your curiosity will find keys. Your courage will climb ladders no one else can see."

"Will I go on an adventure?" Lunibelle asked.

"You are already on one."

She laughed. "That's what Jack said this morning!"

"I did?" Jack blinked. "Well—I was right, then."

"But..." Lunibelle looked down. "Those girls running in the streets, in their twirly dresses and sparkly shoes... they look like the ones from fairy tales. I'm just—me."

"You are more than you look," said the conch. "You shine from the inside, out. One day, you'll wear a dress the wind stitches for you itself."

Willy tilted his head as if he could see it already.

"Will I fly?" Lunibelle asked dreamily. "Or talk to stars? Or bake clouds into cakes?"

"Oh yes," the conch chuckled. "All that and more."

Jack grinned. "That sounds like fun. I hope I get to come too."

"You are part of her story now, Jack," said the conch. "And every story needs a brave heart, a loyal dog, and a question that keeps growing."

Lunibelle clutched the conch close. "Please—tell me more!"

"I've already told you too much," the conch teased.

"Just a little more?" she whispered.

There was a flicker of silence. Then the voice returned, hushed and windswept. "One day, Lunibelle, you will make rivers run backward. You will teach a forgotten letter its name. You will sing a lullaby to a mountain. And yes—you will chase time."

"Chase time?" she echoed. "But... it's so fast."

"You'll be faster," the conch promised, "when your heart runs on wonder."

Lunibelle's face glowed with awe. She looked up to find the sky beginning to change—colors bending and folding like paper cranes. For a moment, it seemed the clouds were spelling something...

But then the conch grew quiet. "I must rest," he whispered, as the pink glow dimmed to pearl gray. "You will remember me when the snowflakes sing."

"Thank you, Mr. Conch," Lunibelle said softly. "I hope we meet again."

"We will," the conch replied, "perhaps when the tide forgets what time is."

Jack gently dug a hollow and placed the conch back into the sand. He smoothed it over with careful hands, like tucking in a sleeping child.

Lunibelle touched the spot gently. "Goodbye."

Willy gave a solemn bark and sniffed once, as if to commit the place to memory.

The wind picked up again, carrying with it a faint echo—whispering wave, or maybe a voice from another chapter.

The three of them stood together for a while, not speaking, letting the quiet curl around them. Somewhere beneath their feet, secrets stirred, and the sand hummed songs.

And far, far away, the clock ticked toward 30 minutes.

Part V: The Footprints That Play in the Sand

Lunibelle was still pondering the words Mr. Conch had just told her.

Jack suddenly remembered something and pulled a crust of bread from his pocket. A seagull spotted it—WHOOSH!—and snatched it midair with a cry.

"Hello, seagull!" Lunibelle laughed, clapping her hands. "May I feed one too?"

Jack broke off a crumb, giving it to Lunibelle; she held it up high. Another gull swooped down—silent, swift, gone in a flash of white feathers.

"They're white!" Lunibelle beamed. "My favorite color! If only I could ride one—imagine gliding on wings of cloud!"

"You'd be the tiniest rider in the sky," Jack said, shielding his eyes to follow the birds. "And probably the sparkliest."

They laughed together, and even Willy barked with joy, spinning in a circle to chase his tail for the sheer fun of it.

"Let's walk," Jack said, pointing down the beach to a jagged black rock in the distance. "We can climb up there and see everything."

"Everything?" Lunibelle echoed, wide-eyed.

"Everything the sea wants to show us," he said with a mystery grin.

So, they wandered farther down the shore, leaving behind three sizes of footprints—two sneakers, four paws, and one impossibly tiny pair that looked as though a snowflake had stepped there.

The rock loomed ahead—tall, dark, defiant against the waves. It jutted from the sand. The sea hurled itself at it again and again, roaring as if a beast trying to crack stone—but the rock held, unmoved.

They climbed it together, until they reached the top. There, they sat side by side, looking out at the rippling expanse of blue.

The wind tousled Jack's hair and lifted Lunibelle's silver dress until it fluttered. The air was salty and wild. Tiny sailboats bobbed far out in the bay. The sky overhead stretched forever.

For a moment, it felt as if time had paused to sit with them.

They were so happy, so full of wonder, they forgot about the clock entirely. But time had not forgotten them.

The clock hands—hour, minute, second—were tireless runners on a circular track, racing forward with merciless precision.

TICK. TICK. TICK.

11:57.

Lunibelle lay flat on her stomach, chin resting on her tiny palms, gazing out. "What's on the other side of the sea?"

Jack squinted into the horizon. "Maybe more sand," he said. "Or mountains. Or a city."

"Is it very, very far?"

Jack nodded. "So far that even a ship takes days and days to get there. And even longer if it stops to pick up stowaway penguins."

TICK. TICK. TICK.

11:58.

"Jack! Look!" Lunibelle cried, her tiny hand trembling as she pointed. A towering jet of water shot into the air, flashing like a fountain of liquid diamonds.

"What is that?" she asked, clutching Jack's sleeve.

"A whale!" Jack laughed. "It's spouting water—they have to come up to breathe, or else they'll get all soggy inside."

"Soggy inside?" she blinked

"That's science!" Jack declared, proud—though clearly improvising.

Willy barked in agreement, which made Lunibelle giggle so hard she almost slid down the rock.

TICK. TICK. TICK.

11:59.

And then, as if the sea wanted to give them one last gift, a pod of dolphins burst from the waves in perfect unison—silver arcs of joy against the backdrop of the sunlit sea. They leapt and spun, flicking their tails with flair. Mid-leap, one dolphin turned its eye toward them and seemed to wink.

"They're waving!" Lunibelle shouted. "They're waving at us!"

"Hello there!" she cried, clapping her hands.

"Hello, Dolphin!" Jack shouted back, cupping his hands like a seashell around his mouth.

Willy barked, tail wagging furiously.

"They're marvelous!" Lunibelle breathed. "So alive! So perfect!"

Jack's smile softened. He looked down at her glowing face.

For a heartbeat, time seemed to pause. Willy sat quietly, eyes half-closed, his tail sketching lazy circles behind him.

Jack felt Lunibelle lean against him, and with it came a sudden sense of responsibility.

He took a breath. A long, quiet one.

And then—his eyes caught something. The distant steeple. The clock face.

He seized Lunibelle's hand—tiny, cold, fragile in his palm. "Lunibelle," he said, his voice suddenly tight, "what time is it?"

And then—

DONG! DONG! DONG!

The church bell struck noon.

Part VI: The Race That Nearly Ends at the Crossroads

They were sitting on the rocks, happily watching the sea, when the church bell struck.

Lunibelle's voice turned trembling and weak. "Jack... I... I don't feel... well..."

Jack's blood turned to ice. The time limit—30 minutes!

He leapt from the rock, heart pounding like a war drum. "RUN!" he cried.

Faster than fear, faster than regret!

THUD. He hit the ground hard, knees scraping against the pavement. Blood welled, but he barely felt it. He scrambled up—two steps—then collapsed again, legs wobbling like loose strings, as though his bones had turned to water.

"What do I do?" he cried, pounding the pavement. "I can't move!"

Willy skidded to a stop, whirled around, dropped flat to the ground with legs tucked beneath him, and barked, "Climb on!"

Jack, arms shaking, ignoring the pain, hauled himself onto Willy's back.

"Hold tight!" Willy growled.

Then—WHOOSH!—they were racing, the wind howling in Jack's ears.

"Jack..." Lunibelle's voice faded. "Thank you... the sea... thank..."
And then—silence.

"LUNIBELLE!"

"Stay with me!"

"GO! GO! WILLY—FASTER!"

"Hold on, Lunibelle!"

"Willy, go!"

In the distance, Jack saw the crosswalk's traffic light flick from red to green—pedestrians began to move—but they were still far away. This was it. The very last chance.

"GO! WILLY!"

And then... time slipped.

The signal light began to flash—blinking like a ghost's eye trying not to be caught.

10: Willy's paws struck the ground, THUMP, like reverberating drums.

9: The world seemed narrowed: no people, no cars, no sky, just numbers floating in the air.

8: "GOOOOO—" Jack's voice was a wind-torn ribbon trailing behind.

7: They were no longer running. They were chasing time.

6: The ground lost gravity. Willy's paws lifted—no push, no leap—just motion untethered, running in the air.

5: Jack looked around. The surrounding scenery blurred into a watercolor painting, like dominoes toppling backward in a rush.

4: "Hold on, Lunibelle—don't melt, not yet—"

3: Every flash of the traffic light was like a door slowly closing.

2: Jack yelled desperately, "WIL—LY!"

1: Willy landed on the other side of the road just as the red light snapped on...

An old policeman dropped his whistle in stunned silence. "In all my forty years..." he murmured, voice trembling, "this... this is the first time."

Willy burst through the front door, panting, his face a mask of sweat and panic.

Jack's hand flew to his shirt pocket—a desperate reflex of habit and hope—but closed on emptiness. There was only a faint, shimmering watermark where Lunibelle had been.

"LUNIBELLE!"

His knees hit the floor, and he didn't feel a thing. Hot tears streamed down his face. "No, no, no," he whispered, the sound broken and helpless.

Willy didn't bark or whimper. He lunged forward, grabbing Jack's shirt and yanking with all his weight. Jack stumbled, but Willy didn't stop.

"The freezer—!"

The thought flashed in Jack's head. He scrambled to his feet and flung the door open. Cold, white air spilled out, whispering. He peeled off his shirt—still warm, still holding her scent—and folded it gently, put it in the freezer.

The latch clicked shut.

Silence.

Then, from inside the freezer, a sneeze. Tiny. Muffled. Impossible. Jack froze, pressing his ear to the frosty door. Silence again.

Then, a chime. Soft. Slow. Hollow. As if someone were knocking from the other side.

Chapter III
Weird Birthday Party

Part I: Where the Light Finds Its Way Home

A. Lunibelle's Returning Radiance

Several days later, Jack was healing quickly. The scabs on his knees had started to tighten, and the worst of the bruises had turned yellow.

Upstairs, he sat at his little desk, pencil in hand, staring down at a math problem that refused to be solved. It wasn't even a hard one. It just looked... untidy.

Willy snoozed peacefully by his feet; his nose tucked under one paw.

"Willy," Jack muttered, tapping his paper, "this one's tricky. Do you think you can solve it?"

Willy didn't stir.

Before Jack could try again, a crisp, cheerful voice chimed above his desk: "Allow me to answer that question!"

Jack spun around so fast that he nearly knocked over the desk.

"Lunibelle!" he cried, his face lighting up.

Jack leaped to his feet—"Ouch!"

He winced and dropped back into the chair, grabbing at his knees.

Lunibelle hovered just above the desk, her glow soft and familiar. She grinned at first, then saw him wince, and her smile faded.

"What happened to you?" she asked, zipping to his side.

"He fell—twice!—racing home from the beach," Willy said from the floor, suddenly wide awake. His ears twitched. "It was awful."

"Oh no..." Lunibelle floated closer. "Let me see."

"I'm fine, really," Jack said, quickly moving his hands to cover up the bandage. "Almost healed."

"Jack," she said gently but firmly, "please move your hands."

There was something in her voice—something calm, steady. Jack obeyed without thinking. Slowly, he pulled his hands away.

The bandages were neat, but underneath, pink scrapes still peeked through.

Lunibelle stared at them. Two small tears welled in her eyes and rolled down her cheeks. "It's all my fault," she whispered. "I played too long. I didn't think you'd run that hard for me..."

"No, no," Jack said quickly. "I just didn't want to be late. I should've watched where I was going."

They sat quietly. The afternoon sun came through the window, making a pale square on the floor.

Jack blinked at her, as if making sure she was really there. "When did you come back?"

"I'm not quite sure," Lunibelle said, drifting on the desk. "It felt like I was sleeping—a long, long sleep. And then one morning... I just woke up, like a light being switched on."

Jack crossed his arms, trying to look serious, though a grin kept sneaking through. "Well, someone took their sweet time. We've been waiting, you know."

Lunibelle giggled. Then her voice softened. "Jack... I think I've grown-up a little."

Jack tilted his head. "In a few days?"

"Well," she said, spinning slowly in the air, "we don't grow by days. We grow by what we learn. That's why my parents sent me to Earth—to learn new things. Back home, you're not really grown-up until you understand more of the world."

She paused. "We don't have seas where I come from. But the sea here—it taught me a lot. That's why I feel just a little taller inside."

Jack watched Lunibelle carefully, wanting to find any differences.

She gave him a small, shy smile, her gaze dropping to her clasped hands. "Not on the outside, of course. I still have my hair."

Jack let out a low chuckle, a sound that rumbled in his chest. "You do have very shiny hair."

"Thank you!" Lunibelle's face lit up, a joyful beam. "I wash it each morning with dandelion dew."

Jack laughed again, a bright, unrestrained sound that filled the air. "I'm glad you're back," he said, the playful light in his eyes softening.

"I'm glad you're still you," she replied, a hint of something deeper in her voice.

B. A Friendship Stitched with Buttons

Jack was so delighted by Lunibelle's return that they were talking without noticing the time. It was the kind of conversation that leaped from one thing to another, full of half-answered questions and bursts of laughter.

"How long do you live?" Jack asked suddenly. "If you don't have years?"

Lunibelle's smile faded a little. "We don't really... die," she said. "That's a human word. But if I act too wildly, or make too many mistakes, I might get called back early."

Jack sat up straighter. "What do you mean, called back?"

She looked down at her hands. "My parents found out about the beach accident. They were very upset. They said if I keep being reckless, they'll call me home at once—no more Earth, no more outside the fridge."

Jack's heart sank. "No!" he said instantly.

Willy, who had been dozing, lifted his head. His tail stopped wagging. He went completely still.

"Don't worry," Lunibelle said quickly. "I promised to be more careful. I'm not leaving anytime soon."

"But... what if they still make you go?" Jack asked, his voice suddenly small.

"They said one more thing..." she whispered, watching his face. "If I make a true friend here—someone who really, truly cares about me... someone who makes me clothes—then I can stay outside the fridge as long as I like."

Jack blinked. "Wait. Clothes?"

Lunibelle nodded. "If I wear human clothes, I'll be almost like a real human. That's what they said."

51

She glanced at her glowing arms and bare feet. "I've always wondered what it would feel like... to wear colorful clothes. Everyone looks so cozy and fancy. I've never even tried on a sock."

Jack's eyebrows rose. "You've never worn a sock?"

"Not even once," she said. "They just look so... soft."

Jack leaned forward. "I'll do it! I'll make you clothes and socks! Or—or Mom will! She's a fashion designer, after all!"

Lunibelle gasped. Her glow brightened slightly. "Really?! Oh, Jack! That's the nicest thing anyone's ever said to me!"

"She's amazing," Jack said proudly. "And I won't tell her they're for a moonlight sprite—I'll just say they're for a doll. Or a puppet. She won't ask too many questions if I sound confident."

Lunibelle's smile wobbled. "But... what if she says no?"

Jack shook his head. "She won't."

"How do you know?"

"Because she's the kind of mom who'd sew a scarf for a snowman if I asked."

That made Lunibelle giggle. Then she clapped her hands together. "Oh! I want a dress! And maybe a belt! And little shoes—no, socks first. Ooh! And buttons! Could I have real buttons?"

Jack laughed. "Absolutely. Buttons galore. You'll have more buttons than the puffiest winter coat."

"I'll be clothed! And warm!" Lunibelle twirled midair, her feet brushing the edge of the desk. "And maybe... maybe even brave enough to step outside longer than ever."

Jack looked at her, heart thudding. "You'd really go outside? Where people could see you?"

She nodded. "Maybe not far. But if I have clothes, I won't feel so... different. Maybe I'll blend in. Just a little."

"You'll be amazing," Jack said firmly. "That's my promise."

Lunibelle floated closer and placed her tiny hands over his. "Then it's mine too. I'll be here. And I'll be the best friend I can be."

They sat like that for a moment, still and quiet. The sun had moved lower in the sky, and golden light spilled across the desk like a blanket.

Outside, a bird chirped; inside, their promise held steady.

It was a small moment. But it felt very, very real. And maybe—just maybe—it would change everything.

And somewhere in Jack's mind, another thought flickered: My birthday is coming soon. Maybe the best present of all would be clothes for Lunibelle.

Part II: Presents the Size of a Whisper

A. A Gift Woven from a Wish

In the dining room, Jack's mom and dad were deep in conversation, their voices hushed but hopeful.

"Jack's recovering fast!" said his mother, setting down a plate and tucking a loose strand of hair behind her ear. She glanced at Jack's father, a smile tugging at her lips. "His birthday's just around the corner. I keep asking him what he wants, and all he ever says is, 'I don't mind.'" She sighed and placed a spoon beside the napkin.

"What are you getting him?"

Jack's father leaned in as though about to reveal a top-secret mission. "He wants a fossil," he whispered, raising his eyebrows with a look of playful pride. "I've already got it. A little fossil fish. Authentic, and small enough to fit in his pocket."

His mother let out a quiet laugh, her eyes sparkling. "A fossil, really? That's so like him. Always collecting odd little treasures." She paused, her smile softening into a crease of thought. "Still... I can't help wondering what he really wants. Something he hasn't said out loud yet."

Meanwhile, upstairs, Jack sat cross-legged on his bedroom floor, a pencil dangling from his mouth. His homework lay forgotten beside him. He was staring at the closet.

How can I ask Mom to sew clothes for a girl who's two inches tall, glows in the dark, and definitely isn't from this planet... without sounding completely out of my mind?

He drummed his fingers against the floor. Lunibelle deserved something proper—a dress that fit, shoes that didn't fall off mid-flight, maybe even a tiny pink sweater with stars on it.

Downstairs, his mother's voice rang out as if a dinner bell across the house. "Jack! Dinner's ready!"

He scrambled to his feet, thundered down the stairs two at a time, and skidded to a stop at the kitchen doorway. The table was overflowing—roast fish with lemon, creamy mac and cheese, crispy broccoli florets, and—best of all—his favorite: warm tomato soup with a swirl of cream.

"Smells amazing!" Jack slid into his chair, eyes wide. "Whoa—this looks incredible!"

His mother watched him with cautious joy. It had been days since Jack had eaten properly—since the fall, he'd barely touched his food. She had tried everything—alphabet soup, dinosaur-shaped pancakes, even a lasagna shaped like a volcano—yet nothing had worked. Until now. Now he was glowing.

Jack ate like someone rediscovering joy. He even ate the broccoli without a single complaint. When dessert came—a little dish of peach cobbler—he didn't just eat it. He licked the spoon and grinned.

As Jack gathered the plates, his mother saw her moment.

"Jack, sweetheart... have you thought more about your birthday present? What you'd really like?"

Jack hesitated, then nodded. "Actually—yes! Thank you!" He swallowed hard. "Could you... make me three suits?"

She blinked in surprise. "Of course! Oh, darling, you finally asked for something! What kind of clothes? A new hoodie? Pajamas?"

Jack hesitated. "Well... not exactly for me..."

B. Mom's Spell for the Tiniest Gift

Jack was very happy when his mother agreed to make clothes as his birthday present.

"They're... not for me." He held his thumb and finger apart, showing a tiny space between them. "They're for someone about this tall."

His mother leaned in. "For... dolls?"

Jack shook his head. "No. For... a two-inch-tall... girl."

His mother nearly dropped a spoon. "I'm sorry—a two-inch-tall what?"

"A girl," Jack repeated, completely serious. "Please, Mom. It's really important."

She stared at him. "Jack... you don't even have any dolls. Why would you want tiny clothes for someone who doesn't exist?"

Jack pressed his hands together, his eyes wide and shimmering with hope. "Pleeease, Mom," he begged, his voice cracking just enough to tug at her heart. "I can't explain it, but... it's everything to me. It's my birthday wish—the only one!"

Then, before she could protest, he flung his arms around her, burying his face in her shoulder like he used to when he was little. "And you're the best mom ever," he mumbled into her shirt. "You always get it. You always fix things. So... you'll do this for me, right?"

He pulled back just enough to flash her a wobbly grin—half sweet, half sly—knowing full well she could never say no when he looked at her like that. "Because you're my mom... and no one loves me like you do."

Willy thumped his tail against the floor. "If it helps, I'll guard the socks once they're finished," he vowed.

His mother gave a short laugh—half confused, half touched. "Oh, Jack. And even Willy's in on it..." She sighed, the towel twisting tighter in her hands. "All right. All right. I'll do it. What kind of fabric are we talking about?"

Jack's grin bloomed like a firework. "Something soft—but it has to keep out rain, wind, and heat! And it needs a hat, shoes, socks, buttons... maybe even a cape?"

She raised one eyebrow. "Color?"

"Pale. Or shimmery. Like moonlight, maybe."

She narrowed her eyes just a little. "Is someone going to wear these?"

Jack nodded. "Yes, Mom. Someone very special."

"Well," she said, slipping into designer mode, "I'll make a sample first. We'll need to test the pattern. Tiny clothes are tricky—can't have them looking sloppy."

"You're amazing!" Jack threw his arms around her. "Thank you, thank you, thank you!"

Later that night, Jack hugged his mom again at the foot of the stairs. "Best Mom ever," he whispered.

His father watched from the hallway, smiling. "I don't think I've heard Jack say 'Mom' so many times in one evening."

She laughed, a little misty-eyed. "I don't know what this is all about, but... if it makes him this happy, I'll sew a dozen tiny coats if I have to."

Then she turned to him with a sudden thought. "By the way—did you order the cake?"

"Done," he said proudly. "Balloons, streamers, glow-in-the-dark stars—the works."

"Perfect," she said. But her thoughts lingered on the strange request. "Clothes small enough to hold a wish," she murmured. "I've never made anything that tiny. Who could they be for?"

But upstairs, Jack was already back in his room—knees bouncing, eyes shining. Tomorrow, he would deliver the news to Lunibelle.

And soon, she'd have something no moonlight sprite had ever had before: real clothes. She can stay out longer!

Part III: Secrets Beneath the Birthday Dress

A. A Girl in Disguise

Overnight, the living room had quietly transformed. Dozens of orange-and-white balloons floated near the ceiling. A big banner stretched across the wall, shimmering faintly in the sunlight: *Happy Birthday, Jack!* In the far corner stood a giant inflatable dinosaur with a comically wide grin, guarding wrapped gifts, their paper rustling softly with every breeze.

But the centerpiece was the cake. It was shaped like a perfect basketball—round and orange Only the rich chocolate aroma betrayed its true identity. Candles, tall and golden, stood on top, waiting for one breath and one wish.

Three o'clock struck.

The doorbell chimed, and the house stirred to life.

Friends poured in—Jack's basketball teammates with high-fives and inside jokes, classmates full of wild stories from school, neighbors carrying baked goods and handmade cards. Laughter filled the rooms, bouncing off the walls and mixing with the smell of frosting and popcorn. Someone turned on music, and the beat added a pulse to the party.

Jack moved from guest to guest, smiling, greeting, occasionally blushing. His cheeks ached from smiling, but he didn't mind. It felt good.

Jack paused on the porch, feeling as though something—or some-one—was missing. The air seemed to hold its breath, waiting.

Then—he saw her.

A girl had just stepped onto the porch. She moved lightly, as though walking didn't quite apply to her. Her golden hair caught the sunlight, bouncing gently with each step. Her dress was a soft, glowing pink, with a green satin bow tied neatly at the waist. The way the light hit her made the edges of her silhouette shimmer faintly.

Jack froze, blinking. She looked familiar—but impossible. His breath caught. "Hi... uh... are you...?" he asked, his voice hovering between awe and confusion.

She leaned in, lips curved into a sly smile. "Lu-ni-bel-le," she whispered, each syllable sparkling.

Jack blinked hard. "But—weren't you two inches tall yesterday? And silver?"

He rubbed his eyes, certain his dreams had spilled into daylight.

She gave a soft giggle and twirled, her dress lifting slightly as she spun. "You didn't think I'd miss your birthday, did you?" she said, teasing, though her eyes held a seriousness beneath the twinkle.

Jack couldn't stop staring. "I—I didn't know you could come out like this. You look... amazing!"

Lunibelle's eyes sparkled as she leaned closer. "Come on, Jack. We can't waste the whole day standing still—there are wonders waiting."

Just then, Willy let out a happy bark and bounded over. His tail wagged. He circled Lunibelle once, then sat beside her as if she were royalty.

"Your mom is incredible," Lunibelle said, touching the edge of her dress with reverence. "She didn't even ask who the clothes were for. She just made them—like she already understood something without needing to ask."

Jack blinked. "She didn't know they were for you."

Lunibelle shook her head. "Nope. But somehow, she got everything right. The fabric, the size... even the way it feels. I think she stitched in something more than thread. Something that helps me stay—keeps me grounded. Real."

Jack's eyes widened. "You mean... this dress lets you stay?"

Lunibelle nodded. "For as long as I want. I'm not just visiting. I'm here."

Jack was excited. "I'll tell her. I'll tell her everything. Well—almost everything."

Lunibelle giggled. "Let's not ruin the mystery."

And with that, the 'y continued—but now, for Jack, the world had shifted slightly. It wasn't just a birthday anymore—it was a moment when the real and the impossible shook hands.

B. The Gown That Lights Up the Party

Jack was standing near the door, talking excitedly to Lunibelle. His hands waved in the air, his words tumbling out. From across the room, Jack's mother looked up from refilling the lemonade bowl—and froze.

There was a girl standing beside Jack—someone she didn't recognize. Someone astonishing.

She wasn't dressed like the other kids. There was a quiet grace about her—something old and new at once. Her pink dress caught the light in a way that made the green satin bow glitter.

Jack's mother narrowed her eyes, puzzled, and dabbed her hands on a napkin.

Jack spotted her. "Mom!" he called. "Come here! You have to meet someone."

He was practically bouncing. "This is Lunibelle!" he said, his voice high with excitement, as if he couldn't believe it himself.

Lunibelle stepped forward, calm and polite, and offered her hand.

Jack's mother reached out automatically. She hesitated for the briefest moment—something about the girl felt familiar in a way she couldn't place—but then she smiled warmly and took her hand.

"Welcome, Lunibelle," she said. "You look... beautiful."

"Thank you," Lunibelle replied, cheeks glowing. "This is my very first birthday party. Ever."

Jack's mother blinked. "Your first?"

Lunibelle caught herself. "I mean... the first one where I've had such a beautiful dress."

Jack's mother looked at her more closely. Something tugged at her memory. The fabric. The stitching. The way the green bow curled just so. Her thoughts raced.

Wait—it was the dress. The one she had made as a joke. The one Jack had asked for with a strange glint in his eye. Clothes for a girl two inches tall. She had laughed, had called it a silly idea, and had still stitched three tiny outfits—just for fun, just to make Jack happy.

She'd never imagined anyone would actually wear them.

Yet here was this girl. Wearing that exact dress. And somehow—it fit!

Jack's mother didn't say a word. She just smiled, her mind quietly cartwheeling. "Come, sit," she said gently, guiding Lunibelle to the couch. "You must be special if Jack invited you."

"I didn't exactly get an invitation," Lunibelle said with a grin. "I just... knew I had to come."

"Are you in Jack's class?"

"No," Lunibelle said sweetly. "Different class. But I've seen him play basketball. He's very fast."

Across the room, Jack pretended not to listen, but one ear turned noticeably pink.

Jack's mother chuckled. "Well, you certainly made an entrance. You really do look lovely in that dress. It fits you perfectly."

"It's the first special dress I've ever worn," Lunibelle said, touching the green bow lightly. "It feels like it knows me. Like it was always mine."

Something shifted inside Jack's mother. This girl—this Lunibelle—was a mystery. But there was something true in her voice. Something gentle. And she wasn't just beautiful. She loved the dress. Not in a showing-off way, but in a way that made Jack's mother proud of every stitch.

Then Lunibelle added, almost in a whisper, "Jack says you make the most beautiful clothes. He says you're the best mom in the world."

Jack's mother blinked. The words landed quietly but firmly. She looked over at Jack, who gave her a sheepish shrug and a grin.

"Well," she said softly, brushing an invisible thread from Lunibelle's shoulder, "any friend of Jack's is always welcome here. And if you ever want to come see one of my fashion shows..."

Lunibelle's eyes widened. "Really? I'd love that!"

Just then, Jack's father clapped his hands. "Next event: basketball shooting contest!"

Children whooped and ran outside. A plastic hoop waited in the grass. Teams formed quickly, chalk lines drawn with dramatic flair. Shouts and cheers echoed through the yard. Jack's team won by a single perfect shot, and he raised his arms in triumph.

Then came the final moment. The cake was carried in and set upon the table. It gleamed with orange frosting, with candles waiting patiently on top. They flickered like tiny suns, wobbling in the air as though nervous to be blown out.

Jack stood tall. Jack's mother lit each candle with careful hands. The room hushed.

"Happy birthday to you..."

The song began. Jack looked around—at the smiling faces, at his parents, at Lunibelle standing at the edge of the circle with her hands folded neatly. She smiled at him, calm and glowing.

Willy barked once, then howled softly, joining the song in his own off-key way. Laughter rippled through the circle, but no one told him to stop.

"Go on," Jack's mother said gently. "Make your wish."

Jack looked once more at Lunibelle. He closed his eyes. Took a deep breath. And blew.

The flames vanished. The room burst into applause.

And deep down, Jack made a second wish—quiet and invisible. A wish not for himself, but for the girl in the dress that changed everything.

Part IV: Pools, Perils, and Sky-Fallen Surprises

A. The Star-Gift That Falls to Earth

The birthday party was a rollercoaster of surprises—and it wasn't done yet.

"Now—it's time for presents!" Jack's father announced, clapping so enthusiastically that his watch flew off and landed in the punch bowl with a gentle plop.

"Awesome!" someone yelled, and everyone gathered around in a noisy, bouncing circle. Wrapping paper rustled. Jack smiled and dove into the gift pile.

First came a stack of books with titles like *Super Brains of the Savannah* and *Math Riddles to Break Your Head*. "Thanks, Aunt Clara!" Jack said, trying not to look terrified.

Next: a basketball signed by every member of his team—including Coach Dale, who'd drawn a tiny whistle instead of signing his name. "That's his signature," one teammate whispered. "He can't spell."

There were video games, robot pens, noise-canceling earmuffs ("For when your sister sings in the shower!"), and a box of glow-in-the-dark socks from a neighbor who always gave socks.

Then Jack reached for a sleek, silver box that looked like it might contain either treasure or a tiny spaceship. Inside: a limited-edition set of trading cards—holographic, numbered, and still smelling faintly of glue and mystery. Jack gasped as though he'd swallowed a trumpet.

"LOOK! QUICK! What's that outside?!" someone shouted, pointing dramatically at the window.

Chaos. Chairs scraped. Cookies flew. Everyone scrambled toward the glass.

In the backyard, something huge and sparkly was floating down from the clouds. It shone silently, gracefully, mesmerizingly.

It descended lower and lower until—SHHHFFF—it touched down softly on the grass.

No one said a word.

It was a swimming pool! A full-sized, glowing-blue, rectangular swimming pool—nearly as big as a basketball court. Water rippled peacefully across its surface, where dozens of helium balloons floated in lazy circles. They weren't tied to anything—they just floated there, politely.

The pool gleamed, a cosmic rectangle stitched into the backyard. Printed in gold letters across the center of the pool were the words: **Happy Birthday, Jack! Signed, L.**

Jack's mother gasped and clutched the nearest person's arm, which turned out to be the mailman. "A swimming pool?" she whispered. "From the sky!"

Jack's father removed his glasses, wiped them with the corner of the tablecloth, then put them back on. "I'm... hallucinating, right?"

he said to no one in particular.

"Did anyone order this?" asked the neighbor who always wore too much sunscreen. "Is this one of those sky-delivery things? Like an airplane stunt?"

Jack blinked. "I—I don't think so?"

"Maybe it's inflatable," offered someone. A kid poked it. It wasn't.

Willy barked once, then tiptoed to the edge of the pool and sniffed the water. He sneezed three times, then wagged his tail to show he liked it.

"Well," said Jack's teammate, hands on hips, "whoever sent that must really like you."

"I mean," added another kid, eyes wide, "it's better than socks."

A beat of silence. Then: "CANNONBALL!" shouted someone, and three kids leaped into the pool fully clothed. Balloons popped, water glittered—and the party erupted into a chaos that could only be called legendary.

B. A Shimmering Borrowed Blue

That night, long after the cake was eaten and the balloons had stopped bouncing, Jack sat in the quiet kitchen, chin in his hands. Lunibelle sat beside him, kicking her legs gently over the edge of the chair.

"Okay," Jack said with a smile. "The swimming pool. That was you, right?"

Lunibelle tilted her head, feigning innocence. "Was it?" she said sweetly. "Or wasn't it?"

"Your... your Doo—it did that?"

"I didn't make it," she said with a delicate sniff. "I... just moved it."

Jack sat up straighter. "Moved? From where?"

Lunibelle gave a tiny shrug. "Somewhere close by. It looked lonely."

"You mean you borrowed it?"

"Yes! That's the word! Borrowed!" she said brightly.

Jack groaned, covering his face. "Lunibelle... on Earth, we ask before borrowing things. Especially a giant swimming pool."

"Oh," she said, blinking. "Where I'm from, things belong to everyone. The stars don't keep the moon, the rivers don't own the fish. If you need something, you use it. Then you put it back."

Jack lowered one hand and squinted at her. "Well... we're definitely putting it back."

Lunibelle nodded solemnly. "Agreed."

"I'll put up signs tomorrow," Jack muttered. He grabbed a napkin and wrote on it: *Lost swimming pool—please claim in backyard, 116 Main Street. Preferably soon.*

"Excellent plan," Lunibelle chirped. "You're very good at Earth things."

The next afternoon, Jack and Willy patrolled the town, taping handmade signs to lampposts and bulletin boards. By evening, they had used up all the tape and every bold marker.

Jack finished posting the last note and returned home. Just as he sat down for a slice of leftover cake—

Knock▢ Knock▢ Knock▢

He opened the door. A tall policeman stood on the porch, holding one of Jack's signs.

"Are you Jack?"

"Yes, sir."

"Did you post this?"

"Yes, sir."

The officer squinted at him. "Well, young man, you've solved a mystery. A very confused man reported his backyard pool missing."

Jack winced. "Would... would you like to see it?"

The officer nodded. "Lead the way."

In the backyard, he stared at the massive floating pool as though he'd stumbled upon a UFO in a vegetable garden.

"Well, I'll be," he muttered. "Never seen anything quite like that."

"It flew here," Jack said honestly.

The officer glanced sideways. "Flew?"

"Quiet as a butterfly."

The officer chuckled. "You've got quite the imagination." Then he handed Jack a slip of paper. "Here's the address. Think you can... fly it back?"

Jack saluted. "We'll try."

"Good lad," the officer smiled. "Try to keep the airspace clear from now on."

C. When the Sky's Pond Rests on the Roof

After the police left and the backyard had returned to its usual stillness, Jack explained everything to Lunibelle over two mugs of warm milk and the final slice of cake.

She twirled a spoon between her fingers. "What time shall we launch?"

Jack glanced out the kitchen window, where stars blinked behind swaying tree branches. "Midnight," he said. "No one will see. Everyone will be asleep—except the moon."

Lunibelle nodded, her glow soft and thoughtful. "I'm sorry," she whispered. "I just wanted it to be... unforgettable."

"It was unforgettable," Jack said softly, reaching for her tiny hand. "Just... maybe next time, with less... airborne real estate."

At midnight sharp, the world held its breath. The moon hung low and full, painting the grass in molten silver. Jack and Lunibelle crouched at the living-room window, noses nearly touching the glass, watching the enormous pool in the backyard.

The wind paused. The trees stilled. The house, even with all its pipes and wires, seemed to go silent.

The clock struck twelve.

With a sigh as soft as moonlight slipping over a sleeping hill, the swimming pool began to rise. Gently, soundlessly, it lifted—higher and higher—until it floated in midair, a luminous blue vessel sailing through a sea of stars.

It looked less like a backyard toy and more like a celestial ark, carrying birthday wishes back to the heavens.

Lunibelle raised one hand slightly, guiding it with invisible strings of thought. Jack watched, utterly still.

Then—BARK! A dog's cry split the night.

The pool jolted. It froze.

BARK! BARK! BARK!

A whole chorus erupted—yowling, yapping, baying. Every dog in the neighborhood had apparently chosen this exact moment to report a suspicious airborne object.

The pool trembled. Its glow flickered.

"It's falling," Jack gasped. "Lunibelle—it's falling!"

She didn't scream. She didn't flinch.

Her eyes sharpened. Her mouth was a tight, determined line. "Call Willy," she said evenly, nudging Jack with her elbow.

Jack snapped his fingers with magician-like precision. "Willy!"

The German Shepherd charged in like a furry thunderbolt, skidding to a stop at Lunibelle's feet.

"What are they barking about?" she asked quickly, crouching to his level.

Willy barked back, "They say there's a giant black monster in the sky—full of mysteries and teeth!"

Lunibelle pressed her palms together. "Tell them it's not a monster—it's a birthday surprise on its way home. And if they hush right now, we'll give them bones tomorrow. Big ones. Meaty. With gravy."

"On it!" barked Willy, and he bolted outside.

Woof! Woof! His voice rang through the night—commanding, musical, and utterly convincing.

And then—silence. Complete, echoing silence.

The swimming pool, which had been sagging perilously just above the rooftop, steadied. A single droplet of water fell, plinking onto a roof tile. Then—slowly, reverently—it began to rise again.

Higher. Higher. Back into the sky it went, gliding through the darkness.

Lunibelle lowered her hands, exhaling softly. Her shoulders, which had been firm and proud, finally relaxed.

Jack let out a sound that was half sigh, half giggle. He shook his head, a stunned smile slowly spreading across his face. "You saved the house."

She smiled. "With a dog. And a promise of bones."

They stood together at the window, gazing upward at the fading glow.

"Lunibelle?" Jack murmured.

"Yes?"

"I'm a little scared to see what you'll do next time."

Her grin sparkled. "You should be."

Chapter IV
The Hockey Games Under the Table

Part I: Parcel and Yellowy Join In

A. The Mysterious Visitor

Jack and Willy had just returned from a walk. From a distance, Jack spotted a small black shape near the front door.

Surprise!—a black cat sat there comfortably, looking impossibly cute. She raised her head slowly, eyes gleaming, and tucked her tiny paws neatly beneath her—round and compact. She meowed softly, as if saying, "How are you?"

It felt almost as if she were the host and Jack the visitor.

Willy trotted up and gave the furry blob a good sniff. The cat blinked once. Then twice. Completely unbothered.

"Are you hungry?" Jack asked, gently reaching down to touch her.

The cat lifted her head, the tip of her tail giving a tiny flick.

Jack went inside and returned with a saucer and a piece of sausage.

The cat nibbled, gulped, then licked her paw with slow, satisfied rhythm.

"Do you need more?" Jack asked.

The cat squinted sleepily and began to doze off.

The next day—lo and behold—the same cat returned, punctual as a postman. When she saw Jack and Willy, her eyes lit up with delight.

Willy trotted out with a saucer in his mouth and placed it before her. Jack added a piece of chicken. The cat ate slowly, stretched with elegance, then slipped away.

By the third day, Jack was no longer surprised. Willy ran inside, fetched a plate, and placed it in front of her. Jack added sardines.

"What's your name?" he asked, crouching beside her.

As usual, the cat said nothing. (She was a proper sort—when she wanted affection, she rubbed against you; but if you tried to touch her first, she remained still and aloof, like a little queen.)

Still, she came right on time every day. Jack chuckled.

"You're like a package," he said. "Can I call you Parcel?"

The cat blinked slowly—perhaps in agreement, or perhaps still savoring the sardines.

One afternoon, Jack found Parcel curled up like a croissant at the doorstep.

"Parcel," he said, petting her velvety head, "are you planning to stay for dinner? And... do you even want a home?"

Parcel tilted her head, her eyes deep with a question she wouldn't ask.

After offering her a saucer of beef, Jack said, "Well, if you're staying, you'd better wait just a pinch." He and Willy stepped back inside.

B. A Feathered Friend in Peril

That afternoon, Jack's mother came home from work, wrapped in the mysterious perfume of a fashion show.

"Jack," she said, pointing toward the door, "what's this about a cat?"

Jack told the tale—how Parcel had appeared like clockwork every day.

"I named her Parcel," he added, proud as could be.

Mom looked like she wanted to say something but instead stirred her tea with a quiet clink.

Later, when Dad got home, Jack retold the saga.

"But what if she doesn't want to leave?" he asked.

"Your mom used to adore cats," Dad said, crossing his arms. His thick glasses caught the light. "We had one long ago. It was hit by a car. She was heartbroken. Ever since, she's been afraid to love another."

Jack peeked into the kitchen. "Mom," he called, "Parcel is really well behaved. Can we keep her?"

Dad joined in. "Seems like she was delivered to us. Maybe it's time to accept the gift."

Mom sighed, then turned to Jack. "You already have a lot of responsibilities. If you really think you can care for Parcel—"

"I can!" Jack shouted before she could finish. "Really! Really, I can!"

Mom smiled softly, a mix of sweetness and sorrow. "Then... we can keep her."

"Thank you!" Jack whooshed out the front door. Parcel was still there, licking her paw. He scooped her up gently, kissed her soft black fur, and whispered, "Welcome home."

Parcel didn't answer, but she purred, slow and steady.

That evening, Jack and Lunibelle were chatting at the dinner table.

"Lunibelle," Jack said excitedly, "we have a new arrival at home today!"

"Parcel?" Lunibelle smiled.

"How did you know?"

"You've been telling me cat stories for several days straight. Who else could it be?" Lunibelle folded her arms, a confident sparkle in her eyes. "I couldn't wait to meet her!"

"Aren't you scared?" Jack asked.

"Don't worry. We'll be friends."

Jack went to the living room, picked up Parcel, and placed her on the table.

"Hello!" Lunibelle greeted.

MEOW—Parcel blinked slowly.

"What's your name?"

"Parcel."

"Interesting! I'm Lunibelle."

"Who delivered you here?" Lunibelle asked with a curious smile.

"I think..." Parcel closed her eyes as if remembering something deep, "my baby."

"Your baby delivered you here?" Jack asked, feeling like he'd just stepped into a philosophy class.

Parcel didn't answer, but her face held something—happiness and longing.

"How old are you?" Lunibelle asked, gently stroking the cat's glossy fur.

"Two years old," Parcel said, her voice growing bolder. "And you?"

"Oh, before the Big Bang."

"Before the Big Bun?" Parcel repeated, puzzled.

"That means very, very long ago!" Lunibelle laughed.

From then on, whenever Jack and Willy went out for a stroll, Parcel padded behind them—no leash, no coaxing. She followed like a quiet shadow.

Once, they were walking through the woods.

Without warning, Parcel leaped.

CRUNCH! went the leaves. THUMP! went Jack's heart.

Parcel crouched low, staring into the grass.

"What is it?" Jack stopped, dropping to his knees and parting the grass.

Cradled under golden leaves lay a bird, fragile as a cracked glass ball—a canary. Its feathers shimmered gold, messy and ruffled. One wing drooped. Its glossy black eyes blinked in fear.

It tried to hop—once, twice—each time stumbling. After a few brave flutters, it collapsed into the grass, its chest rising and falling as it gasped for breath.

"Oh, you poor flutter," Jack whispered. He gently placed it in his hand. The bird didn't resist. Jack felt its trembling bones and fast, frightened breath. "Don't worry," he whispered. "We'll look after you."

That night, the golden canary joined their little household.

Jack named the golden canary Yellowy.

Under everyone's gentle care, Yellowy's wing healed quickly. Soon, she was perching on the chandelier, singing off-key opera with delightful drama.

Sometimes, Yellowy would land on Willy's head, covering his eyes with her wings as he wandered in circles looking for meowing Parcel. He whirled like a wind-up toy unleashed until he flopped over, dizzy.

Everyone laughed.

Part II: A Cradle of Whispers and Wonder

A. The Meows Are Born

Parcel, Willy, Yellowy, and Lunibelle had become fast friends. Then one day, Parcel's belly began to look... rather balloonish.

"Mom," Jack said, eyes wide as teacup saucers, "is Parcel going to—?"

"Yes, dear," Mom replied with a knowing smile. "She's going to be a mama cat. Time to get ready."

When Jack told her, Lunibelle clapped her little translucent hands. "I love baby kittens!" she squealed. "They look like little clouds just learning how to float!"

Then came the day—Yellowy's squawk-tweet-screech woke Jack from a perfectly respectable dream about kittens.

Jack tiptoed to Parcel's box. It wasn't empty anymore.

Count them: one, two, three, four kittens. Their eyes were closed, their ears fluttered, their fur was sparse and soft.

Parcel was licking them gently.

Jack said nothing, afraid to startle the new arrivals. He simply nodded, solemn as a knight at the coronation of four furballs.

Later that day, Lunibelle came bouncing into the room. "I visited the nursery!" she chimed. "Parcel says the babies are named Meow1, Meow2, Meow3, and Meow4. It's a very efficient system."

Jack raised an eyebrow. "It is... simple. Do cats always name them like this?"

"We must always respect a mother's naming rights," said Lunibelle.

One afternoon, Lunibelle bounced over to Parcel's cozy corner for a visit. The kittens were nestled together in a heap, snoring gently.

"They're growing so fast!" Lunibelle exclaimed, eyes twinkling.

"All they do is eat and sleep," Parcel said with a sigh and a grin, her eyes brimming with that kind of love.

Suddenly, Lunibelle pointed. "Look at that yellow kitten! Her eyes are open! She's peeking at me like she knows all my secrets!"

"Oh, that's Meow1."

"Hello, Meow1!" Lunibelle waved like she was greeting a tiny queen. Then she paused. "Wait a minute... didn't you tell me yesterday that Meow1 was gray?"

Parcel leaned in close, whispering. "Yes. And now comes the mystery. I've discovered... kittens change color! They roll in dreams at night and wake up wearing new coats," Parcel added mysteriously.

Lunibelle gasped so hard she almost swallowed her own giggle.

"Really? Then how do you tell them apart? Do you sniff their souls?"

Parcel shrugged with motherly majesty. "I don't know how. But I always know who's who. Maybe it's my magical mother radar. Or maybe it's simply the way Meow2 snores in lowercase."

Lunibelle clapped her hands with delight. "When they grow up, you must put up a sign every morning," she declared, "that reads:

Ladies and gentlemen! Behold today's Kitten Colors and Patterns!
Meow1 is a tiny gray thundercloud.
Meow2 is a ginger firecracker with sideways tiger stripes.
Meow3 is a midnight cupcake, splattered with white polka dots.
Meow4 is pure snow, except for one smudge on her ear.

She pointed at the kittens and said, "Oh, and did you know Meow3's stripes only appear when she sneezes, and Meow4's ears are full of ghost whiskers that wiggle when nobody looks?"

Parcel burst into laughter, her tail flicking with joy. "They're not that complicated! They're just walking mysteries wrapped in fluff and mischief."

B. First Words in the Nursery

Since Parcel gave birth to four cute babies, Jack's home now housed eleven beings: Jack, Lunibelle, Mom, Dad, Willy, Parcel, four little Meows, and Yellowy. (Twelve, if you believed the refrigerator was magic—and Jack absolutely did.)

At dinner, Mom raised a forkful of salad and said, "Parcel needs her own quiet room now, just until the kittens grow a bit. Willy's a lovely dog, but he's also a bit... enthusiastic."

"But, Mom," Jack protested, "Parcel will feel lonely! Willy's her friend! And Yellowy sings to them every morning!"

Mom sighed. "I know, Jack. But new mothers can be nervous. We just want everyone to be safe. If someone's always home to supervise, maybe it's okay."

That night, Jack and Lunibelle hid in his bedroom. "Mom says we might need to separate Parcel," he said.

"I'm home all day, so I can watch over them. Let's test it for a few days. If everyone behaves like civilized animals, maybe we won't need to move anyone." Lunibelle said.

So Lunibelle became the nanny of the household.

Under her watchful sparkle, the kittens played, slept, and occasionally sneezed on each other. Willy behaved like a gentleman. Yellowy oversaw daily roll calls from the curtain rod. Parcel purred with the contentment of a cat who knew all her babies were adored.

Kittens grow fast. Soon they wobbled about on soft legs, looking like tumbling sock puppets in a comedy club.

One day, Meow4 suddenly blurted out the first sentence of his life: "Why am I Meow4 and not Meow1?"

Parcel was utterly speechless. A riddle from a kitten! She blinked slowly, her mind searching for an answer beyond the simple truth of numbers. She looked into his wide, searching eyes and knew her reply had to be more than just an answer; it had to be a story.

"Because you're Meow4, so you're Meow4," Meow1 cut in with her very first words, as if terrified Meow4 might steal her name.

"Because you were the last one born," Parcel finally said, counting her paws. "One, two, three, four—you popped out fourth."

"But why was I the fourth one out?"

That stumped Parcel.

Lunibelle was flipping through a picture book, glanced up. "Maybe you just snoozed a little longer in your mommy's tummy."

"Mommy! next time, you have to wake me up first!" Meow4 declared solemnly.

"Too late—you'll have to wait for the next time!" Meow1 lifted her chin triumphantly. Then she glanced down at herself. "Mama, I need a bath!" (Which, for kittens, meant being licked from head to tail.)

The commotion woke Meow2, who immediately made the first announcement of his life: "Mummy, I want a basketball!" (Heaven only knows how he even knew that word.)

"Hold on!" Lunibelle set her book aside. "I'll go find one."

Meow3 stretched with a lazy yawn.

"You're kicking my head!" Meow4 squeaked. "The youngest always gets bullied!"

Parcel was about to offer comfort when a slow, deliberate voice oozed out from the tangle of kittens.

"I am think..." Meow3 said.

Everyone froze. Had they heard that right?

"What did you say?" Yellowy fluttered down from the chandelier, landing lightly on the box.

"I am think..." Meow3 repeated.

"What are you thinking?" Yellowy blinked. Since when, exactly, did Meow3 think?

"What am I think?" Meow3 squinted. "I am think... about what I am think."

"Good gracious!" Yellowy's feathers puffed. "The more you talk, the less I understand!"

"She's philosophizing," Willy said, as if recalling some deep moment from his own youth.

Parcel was already feeling dizzy from the intellectual gymnastics when Lunibelle returned, a tiny glass ball cradled in her palms.

"Quick!" she smiled. "We'll need a philosopher's chair immediately! Rule number one of the nurseries: no kitten may philosophize without brushing their whiskers first!"

She paused in the doorway, eyes twinkling as she took in the pandemonium: the tangled kittens, Yellowy flapping feathers, Willy's shining eyes, and Parcel's frazzled fur.

With a graceful hop, she stepped into the room. "I'll take Meow2—he wants to bounce, right?" she said. With a practiced flick, she sent the glass ball sailing, catching it mid-spin.

"Willy, you're on Meow3 duty. Yellowy, Meow4's all yours." She turned to Parcel with a warm wink. "That leaves you free to give our royal Meow1 her bath."

In a blink, the chaos turned to choreography—each of them moving into place, Lunibelle at the helm.

Part III: Hockey in the Forest of Chair Legs

A. A Whirlwind Starts

One day at noon, in the living room, Willy squatted motionless as though a sphinx, pondering problems that didn't need pondering. Yellowy hung upside down from the chandelier, swinging gently like an ancient pendulum. Parcel wore glasses as she mended clothes, occasionally tossing love to the kittens with a glance above her lenses. The four kittens rolled across the floor like fuzzy, bouncing tennis balls.

Lunibelle had just ended a heartwarming conversation with her parents, who were overjoyed to hear she'd found a genuine friend and now had such beautiful new clothes. Their excitement bubbled over—they couldn't wait to visit and see her model her stylish outfits! With cheerful reassurance, they told her she could stay outside as long as she wanted, dressed up or in human clothes, as long as she was happy. Her presence in the living room was like a cool breeze drifting through dull woods.

"I've got an idea—a wonderful idea! How about we play a game?"

"Yay! Yay!" squealed the kittens.

"Let's play hockey!" Lunibelle hopped onto the cabinet, swinging an imaginary stick. "A real one!"

"I can eat lots of ice!" Meow4 declared.

"Hockey! Not an ice-eating contest!" Meow1 huffed. (Meow1 always refuted Meow4.) "You never listen properly!"

Meow4 opened his mouth to retort—

"Yellowy will be the referee, and I shall be the scorekeeper," Lunibelle announced, brandishing a notebook and a pencil. "Willy, Meow1, and Meow3 on Team One. Parcel, Meow2, and Meow4 on Team Two. The arena shall be... the dining room!"

"But the dining room's got too many legs—table legs, chair legs, human legs—wait, not human legs now," Willy pointed out.

"Exactly!" chirped Yellowy. "Four table legs, twenty-four chair legs. Twenty-eight obstacles!"

"This match will take place between the legs," Lunibelle confirmed. "That's what makes it fun!"

She retrieved a puck of ice from the refrigerator. "Each player strikes it with their tail. The ice leaves a wet trail. Only straight lines count. If it hits a leg, we stop the tape!"

"Where are goalposts?" Meow2 gestured with his two paws.

"Good question! This game is about distance, not destination."

"What if it melts?" Yellowy flapped her wings.

"I've got plenty in the refrigerator," Lunibelle replied. "I'll change it often."

"Official pre-match clarifications," Yellowy intoned, suddenly very grand. "One: points are measured in centimeters of glide. Two: straighter trails earn prouder chirps. Three: if the puck melts mid-glide, the ghost of the line still counts—because science."

Lunibelle clapped once. "And four: any dramatic meowing must be submitted to the referee in triplicate."

The kittens gasped as though paperwork were spookier than ice.

"Team huddle!" Willy barked softly. "We chase calm. We do not chase chairs."

Parcel nodded, adjusting her invisible coach's cap.

B. Beautiful Chaos

In the dining room, under the table, everyone had already taken their positions. They were very excited and ready to start this unprecedented competition. The game was about to begin; every tail was raised high, just waiting.

Lunibelle stood at the table corner, and Yellowy hovered with the puck.

"Ready!"

"Three... two... one... DROP!"

The puck fell.

Meow1 charged—but missed, tail slicing air. "Oops," she muttered.

Meow4 skidded forward, bumping into Meow2. "You're on my team!" Meow2 yowled.

"Oh no!" squeaked Meow4. "I forgot!"

"First strike—nothing! Second—collision! Third—uh-oh!" Yellowy quickly called.

Parcel nudged the puck with a flick. "Six centimeters—recorded!"

"First score! Or... maybe not!" Yellowy's voice rose an octave.

Willy leaped in, but his tail swept the puck under a chair.

"Out of bounds!" Yellowy raised one wing.

Meow3 tapped it lightly. It spun in a slow spiral. "Three centimeters," Yellowy shouted.

It went on like this: Meow1 hit the puck backward. Meow2 sat on it. Meow3 struck it, only for it to bounce off her paw. Meow4 tripped over Meow1. Parcel kept yelling, "Other way, kittens!" More than once, Meow2 cheered—only to realize the puck hadn't moved.

Willy tried to help. "Left, Meow1! LEFT!" But Meow1 turned right.

"Everyone's in the wrong place!" moaned Yellowy. "This chaos needs a shape!"

"Formation?" Meow4 asked. "Is that a snack?"

Despite the mayhem, a few decent strikes occurred:

"Parcel—eight centimeters!"

"Willy—seven!"

"Meow4... blocked her own teammate!"

"Meow1—nice flick! Five centimeters!"

There were collisions. Meow-outs. Long pauses when no one remembered whose turn it was. Yellowy zipped around, wings fluttering.

"Team Two—four centimeters!"

"Team One—six!"

"Team Two lost the puck behind the plant!"

"I found it!" Meow2 cried, holding it in his mouth.

"No teeth!" Yellowy scolded.

Lunibelle scribbled furiously. "Note to future historians," she announced. "Match One proves that rules are suggestions, chairs have gravity, and Meow2 believes pucks are snacks."

After what felt like both ten minutes and forever, Lunibelle shouted, "Time's up!" Everyone collapsed, fur and feathers strewn like confetti.

Yellowy fluttered to Lunibelle's notebook. "Final score," she announced. "Team One: twenty-four centimeters. Team Two: twenty-five centimeters."

The kittens blinked.

"That's... it?" Meow1 thought she herself got more points than that.

"I am think..." Meow3 offered. "We tried our best!"

"That was just the first match," said Lunibelle kindly. "Next time, you'll know how it works."

Willy wagged his tail. "Let's do it together. We'll get better."

"And next match," added Yellowy, "no sitting on the puck."

Everyone nodded.

Yellowy lifted off and declared, "Let it be recorded in the official Hockey History: Team One—twenty-four points. Team Two—twenty-five points. The closest of games, in the most tangled of forests!"

Parcel purred and licked Meow2's forehead. "It was beautiful chaos," she said with confidence. "And the next game will be even more beautiful."

Part IV: Knotted Tails and Tug-of-War

A. The Tangled Tails Incident

Before the second game began, Yellowy cleared her throat. "In order to improve reporting speed and accuracy," she declared, "there will be no more 'Meow' before numbers. So: 1 is Meow1, 2 is Meow2, 3 is Meow3, and 4 is Meow4."

"So... are we still cats?" Meow4 asked, scratching his head.

"Call you Woof4, and you'd still be a cat," Meow1 muttered, rolling her eyes.

The match began with a tail-thwack—Meow2 struck the puck. "Six centimeters on the record!" Yellowy chirped.

"Following the first match," she added with professional flair, "the players have dramatically leveled up! They judge the puck's path better, dash quicker between chair legs—especially 1, 2, 3, and 4! And let's not forget Willy and Parcel, swift as shadows on the outer edge!"

"Look at that puck!" she exclaimed. "It's bounced off three legs and changed direction thrice—as if it had a mind of its own and didn't fancy being hit. 1 finally catches up—strike! Seven centimeters! Super cool!"

Meow3 and Meow4 zipped from opposite sides to pounce—but just as they leaped, the puck clipped a table leg and flew through the gap between them. The kittens spun like mismatched gears in a clock gone silly, struck—and tangled.

Their tails had twisted into a perfect bowknot.

"STOP!" cried Yellowy, flapping wildly. "This is a first in ice-hockey history—tails entangled mid-match! I repeat: entangled tails!"

The two kittens waddled in opposite directions—you in, I out—but the knot only tightened.

"Relax! Relax!" Yellowy instructed. "3 to the left! 4 to the right! No, no—the other right!"

The others gathered around in a flurry of suggestions.

"Pull to the center!"

"No, spin like a top!"

"Climb the table leg!"

"Dangerous! Roll like dough!"

Meow3 and Meow4 squirmed, spun, slumped—but their tails remained knotted. Exhausted, they flopped to the floor.

"Mooommy," mewed Meow4 tearfully, "am I... turning into Meow3?"

"Muuum," mewed Meow3, "I am think... but I don't want to be Meow4!"

Parcel gently patted both of them. "You'll always be yourselves. Meow3 is Meow3. Meow4 is Meow4."

Yellowy crossed her wings solemnly. "This is an event of historical magnitude. Never before seen!"

Lunibelle knelt beside the knot, eyes shining. "Identity may tangle," she whispered, "but names never leak. We'll unknot the problem and keep the kittens."

Willy saluted with his tail. "Coach, say the word."

Parcel adjusted her imaginary whistle. "Team, prepare for silliness and science."

B. You Are Still You

During the game, the tails of Meow3 and Meow4 were unfortunately—and spectacularly—tangled together. It was less of a tangle and more of a declaration of tail unity, as if their fuzzy limbs had decided to be one.

After several failed attempts to separate them, Lunibelle stepped in with a clipboard in her hand.

"Operation: De-Tangle is now in session," she declared. "Codename: Fuzzy Tug-o'-War!"

Parcel tilted her head. "What happened to Codename: Nap Time?"

"That was scrapped due to tail complications," Lunibelle replied. "We need strength, coordination, and questionable logic. Everyone, into position!"

She gave instructions. "Meow2, hug Meow4! Parcel, hug Meow2! Meow1, you hug Meow3!"

"What about me?" asked Willy, paw in the air.

"You hug Meow1."

"What if I want to hug Meow2?" Meow1 asked.

"You can switch at halftime," Lunibelle said.

Yellowy zipped to the ceiling and raised one wing. "On my count! Everyone ready?"

"I was born ready," said Meow1.

"I was born to nap," said Meow3. "But I am think... I'm ready."

"GO! Three... two... one... PULL!"

Everyone yanked.

POP! Meow2's paws slipped, Parcel fell backward into a chair leg, and Willy accidentally smooched the flower vase. The vase swooned, tipped, and landed in Meow1's lap like a fainting diva.

"Reset!" Yellowy trilled.

New positions.

"Let's revise the lineup," Lunibelle said, consulting her clipboard. "Parcel and Willy, you're the anchors—strong, fluffy, and occasionally sensible."

"Thank you," said Parcel and Willy in unison.

"Meow1, hug Willy. Willy hugs Meow3." Lunibelle ran to this side. "Meow2, hug Parcel. Parcel hugs Meow4." Lunibelle ran to that side. "That makes a purring-pulling pattern. Got it?"

They all nodded.

Yellowy raised her wing once more. "Ready! Set! TUG!"

They pulled with gusto.

SNAP!—not of the tails, but of the curtain rod, as Yellowy flapped too hard from excitement. The curtain landed over Meow4, who shouted, "I'm lost in the fog of war!"

Lunibelle rescued him with a single swoosh of her pinky finger.

"Last try! No hiccups, no distractions, no theatrical curtains!" she cried.

Everyone took their place again, more determined than ever. A hush fell.

"Three... two... one... PUUUUULLLLL!"

They swayed as if a wobbly bridge in a windy canyon. Everyone leaned, grunted, gasped, and growled in adorable effort.

Suddenly—POP!

The tails untwisted so forcefully that Meow3 and Meow4 flew backward like startled frogs. They rolled, bounced, and finally flopped into a heap of triumph and tail freedom.

"I'm not her!" shouted Meow4.

"I am think... I'm me again!" shouted Meow3.

Everyone burst into cheers.

"Celebrate with sardines!" yelled Meow2, who hadn't actually done much but felt celebratory anyway.

Yellowy flapped triumphantly and scribbled in her scroll with her beak. "Let the official records state: *Tail Entanglement Resolved by Collective Wiggling, Round Three.*"

Parcel licked Meow4's ear with relief, and Lunibelle patted Meow4.

"Match resumes!" Yellowy declared.

The players raced back into place, slightly dizzy but determined. The puck zipped past chair legs.

Team One struck—ten centimeters! Team Two answered—eleven!

Whiskers twitched. Tails swished. Even Meow3 temporarily

stopped philosophizing long enough to chase the puck with abandon.

When the final whistle blew—actually Yellowy yelling "THE END!" as loud as possible—they collapsed into a joyful heap once again.

Yellowy descended slowly. "Final score for round two: Team One—thirty-two! Team Two—thirty-one!"

A gasp. Then—

"WE DID IT!" howled Willy.

"ONE POINT! VICTORY BY A WHISKER!" shouted Meow1, literally measuring a whisker against the scoreboard.

Parcel purred, tail lifted high. "This game had everything—strategy, knots, synchronized tumbling, and at least two logical crises."

"And let it be known," Yellowy trilled, "that in the heart of the dining-room forest, with twenty-eight legs and zero logic, a game was played. Tails were tested. But triumph—triumph wagged its tail and won."

Lunibelle closed the notebook with a satisfied snap. "Post-match note," she said. "Identity crisis: solved. Team spirit: upgraded. Curtain rods: status uncertain."

Part V: The Vanishing Puck and the Final Laughter

A. The Fastest Game on Earth

The chaos had settled—for now—but magic, like ice, has a way of slipping away when you least expect it. And so, the final match began.

No one announced it. No one even blew a whistle (except Yellowy, who occasionally tooted into a straw just for flair). But everyone knew this was the one—the last game, the grand finale, the spectacular conclusion to the most tangled, tail-thwacked tournament anyone had ever seen.

The players took their places. Tails high. Eyes sharp. Paws itchy with anticipation. Yellowy hovered above the table.

"Final match! All paws on deck!" She dropped the puck—a fresh, shining disk of ice—and it spun through the air.

"GOOOOOOO!" shouted Lunibelle, holding her pencil like a sword. "Game on!"

Meow1 was first to launch—tail flicked like a slingshot, and the puck zipped forward.

"Eight centimeters!" Yellowy chirped. "Spectacular opening strike!"

It bounced off a table leg—PING!—ricocheted left and darted toward Meow2. He bolted, zigzagging between two chair legs.

A swipe!

"Oh no! Missed!" Yellowy called, spinning midair.

Meow3 slid in sideways. "Incoming!" she shouted and—WHACK!—six centimeters! The puck hissed across the floor.

Willy pounced. Tail—THWACK! "Five centimeters more!" yelled Lunibelle.

The puck flew like a comet. Meow1 leaped into action. Meow4 bounded after her, tripping over his own paws. Meow2 joined in, bumping into both.

"Such reflexes!" Yellowy cried. "If a mouse showed up, it wouldn't stand a chance!"

The puck danced between chair legs. It bounced once, twice, changed direction, and zoomed under the china cabinet.

"I've got it!" shouted Meow4. "No—I lost it! Wait—I sat on it!"

"Puck location confirmed," said Yellowy. "Please do not use your butt as storage!"

Meow4 stood, and Meow3 immediately struck it again—seven centimeters!

"I haven't even had a turn!" Meow2 shouted, chasing after the puck.

"Then hurry!" yelled Meow1. "I just spun three times for nothing!"

The puck rolled toward Parcel, who sat poised and graceful. Her tail snapped—

"Eight centimeters!" Yellowy trilled. "Parcel performs with elegance and danger!"

Lunibelle clapped. "Marvelous strike! That one gets a sparkle on the scoreboard!"

Willy barked once, a bark of righteous determination. He crouched low, legs twitching.

"Go, Willy!" Meow1 cheered.

He charged. Tail—THWACK!

"BOOM!" cried Yellowy. "Five centimeters—plus a magnificent skid!"

Willy spun in a triumphant circle and bumped into the plant.

"Foul on the fern!" Lunibelle called, giggling.

Yellowy zipped back and forth overhead. "This is the fastest game on Earth! Possibly the fastest game in the solar system! Faster than the legendary Teapot Olympics of 1842! The puck is now under Chair Two—no, Chair Three! No—Chair Five!"

Meow3 zoomed through the chair legs. She leaped, tail slicing the air—WHAP!

"Seven centimeters!" yelled Lunibelle.

Meow2 dove and missed, rolled, stood up, and shouted, "I'm on defense now!"

"You were always on defense," said Meow1.

"No, I was in denial!" Meow2 replied.

The puck slipped past everyone and headed straight for Meow4, who froze. The puck gleamed. Meow4 twitched. Then—WHACK!

"NINE CENTIMETERS!" roared Yellowy. "Speed! Precision! Complete surprise!"

Meow4 blinked. "Did I do that?"

"Yes," said Parcel, eyes wide. "And you didn't sit on it this time."

The puck shot out the other side of the table, zipped past Lunibelle's footstool, rolled through a napkin fort, and rebounded off a spoon.

"Physics has left the building!" cried Yellowy.

"Forget physics!" Meow3 shouted. "I'm chasing chaos!"

Lunibelle could barely keep up with her notes. "They're playing faster than I can write! My pencil is melting!"

Everyone surged toward the final strike. Meow1 lunged. Meow2 dived. Meow3 twirled. Meow4 slid in backward, squealing. Willy launched. Parcel glided.

The puck flew straight up into the air—and vanished.

Just like that. Gone. No trace.

Everyone froze. A full second passed.

"Did it melt midair?" Meow2 whispered.

"Did I imagine the whole thing?" said Meow1, blinking.

"Where's the puck?" said Parcel.

And just like that, the fastest game on Earth had ended—not with a goal, not with a cheer, but with the puck vanishing into thin air, as if it had played its part and slipped away forever, retiring into mystery.

B. Three Winding Centimeters

At the most crucial moment of the third game—the puck suddenly vanished. Not melted. Not shattered. Not sneakily licked up by Meow4. Gone. POOF.

Yellowy froze midair, flapping so hard.

"Where's the puck?!" cried Parcel.

Willy sniffed the floorboards, the sofa legs, even his own tail (twice), just to be thorough.

Lunibelle flipped through her notebook, as if the puck might be hiding between its pages.

"It's not under Chair Two," announced Meow2, who was lying on his back, staring at the ceiling. "Unless it's hiding up."

"Hiding up?" Meow1 squinted.

"Upside-down hiding," he said with great authority.

Yellowy looped through the air. "This is the strangest event! The puck has... disappeared! I swear by my golden tail feathers—it was right there a moment ago!"

"The puck has been taken by invisible spirits!" Meow4 wailed dramatically, flopping onto his side.

"Don't be ridiculous," Meow1 retorted. "Spirits don't play hockey. They play checkers."

"I am think..." said Meow3 huskily, blinking slowly. "I... I may have... swallowed it."

Silence.

Then Yellowy, voice trembling, asked, "Swallowed... what?"

Meow3 tried to sit up straight but hiccupped instead. "I am think... it was mid-flight... the puck bounced off Chair Five... shot into my mouth... and then..." She gulped, dramatically. "Right into my throat. No stops. No layovers."

Everyone held their breath.

Lunibelle rushed over and tapped Meow3's tummy. "Any ice noises in there?"

"I am think... I feel... slightly chilled."

Yellowy flapped higher, drawing a formal scroll from her feather pouch. "This is an official moment in Hockey History. Write this down! The puck has entered Meow3's digestive system. Unprecedented! Unseen! Unchewable!"

"I am think..." Meow3 raised one paw proudly. "Does the distance from my mouth to my belly count as three centimeters?"

Lunibelle and Yellowy exchanged glances.

"Sadly," Lunibelle said, "that's not a straight line. It's got... digestive curves."

"No score for Meow3's belly," Yellowy confirmed, scribbling in her scroll.

"I am think... this was the most unusual goal in hockey."

"Bah!" grumbled Meow4. "My mouth is just as good at swallowing. I could've done that with my tongue tied and my eyes closed."

"You try next time," Meow1 replied calmly. "But I recommend chewing first."

C. Awarded Glories

With the puck now irrevocably inside Meow3's stomach, and all freezers emptied of spare ice due to overuse and an earlier ice-sculpture experiment involving a carrot and a shoe, Lunibelle stood atop a footstool.

"Game over!" she declared. "And what a finale!"

Yellowy fluttered to Lunibelle's shoulder. "Final score for this round: Team One—thirty-six, Team Two—thirty-six!"

The kittens sat up straight.

"A tie?" said Meow2.

"A double victory!" Yellowy trilled.

"I am think..." said Meow3 wisely. "Which is better than a triple defeat."

"And less confusing than a quadruple sneeze," Meow4 added.

The entire room burst into applause. Tails slapped the floor, paws waved in the air, and Yellowy tooted a note on a miniature whistle made of a pasta noodle.

Lunibelle stepped forward. "Now, let the Official Awards Ceremony begin!"

Yellowy opened a tiny golden envelope and read:

Meow1 — Best Corner Turner Award

Meow2 — Most Frequently Toppled Player Award

Meow3 — Most Likely to Swallow a Puck Award

Meow4 — Most Tangled Tail Award

Parcel — Best Right-Side Outer Player Award

Willy — Best Left-Side Outer Player Award

Yellowy — Fastest Commentator in the Universe Award

Lunibelle — Most Devoted Spectator with Excellent Fashion Sense Award

"I want..." Meow4 just began, but his words were lost in the swell of cheers.

The cats, the dog, the bird, the alien, and the magical moment all curled together beneath the table—an arena of legs, laughter, and legends.

Above them, the chairs stood still, and the air glittered with memory. And though the puck was long gone, its icy spirit lingered.

"Lesson of the match," Lunibelle announced. "When you tie tails, you untie hearts—and when you swallow the puck, you still win."

Chapter V
The World Without Math

Part I: The Day the Numbers Wave Goodbye

After walking his loyal dog, Willy—who was not just a dog but occasionally a philosopher—Jack returned home with wind in his hair and mud on his socks. His shoes squelched as he stepped into the hallway, leaving tiny muddy footprints.

As was his ritual, he plucked a bright orange sticky note from the refrigerator—where messages tended to stick like weird thoughts.

Yogurt is in the fridge, don't forget to eat it.—Written in Mom's usual script: graceful, loopy, and not unlike the handwriting of a ballerina tiptoeing across the page.

Beneath that, in bold, tilted letters, was Dad's Daily Riddle.

"Addition, subtraction, multiplication, and division—who invented these strange symbols?" Jack thought. "They give me a headache." He frowned, grabbed a pencil, and snatched up a crumpled bit of paper. "Let's see... one... no, wait—two... or is it zero?!" he exclaimed. "Three different answers! How wonderfully frustrating!"

He fluffed up his hair (which didn't help at all) and called out, "Willy! Come quick! I need your brilliant brain!"

"I was just stretching my thinking paws," said Willy, flopping loyally beside Jack with an expression that clearly said: *Professor Willy is on the case.*

Jack leaned in, eyes wide. "I've already gotten two riddles wrong this month. I promised Dad I wouldn't miss five—and this one's looking awfully tricksy. I need you."

Willy tilted his head—first left, then right, then in a perfect circle, as if stirring ideas with his ears.

Just then, a crisp, chiming voice piped down from the top of the refrigerator: "Good day, Jack! Hello, Willy! Are you decoding secrets again?"

With a flutter and a poof, Lunibelle appeared, leaping down from her perch atop the refrigerator. She landed perfectly in the center of Jack's palm.

She had a silvery glow, soft and luminous, with two jet-black eyes and a smile so gently curved it seemed to have been sketched by a playful hand.

"What's all the scribbling?" she asked, peering at the paper.

"It's a math puzzle," Jack sighed, pointing at the string of tangled numbers. "Dad writes one every day. If I get it right, I earn three chocolate buttons!" He gestured dramatically to a jar of glittering candy.

"Oooh, that explains it!" Lunibelle said with a grin, twirling midair. "I ate the buttons yesterday. Sorry, Jack! They tasted like secret equations—delicious but a bit crunchy."

"It's all right," Jack muttered, cheeks pink. "The buttons were innocent."

"Do you find math tricky?" Lunibelle asked, tapping her foot in the air.

"Not... really," Jack replied.

"Then why don't you like it?"

"I don't think it's hard," Jack said. "I really don't like it. It's all too... mathemagical."

"Too what now?" Lunibelle giggled.

"Mathemagical! You know—mysterious symbols, secret rules, invisible lines. It's like a magician's spellbook written in numbers."

"So that's why you summoned the noble brain of Sir Willy?"

"If I could live in a land where math didn't exist," Jack said wistfully, "I'd be very happy. I'd hand in a test with absolutely nothing on it and say, 'There are no numbers on the paper because math doesn't live here!' And I'd get full marks for honesty."

Lunibelle asked, "Would you really like to visit a place like that?"

Willy, who had been sniffing Jack's socks thoughtfully, nodded vigorously.

"Well then," Lunibelle mused, "we should bring Willy, Yellowy, and the Parcel family."

"Where are we going?" Jack asked, eyes widening.

"To the land without math," Lunibelle said, patting Willy. "Go fetch Yellowy and Parcel's family."

Willy bounded off.

"Really?" Jack asked, excitement bubbling. "For how long?"

"Long enough to forget about multiplication tables," Lunibelle replied.

Soon Willy returned, Parcel's family padding in behind him, and

Yellowy fluttering down to perch on Jack's shoulder.

"Okay," Jack said, sitting cross-legged on the floor. "What now?"

"Everyone sit down," Lunibelle said seriously. "And don't move!"

A gust of wind blew in. Then came a white fog—a swirl of starlight—and the mist grew thicker and thicker.

The refrigerator let out a soft chime. The sticky notes fluttered, waving goodbye.

The air filled with a light, floral scent. Everything beyond the fog vanished. Jack felt a tug behind his belly button, as if the universe had looped him on a yo-yo string and flicked him away with its wrist.

After a moment, the white mist began to thin.

The kitchen vanished. So did the refrigerator. And the sticky notes. And the tangled math riddle. All gone. All replaced by something altogether... otherworldly.

And so, begins the adventure.

Part II: The Wobbly House of Hoofys

Jack opened his eyes and blinked—then blinked again. The world was warped.

This place was deeply strange. An irregular square sun blazed in the sky. The clouds were unequal triangles. A clock floated, ticking backward. A stream burbled past, its water flowing uphill and singing a skipped-number alphabet.

"Where is the kitchen?" Meow4's eyes went wide. "Oh no—where are we?"

Silence.

"I am think…" said Meow3, turning her head slowly. "We are precisely where we stand."

They faced the gates of a peculiar park, its iron bars woven with impossible shapes—circles that never closed, spirals that twisted into themselves. A whisper hung in the air: "Here, there are no counts, no sums, no chains of reason." Beyond those bars lay a world where time frayed at the edges, and the very air resisted the tyranny of numbers.

A banner hung above the gate: ***WELCME TO HE WRLD WITHOT MAH!***

"Strange!" Yellowy fluttered around it, frowning. "Is this even English?"

"I guess," Willy replied like an ancient archaeologist, "it means: *WELCOME TO THE WORLD WITHOUT MATH!*"

"I'm finally here!" Jack grinned.

"Aha!" Lunibelle's eyes twinkled. "Let's take a peek inside, shall we?"

And no sooner had they stepped forward than—CREEEEEAK!—the gate swung open all on its own.

Beyond it, soft blue grass stretched into the distance. Trees walked from place to place. Flowers changed color in a flash. Signs spun like gyroscopes, their arrows looping endlessly.

They wandered carefully into Whimblewood Forest, where trees mumbled nonsense, Butterflies flitted about with one wing shaped like triangles and the other like rhombuses. and squirrels napped upside down on branches.

This was a grand adventure to nowhere in particular—the very best kind.

Suddenly—THUNK! Followed by a KER-SPLOINK! A crashing noise ripped through the trees.

"Did you hear that?" Jack asked.

"Like a big tree being chopped down," Lunibelle nodded.

They tiptoed closer, peeking through a curtain of candy-vine leaves.

What they saw made them blink twice and rub their eyes, just to be sure.

Three plumpish creatures—round as marshmallows, bouncy as rubber balls—were tumbling over heaps of wood, saws, ladders, and a collapsed roof. They were blueberry-colored, wearing yellow tool belts, covered in sawdust, and thoroughly confused.

These were the Hoofys. And they were very busy being busy.

"Hoofy Two! Your pillar is much too short!" shouted Hoofy One, pointing a stubby finger at a drooping post.

"It's not my pillar that's short," huffed Hoofy Two. "It's your beam that's too short!"

"Your materials are always the wrong kind of wrong!" Hoofy One retorted, waving a banana-shaped plank.

"Can you make one straight beam?" snapped Hoofy Two.

Before the argument could reach maximum fluster, Hoofy Three—who had been hammering a door into the middle of a wall frame—looked up.

"Stop all that arguing and get back to building! Except..." He held up the door and frowned. "...why doesn't this fit?"

"This place is weird!" Meow4 pointed at the structure. "That's just half a house!"

"I am think..." Meow3 predicted gravely, "it will collapse if the wind blows."

At that moment, the leaves began to rustle. The wind rose. The branches trembled.

Then—

The house began to shake.

"Hold the house!" Hoofy One shouted. They dropped the boards and pressed their backs against the shuddering wall.

The wind howled louder. "You two stay here!" Hoofy One called out, hair flying. "I'll go over there!"

"We go together!" Jack was already running.

Lunibelle charged after him. Willy barked and bounded behind them. Parcel and the four kittens followed. Overhead, Yellowy zipped through the air.

When they reached the swaying wall, they braced themselves against it.

"Push!" Lunibelle shouted. "We hold it—until we can't!"

The wind slammed against them. WHOOSH—WHOOSH—WHOOSH! CREAK! CREAK! The wall lurched again, more violently this time.

"Mommy!" Meow4 screamed, voice full of terror.

"Take the kittens and get away!" Jack cried out. "Now—go!"

"Follow Mommy!" Parcel yowled, her voice whipped thin by the wind. She waved her wings frantically, rounding up the kittens.

They ran.

CLANG! A board snapped off the roof and crashed to the ground.

"The house is going to fall!" Hoofy Two cried out.

"EVERYONE LISTEN!" Lunibelle shouted, her voice cutting through the wind. "When I count to one—we run. No waiting. No questions!"

The Hoofys nodded. Jack nodded. Willy growled low and steady. He nodded too.

The wall tilted sharply. The window frame fell with a crash. The door split in half and hit the ground with a thud.

"LUNIBELLE! JACK! WILLY!" the kittens called out from the hill.

"Run! Please run!" Parcel hugged them close.

Lunibelle's eyes narrowed. "Three..." She locked eyes with Jack. "Two..."

Yellowy braced herself on Jack's shoulder, wings trembling.

Suddenly—

The wind stopped. The trembling halted.

Silence.

The house stood—barely.

The Hoofys collapsed in a heap, panting.

"Almost the thirty-first time," Hoofy Three muttered, wheezing. "Almost the thirty-first time!"

Lunibelle and Jack approached them slowly, hearts still pounding.

"Thirty-first time what?" Lunibelle asked gently.

Hoofy Two sighed. "It's already fallen thirty times."

Jack blinked. "What! How?"

Hoofy Three sat up. "Since our great-great-great-Hoofy hammered the first splinter," he said, "we've been building this house.

Over and over again. And it keeps falling."

"But... why?" Jack asked.

"We're building a house!" declared Hoofy One proudly, as it were the most obvious thing in the world.

"We've always been building it," added Hoofy Two, rubbing a scraped elbow.

Jack nodded slowly, still puzzled—but more curious than ever.

Part III: The Second Time Is the Charm after the Thirtieth Fall

Lunibelle examined the structure. If it were a hat, it would fall off your head. If it were a cake, it would slide right off the plate.

"It's got three walls, one corner, half a staircase, and no roof," she observed.

"And the staircase goes sideways," Jack added, walking forward, carefully avoiding it with his foot.

"That's the feature wall!" Hoofy One said proudly.

"It features... a wall," added Hoofy Two.

Hoofy Three nodded with great wisdom. "It's modern design. Very advanced."

"But... why is it all lopsided?" Lunibelle pointed at the tilted beams.

"It's fallen over thirty times," sighed Hoofy Two. "If it didn't keep falling, we'd be living in it already."

"Don't you measure the wood before you build?" Jack asked, holding up a plank shaped like a crescent moon.

"We don't use numbers here," said Hoofy Three.

"We use the ancient art of guessery," said Hoofy One, striking a heroic pose.

"We squint and guess like champions!" said Hoofy Two, shutting one eye and holding a plank to the sky.

Lunibelle blinked. "So... no rulers? No blueprints? No plans at all?"

The Hoofys looked at one another, then at Lunibelle.

"Plans? Blue? Rulers?" they said in perfect unison. "Never heard of them. Are they tasty?"

"No," Jack said, trying not to laugh. "They're tools you use to make sure things are the right size and shape."

"Can you show us?" Hoofy One asked, wide-eyed with curiosity.

"We'd be ever so grateful," said Hoofy Two.

"And we might even make cookies afterward!" promised Hoofy Three.

Jack and Lunibelle nodded.

Out came pencils and paper, rulers, and string. Jack sketched a proper blueprint, while Lunibelle taught the Hoofys how to measure twice before cutting once.

There were hiccups, of course. Hoofy Two used the ruler as a sword and challenged a squirrel to a duel. Hoofy Three tried to eat the pencil. Hoofy One kept holding the blueprint upside down and insisted it was a treasure map.

But eventually, they got the hang of it. They measured. They marked. They cut straight planks. They began building straight walls.

The cats joined in to help. They stretched ropes taut so the walls could line up properly.

After a while—

"Let's jump rope!" Meow2 (he is very sporty) declared, full of energy.

So the kittens began to jump rope, chanting:

Meow1 runs, Meow2 spins, Meow3 jumps, Meow4 grins,
Whiskers twitch and tails fly high,
Kittens leap beneath the sky!

They were having such fun, they completely forgot about the construction.

"Straighten the rope!" Willy barked, supervising like a general. "No more jumping—hold that line straight!"

At last, when the final nail was hammered in, the Hoofys stepped back and gasped.

"Our house!" cried Hoofy One.

"It's not falling over!" squealed Hoofy Two.

"And the door opens in only one direction!" Hoofy Three shouted in amazement.

The three of them bounced and spun in dizzy circles, chanting, "Our house! Our house! OUR HOUSE!"

Tears welled in their eyes. After so many generations, the house was finally standing. Not only standing—but standing tall.

They invited Jack, Lunibelle, and all the animals inside for a grand tour.

There was a wibbly-wobbly painting of a turnip on the wall, a staircase-slide (on purpose this time), and a chandelier made entirely of glass cups.

"We even made a room for blueprints," Hoofy One said, proudly showing it off.

"And a room to measure sock-length in giggles or gummy bears," added Hoofy Two, practically glowing.

"And a room where we guess what each room is for!" exclaimed Hoofy Three with delight.

Everyone burst out laughing.

"Congratulations!" said Lunibelle.

Part IV: The Singing Corn That Vanishes

After the grand success of helping the Hoofys build their first-ever upright house, Jack, Lunibelle, and the pets wandered merrily along a curving path that wriggled through Whimblewood.

Before long, they came upon a golden sea of corn stretching so far it tickled the horizon. Standing solemnly at the edge of the field were three tall, spindly creatures—yellow as buttered popcorn and shaped rather like corn cobs themselves. Each wore faded overalls, frayed straw hats perched atop their heads, and frowns etched deep with worry.

One held a hoe. The second clutched a rake. The third carried a woven basket with only three lonely kernels rattling inside.

"Hello!" Jack called out, stepping forward.

"Oh... greetings," the tallest of the trio replied gloomily.

They all looked rather tangled in thought.

"What are you doing here, looking so glum—and glummer?" Jack asked.

"Is something amiss in this golden kingdom of corn?" added Lunibelle.

The tallest corn-cob creature gave a long, leaf-rustling sigh and pointed a finger toward the glowing field.

"It's the corn," he claimed. "Always the corn."

"It's gorgeous!" Lunibelle gasped. "Look how it shimmers—it's like a treasure made of sunshine!"

"We are the Qoofy Brothers," said the tall one. "Farmers of corn from a line as long as a dragon's tail. Our ancestors planted this field, and we live for the corn."

The second Qoofy, who was balancing a particularly shiny cob in his palm, added, "Look at it! Golden and plump, each kernel like a tiny gold coin. Smell it—it's sweeter than any perfume!"

The third Qoofy gazed out lovingly over the swaying stalks. "The corn loves us too—for when we walk among them, they sing. Would you like to hear their song?"

And with that, the Qoofy Brothers began to sing in soft voices, like the rustle of dry leaves.

WHISH-A-WHOOSH, WHISH-A-WAY,

Here comes the sun, and so we sway.

We grow up tall, with kernels round,

We fill the bins with a rusty sound.

WHISH-A-WHOOSH, WHISH-A-GLEE,

We fill the barns so happily!

A scarecrow at the field's edge waved its head along with the rhythm.

"We harvest every day," said Qoofy Two, swelling with pride.

"And carry it to the old barn by the edge of the field," added Qoofy Three.

"We work hard," said Qoofy One. "We dreamed of corn mountains, reaching for the rafters. But alas—" he paused dramatically.

"Alas!" all three cried together.

"The corn disappears!" Qoofy Two pounded the ground with his hoe.

"A thief in the night!" shouted Qoofy Three, shaking his rake.

"A corn criminal!" bellowed Qoofy One, stomping his boot.

They told their tale in tumble-jumble.

"We found a strand of gray hair," Qoofy Two murmured, his voice tight with suspicion. "Right here—not far from the old barn. Looks like Old Gray Wolf's."

Qoofy One snatched the hair from his fingers, rolling it between his own calloused thumb and forefinger. His nostrils flared. "It is Old Gray Wolf's!" he barked, as if the very idea of doubt offended him. "Who else around here has hair like this? Coarse as wire, gray as storm clouds—it's him, no question!"

Qoofy Three leaned closer, his voice dropping to a conspiratorial whisper. "Then it's just as we thought. Under cover of night—when the shadows were thick enough to hide a ghost—he slithered in."

His fingers mimed a creeping motion. "Stuffed his bag full... and ran away."

The three of them fell silent, the weight of the discovery settling over them. Somewhere in the distance, a crow cawed—a sharp, mocking sound.

At their feet, a line of kernels pointed one way, while their husks pointed the other, as if the field itself couldn't agree on directions.

"We confronted him," Qoofy One continued, "but he asked me, 'Where are your records? Where is your evidence?'"

"We don't do numbers!" cried Qoofy Two. "We feel the corn!"

"We listen to it!" added Qoofy Three.

"So we took him to court," said Qoofy One.

"But the judge asked for evidence," added Qoofy Two. "How many did you harvest? How many were stolen? Where are your records?"

"We had none!" shouted all three at once.

"The wolf smirked. The judge shrugged. He was declared—"

"—Innocent!"

Part V: Gavel Raises in the Pumpkin Court

The court's decision had emboldened Old Gray Wolf.

"He still steals corn," whispered Qoofy Three, eyes brimming. "And now he steals even more!"

Jack clenched his fists. "We can't let this stand—not on our ears, our noses, or even our toes!"

"What can we do?" asked Qoofy One, raising hopeful eyes.

Lunibelle straightened her shoulders. "From this day forward, I shall record every harvest! We shall have numbers, and tallies, and the mighty strength of math!" She lifted her tiny quill.

"And we'll be your witnesses," Jack added.

The Qoofy Brothers cheered, twirling their straw hats with delight.

That very day, they harvested 110 ears of corn. Lunibelle wrote the total on a scroll of corn-colored parchment.

The next day: 110 more. The third day: another 110. She kept the numbers tallied and tidy, tied with ribbon and tucked neatly into Jack's satchel.

But on the fourth morning, disaster struck. The barn, once golden and gleaming, was half empty. Lunibelle gasped. "Only 150 ears remain!"

Jack did the math. "We should have 330. That wolf stole—180!"

"Willy! Yellowy!" Jack commanded. "Start from the barn. Follow the thief's trail!"

"This is what I'm best at!" Willy's ears pricked up as he dashed off. Yellowy fluttered into the sky after him.

Not long after, they returned.

"I found the path the thief used," said Willy confidently. "It runs from the barn straight to the wolf's den."

"I saw a pile of stolen corn hidden in the backyard!" Yellowy chirped. "Clear as day from the air!"

Lunibelle drew the route on a scroll and documented the evidence. Her map ink curled into tiny ears of corn, while the wind tried to blow the arrows backward—as if the world disliked being directed.

With scrolls in hand and facts on their side, the Qoofy Brothers would march Old Gray Wolf to court—again.

They agreed to meet in court at nine o'clock sharp the next day. Before parting, Jack asked for directions.

"Easy," Qoofy One said, waving a hand. "Go south, then east, then south again—you can't miss it."

At dawn, Jack and his group set out, shoes crunching on frost-hardened earth. "This time," Jack muttered, "that cunning wolf won't slip away."

South. East. South again. No court. Only empty fields and a sinking dread.

"Where—?" Jack's voice frayed at the edges. Then—footsteps.

Hoofy Two appeared, blinking at them.

"The court?" he asked, a strange feeling creeping into his gut. "You're going the wrong way!"

A heartbeat of silence. Then the horrible truth struck—directions here were reversed from Jack's world. South was north. East was west. The signpost at the crossroads confirmed the truth by pointing in the exact opposite direction of its destination.

Somewhere, a bell tolled. The session was starting.

"Follow me!" Hoofy Two sprinted ahead, the others stumbling after him in desperate haste.

This time, the courtroom was a grand affair: a circular hall carved from a giant pumpkin, with buttery golden light filtering through its skin. Its doors opened only after three and a half knocks—an impossibility that nonetheless occurred.

The judge was the wisest orangutan in the land, sporting a monocle. The jury included a possum in pinstripes, a jittery duck, and a drowsy tortoise.

"I didn't steal two bags of golden corn," the wolf said, his voice dripping with false calm. "Last time, they had nothing. Do they have proof now—or just more lies?"

"Your Honor," Qoofy One declared, gripping the stand, "this time, we have evidence."

"We have witnesses!" Qoofy Two blurted.

"Call the witnesses," the judge commanded, his voice echoing off the courtroom walls.

Silence.

The Qoofy Brothers shifted on their feet.

"Call. The. Witnesses," the judge repeated, louder.

Still nothing. The crowd murmured, eyes darting. Sweat glistened on the brothers' reddening faces.

"No witnesses at all," Old Gray Wolf drawled, picking his teeth. "Lock these liars up."

"Final call for witnesses!" The judge's monocle flashed, the glare pinning the brothers like a spear.

The courtroom buzzed. The Qoofys swayed, knees buckling.

With a sigh, the judge raised his gavel—slow, inevitable.

The wolf's smirk widened.

Part VI: The Final Test of the Sly Wolf

The air in the courtroom was thick with the weight of Jack's failure.

He and his group had lost their way, burning through precious time. The judge raised his gavel with excruciating slowness, his eyes darting toward the door as if praying for a miracle.

Yellowy shot through the door like a comet. "I'm a witness! Me—me!"

The gavel froze midair. The wolf's grin turned to ice. Jurors jerked upright.

"Witnesses present!" the judge boomed, delighted.

"There's more!" Yellowy panted, perching on the railing of the witness stand.

Jack and the others burst in, gasping.

"Let the witnesses speak!" the judge happily declared.

"We do have evidence!" said Lunibelle, raising her scroll. "Each harvest, carefully recorded!" Numbers shimmered down the parchment.

Jack stepped forward. "The Qoofys harvested three hundred thirty ears of corn in three days, but on the fourth day, only one hundred fifty remained."

The orangutan adjusted his monocle. "Hmm. Solid evidence."

Old Gray Wolf frowned. "Perhaps it was raccoons—or a particularly peckish porcupine?"

The possum gasped. The duck flapped its wings in panic. The tortoise blinked once—very, very slowly.

Lunibelle unrolled a second scroll—complete with paw-print sketches and a trail of corn leading directly to the wolf's den.

"We still have other witnesses," said Jack. "Willy and Yellowy."

"Can you confirm this route?" asked the orangutan, peering at the map.

"Yes, Your Honor," said Willy, standing tall. "I tracked it with my nose. It leads straight to the wolf's den."

"I saw the stolen corn from the air," Yellowy added. "It was piled up under the old elm tree in his backyard."

Old Gray Wolf stammered. "I... may have... accidentally borrowed..."

"Can you produce a corn-certified invoice?" asked the judge.

"A... corn receipt?" the wolf blinked.

"Exactly," said the judge. "No receipt, no excuse."

The bailiff—an earnest badger—held up a feather-scale and declared, "Truth must weigh more than excuses."

The jury huddled, whispered, and nodded.

The orangutan cleared his throat. "We declare Old Gray Wolf guilty of corn theft! The sentence: one year of labor in the cornfields—under the supervision of the Qoofy Brothers."

The courtroom erupted in applause.

The wolf groaned. "I'll need gloves."

"And a better attitude," said Qoofy One.

"And perhaps a songbook," added Qoofy Two cheerfully.

Jack, Lunibelle, and the pets strolled merrily out of the pumpkin-shaped courthouse, where justice was served—warm and buttery.

Back at the cornfield, Old Gray Wolf—his straw hat far too small for his head—hacked weeds, hummed a tuneless corn song in a sullen mood, and handed baskets to the Qoofy Brothers. A tiny ledger peeked from his pocket. From time to time, he made a reluctant tally.

The friends waved goodbye.

"Justice tastes nearly as sweet as corn," Jack said with a grin.

"And with a bit of math," Lunibelle added, "it sings even louder."

The corn swayed in the breeze, singing once more:

WHISH-A-WHOOSH, WHISH-A-GLEE,

The corn is safe,

And so are we!

"Math helped the Hoofys build their house," said Lunibelle, skipping a little skip, "and helped the Qoofys win their court case too!"

"I think I'm starting to like math," Jack said, his smile bright.

"I'm starting to like math too!" meowed Meow4, tail high.

"Math is not as simple as a jump-rope rhyme!" Meow1 teased. "You have to use your brain!"

"You need 'I—am—think...'" added Meow3, stretching the words like bubblegum.

"I shall begin to 'I am think...' forthwith!" said Meow4, scratching his head.

Everyone laughed.

"Then it's time to go home," Lunibelle said, her eyes twinkling. "Everyone, close your eyes and say, 'Take me back to the place where math lives!'"

They all squeezed their eyes shut and chanted in perfect unison: "Take me back to the place where math lives!"

Part VII: The Math Is Not Only Math Anymore

When they opened their eyes—POOF!—they were standing right

back in the house. The refrigerator purred as if it had just finished a lullaby, pleased with itself, while the air smelled faintly of peanut butter and toast.

Everything looked just as Jack had left it. He turned slowly in place, half expecting a trail of golden corn kernels—or a Hoofy peeking from behind the couch.

But there was only the soft tick of the clock... and the gentle buzz of the ceiling fan.

He tiptoed to the refrigerator. There, where he'd left it, was a new orange sticky note:

Dinner's in the oven. I made your favorite apple pie. I might be a little late tonight—Mom.

Beneath it was Dad's daily riddle:

I don't belong to you, but you use me all the time. What am I?

Jack grinned. "Your name," he whispered, and gave the sticky note a little salute.

That Friday, after lunch and before the vacuum cleaner made its weekly song, Jack's dad came home from work. He loosened his tie dramatically, took a mighty sip of water, and reached for Jack's homework notebook.

"Let's see what new mischief you've cooked up—"

He flipped a few pages, then stopped. His voice shifted from playful to pleasantly stunned. "Whoa-ho-ho! Great job! Jack, you've had five days in a row without a single mistake!"

Jack beamed. "High five!"

CLAP! Their high five crashed like a pair of circus cymbals.

Dad chuckled. "So, who taught you the secret? Was it your

teacher? A clever squirrel? A traveling mathematician?"

"It was Lunibelle," Jack replied.

"At your birthday party," Dad nodded. "I met her. A smart and beautiful girl! With a perfect scientific mind!"

Jack smiled mysteriously and said nothing more—for how could he explain a sparkly, skipping fairy from the top of the refrigerator who had carried him into the Land Without Math?

Some things are better left just curious enough.

Later that evening, while the moon painted soft brushstrokes across the windowsill and Willy snored gently in his sleep (his paws twitching as if he were walking purposefully down a corn-thieving trail), Jack tiptoed back to the refrigerator.

He placed a small box—handmade with great care—on the top shelf. Inside lay three perfect chocolate buttons and a folded note:

Thanks, Lunibelle. For everything.

And as he gently closed the fridge door, he thought he heard it—a faint tinkle.

The next morning, the box was empty. In its place: a tiny golden ruler and a note written in elegant, swirly script:

Dream big. Measure twice. L.

Jack paused, holding the ruler. For a moment, he almost believed it glowed. Then he tucked it into his pencil case... and the note into his heart.

He knew math hadn't magically become easy overnight. The numbers still danced out of reach. The equations still curled like riddles.

But somehow, impossibly, it had transformed.

It felt like stumbling upon a hidden kind of magic—shimmering beneath the surface of every problem. No longer just a struggle, math had become something richer. Something more. A secret language. A shared wonder. An invisible thread between him and Lunibelle.

Each solved equation was not merely a victory—it was a treasure, glowing brighter because she was there to uncover it beside him.

And from that day on, whenever Jack sat down to solve a riddle... or crack a code... or figure out how many steps it would take to reach the moon...

He would always glance at the top of the refrigerator.

Just in case.

Just in case Lunibelle, with twinkling eyes and a bag full of wisdom, happened to be watching.

Chapter VI
To Save One Fish

Part I: The Fossil's Tear and the Promise

A. The Little Fish Who Longs for the Sea

It was a lazy afternoon—the kind that makes clocks yawn and windows blink slowly in the pale gold of sunset. In Jack's room, everything was still, except for two minds fizzing with questions.

Jack lay sprawled on his belly, flipping through a book of dinosaur fossils, while Lunibelle knelt beside him, pointing at a picture of a very pointy Stegosaurus tail.

"It seems like creatures on Earth went from big to small," Jack observed, turning the page, "and from simple to clever."

"Then back again from clever to confused," Lunibelle said, matter-of-factly. "Depending, of course, on how you define clever or confused."

Jack opened his mouth to ask what she meant, but Lunibelle suddenly held up one finger and pressed it to her lips. "Shhh! Don't speak. Just listen."

The room fell into a hush so deep that even the sunlight seemed to hold its breath. Time itself tiptoed out, finding a secret corner to hide in. The curtains, usually so eager to dance in the breeze, hung motionless and still.

Jack cupped one hand like a banana behind his left ear, tilting his head like a detective—a dog listening for clues. Nothing. He switched to his right ear. Still nothing. Not even a tick from the wall clock—which might have gotten bored and wandered off.

Willy, who had been sleeping on the floor, opened one of his eyes and then closed it again.

On top of the wardrobe, Yellowy froze mid-preen, her bright eyes scanning the corners of the room as if she expected the ceiling to sneeze.

Jack frowned. "Lunibelle, I don't hear a thing. Are you sure—"

"Shhh! Wait," she whispered urgently. Her eyes glittered with certainty, though Jack's brows remained knitted in doubt.

Just as he was about to insist there was nothing there, Lunibelle tiptoed across the desk to the small fossil lying on the bedside table—a fish. It was Jack's birthday gift from his father, who had proudly declared it was "two hundred million years old, give or take a Tuesday."

Jack followed her, muttering, "It's just a rock—a really cool rock—but still—"

Then the impossible happened.

Lunibelle crouched and gently pressed her head against the fossil. "Hello, little fish," she whispered.

"Hello," said a voice—so faint it might have been no more than a spider thread in the breeze.

Jack jerked back, eyes wide. "No way. Did you hear—?" He leaned close again, this time holding his breath as though silence itself might help him catch the sound.

From the fossil's single tiny eye, a gleaming tear trickled out and rolled over the stone like a pearl with a purpose.

"Why are you crying?" Lunibelle asked, her voice gentle as a lullaby sung underwater.

"I miss my mamma," the fish replied with a sniffly gurgle.

"Where is she now?"

"She lives at the bottom of the sea."

"What happened? How did you get separated?" Jack asked, his doubt melting into awe.

The little fossil wriggled slightly, the stone flaking ever so faintly with the motion of memory. "It was a long, long time ago," the fish said with a choked voice. "I was playing hide-and-seek with the other fish. I hid behind a swirly bit of seaweed. Then... I heard my mamma shouting, 'Run, little fish, run! The volcano!'"

The fish trembled, stone and all. "I didn't even get to swim. The sea began to shake. Then came a roaring, rumbling, growling sound. Suddenly, fire and black smoke rushed through the water. Everything went dark. The rocks rained down, and then—"

She paused. "We were buried. I guess we became... fossils."

Jack and Lunibelle sat very still. Willy opened both eyes without blinking. Even Yellowy had nothing to chirp.

B. Lunibelle's Enduring Vow

After listening to the story told by the small fish, no one spoke for a long moment. The room felt wrapped in something sacred. Jack's fingers rested beside the fossil, not quite touching it, as if too much pressure might break the silence or the spell. Lunibelle's eyes shimmered, reflecting a memory that wasn't hers but which she somehow understood.

Willy looked at Jack, then at Lunibelle, waiting for instructions.

Yellowy blinked slowly, fluffing her feathers with quiet resolve.

Finally, Jack whispered, "But how did you end up here on my desk?"

"One day, I was lying on the seabed—probably sighing—when a net scooped me up. A fisherman found me and sold me to a shop." The little fish thought for a while. "Then a man—maybe your dad—bought me for your birthday," she said with a sigh. "But—I miss the sea. I miss my mamma."

Silence.

The fossil glowed like a web of longing woven from millions of years. It was like the sea itself—always rising and falling.

Jack rubbed his forehead. "But... how could we help? You're—" He stopped, unable to say the word *fossil*. "I mean, you're stone, aren't you?"

Lunibelle tilted her head. "Stone can still remember. And remembering is half of being alive."

Jack hesitated—torn between logic and compassion. Part of him wanted to laugh at the absurd idea of saving a fossil, but the little tear shimmering on her cheek made his throat tight. "All right," he said softly. "If there's even a chance... we'll try."

"Do you remember where you lived?" he asked more firmly. "Maybe we can help."

"I remember beautiful coral... long, wavy seagrass... glittery shells... and pearls. It was blue there. Very blue."

That night, the moon slipped through the window blinds and painted stripes of milky white on the floor like layers of sea waves.

Jack was fast asleep, snoring softly.

Lunibelle crept in, her body glowing faintly silver, her tiny feet silent as thoughts in the dark. She stood by his bed.

"Jack," she whispered. "Jack!"

No response. Jack snored louder.

With a sigh, Lunibelle tugged on his ear like someone trying to pull a stubborn carrot out of the ground.

"OW—huh?! Lunibelle?" Jack blinked, rubbing his eyes. "Is something wrong?"

"We're going to the bottom of the sea," she said in the tone of someone announcing tea with the Queen of Jellyfish. "We're going to save the fish who were buried by the volcano."

Jack froze, the absurdity jolting him fully awake. "Wait—save who? From millions of years ago? Lunibelle, that's—"

"No time! I'll explain on the way!" she insisted.

Jack exhaled and gave a crooked smile. "All right. If you say so. But don't expect me to explain this to my parents."

He bounced out of bed like a spring. "Should I bring my swimsuit? Diving goggles? Flippers?"

"Nope," Lunibelle said crisply. "Bring the fossil. That's all we need."

They sneaked down the stairs, and Jack eased open the front door.

"Take me with you!" chirped Yellowy, swooping down to land on Jack's shoulder.

Behind them came a familiar sound—tap, tap, wag—from the hallway. Willy trotted forward with his tongue out and his tail swinging.

Jack looked at Lunibelle. "Them too?"

She nodded.

The clock on the wall struck twice. Jack looked up. It was two in the morning.

The night outside smelled of stars and secrets. The sky was a colander of stars, and the buttery moon followed them like a nosy neighbor. As they tiptoed down the moonlit path toward the beach, Jack asked, "Do you remember our first trip to the ocean?"

"I remember—it was perilous," said Lunibelle, her long hair fluttering in the breeze. "Willy ran so fast, he practically flew."

"We almost—" Jack stopped short. He didn't want to say it.

"I won't die," Lunibelle said simply. "Because I don't live in Time. Not quite."

At the beach, the waves whispered to the sand, and the wind offered everyone a salty kiss.

"Everyone closes your eyes," Lunibelle instructed, her voice oddly formal. "Don't open them until I say so."

Jack, Willy, and Yellowy obeyed.

And Lunibelle began to count.

"Ten... nine... eight... seven and a wiggle... six and a half... five... half a seashell... four... three... two... one..."

Part II: Currents as Maps

A. Echoes the Fish Can't Remember

Jack blinked. Yellowy blinked. Willy blinked—first one eye, then the other. (Dogs can be oddly dramatic about these things.)

And what they saw made their blinks stick.

And the colors—oh, the colors! Coral reefs blushed in pinks and oranges. Seaweed swayed like fluttering green ribbons. Jellyfish puffed their glowing umbrellas, trailing sparkles like absent-minded little fireworks.

"I feel like I'm dreaming," whispered Jack.

"You probably are," said Lunibelle. "But we're all dreaming the same dream, so it's all right."

"Whoa," said Willy—and dogs don't say that lightly.

"I want to build a nest on that beautiful coral!" Yellowy flapped, already scouting her future home.

"Wouldn't the egg hatch into a fish?" Jack teased.

Yellowy paused. "As long as it doesn't meow, I'm fine."

They floated above the coral garden, dazzled. Pearls nestled like sleepy stars inside open clams. The sea anemones had curled up for the night, their tentacles glowing like pearl-draped fingers. Glimmering worms wrote twinkling loops in the water. Even the darkness was beautiful—mysterious, velvet, full of friendly shadows.

Then Lunibelle grew serious. "Jack, take out the fossil."

Jack carefully pulled it from his pocket. It gleamed faintly in the undersea light.

"I'm finally back to sea!" the fish gasped.

"Little Fish," Lunibelle asked gently, "do you remember what your home looked like? Any clues?"

The fossil stirred slightly in Jack's hand, as if searching for the answer in memories accumulated over millions of years.

"I remember... beautiful coral... long seagrass that tickled my fins... glittery shells... and the water was blue—so blue it made other blues jealous."

"That's very poetic," said Lunibelle, smiling faintly.

"But... where?" Jack asked. "How far?"

"How far is the ocean?" the fossil said. "That far."

Jack sighed, torn between logic and hope. "That's not much of a map. But we'll keep going."

Yellowy rolled her eyes. "Helpful."

Willy muttered, "It's like asking a cloud for a compass."

"I'm sorry," said Little Fish. "I was so small when it happened. I didn't know how to measure anything—except the loudness of my mamma's voice when she was scared."

Just then, something large and slow drifted above them, casting a swinging shadow.

B. Grandpa Current Whispers the Way

Just when the fish couldn't give an answer, a shadow of wisdom moved through the water above. The group looked up and saw what could only be described as an ancient floating island—until it blinked.

It was a sea turtle. A very old one. Possibly the oldest creature Jack had ever seen. Cracks filled its shell. Its flippers moved in grand, slow strokes.

"Yellowy," Lunibelle said, "fly up and ask if he's willing to come down."

Yellowy zipped up and landed delicately between the turtle's eyes. "Excuse me, ancient sir! Might we have a word?" She pointed down.

The sea turtle squinted. "A bird on the forehead," he said. "That used to mean good luck—or dandruff. Can't remember which."

He slowly tilted his flippers and glided down toward the group, trailing bubbles.

"Good evening, Mr. Turtle," Lunibelle said with a bow. "Might we ask you a few questions?"

"Young folks are always full of questions," said the turtle. "Back in my day, questions were slower—you had to mail them to the Coral Council. Anyway, proceed."

"How old are you, sir?" Jack asked, wide-eyed.

"Older than yesterday, younger than the moon. But if you must know, I use the N + 1 method. You can call me Grandpa Current, though—every current eventually loops back to me."

Yellowy perked up. "You mean... your age is always N + 1?"

"Exactly." The turtle tilted his head. "N is the number of years I've already lived. I add one every year. So it's always correct, even when I forget the number entirely."

Jack whispered, "That's genius."

"No, just convenient," said the turtle. "Wisdom isn't knowing everything—it's knowing how to make up for what you've forgotten."

Lunibelle smiled. "Dear Grandpa Current, do you, perhaps, remember anything about a volcanic eruption under the sea?"

The turtle frowned so slowly it took several seconds to finish. "A volcano... ah, yes. There was a volcano. I think. Or was it just a particularly spicy lunch?"

"No, definitely a volcano," Jack assured him. "You can't eat fire."

"Yes, yes," the old turtle rumbled, his head bobbing in a slow, deliberate motion. "My grandfather told me of a time long, long ago when the sea itself was so frightened it trembled, every fish darted about in a panicked silver flash, and the tiny shrimp, trembling too, burrowed deep into the sand, hiding from a terror they could not name."

"Just that one," Lunibelle said, her eyes bright with anticipation. "Can you tell us where it was?"

Grandpa Current paused. "Where was it? Hmm... Oh! I was just a hatchling, floating on the current."

"You mean the current brought you there?" Lunibelle nudged gently.

"Oh yes," said the turtle. "We turtles love a good current—it's like an escalator, only wetter. No need for paddling. You just hop on and off. Shame you

land-creatures don't have them."

"I have a creek near my house," Jack offered, then chuckled at how small it sounded.

"Not the same." The turtle shook his head. "No dolphin dance."

"Do you remember where the volcano was?" Lunibelle pressed gently.

The turtle blinked. "Let me think," he said. "Time is mostly nostalgia—bittersweet and terribly easy to forget."

He began to spin—very, very slowly—in place, his flippers pointing like the hands of a sleepy clock trying to remember where noon went. But after only half a turn, he stopped and sighed. "Ah yes—west, toward the Endless Plains, beyond the Coral Forest. That way."

The group thanked him profusely.

"You're welcome," he said. "Now, if you'll excuse me, I need to forget what I just said so I can learn it again tomorrow. But remember: if ever you're lost, just follow the flow."

Yellowy, inspired, burst into song as they swam forward:

The turtle is wise, with a shell full of tales,
His years are all secret, like sand grains untold.
He counts with an N, then adds one with glee,
And follows the currents wherever they be!

As the friends swam toward the direction the turtle had pointed, the ocean began to grow darker, deeper, and more mysterious. The coral faded behind them.

But they were not afraid.

Because somewhere ahead—hidden in time, buried in mystery—was a volcano that had swallowed the past.

And maybe... just...

Part III: The Dance of Trust and Proof

A. Yellowy Gets Eaten Politely

Just as the sea grew darker and the group began wondering if they'd accidentally fallen into the deep end of a forgotten world, two glowing blue orbs appeared ahead—blinking, bouncing, and bobbing. Jack shielded his eyes, unsure if they were beacons or bait.

"What in the watery wonder is that?" Jack whispered.

"I vote we follow them!" Yellowy declared. She zoomed forward before anyone could vote otherwise.

"Yellowy, wait—!" Lunibelle called, but the canary was already flitting ahead, drawn like a moth to a glow stick.

For one tense moment, Yellowy darted between the two orbs, circling them as a child chasing lanterns at a fair.

Then—GLOMP! Something squishy and suspiciously soft sucked her right in. She flailed once, twice, and vanished into a glowing blue pouch.

"Yellowy!" shouted Jack, running as fast as he could.

They arrived just in time to see the last flutter of yellow feathers disappear into... a translucent, glowing sack.

"Oh, squids and sunfish," muttered Lunibelle. "She's been swallowed by a luminescent octopus!"

The octopus in question was quite the spectacle. Its eight arms curled and twitched with purpose. Its body shimmered with bioluminescent spots—as though a galaxy had been glued to its skin. Two arms had blinking blue tips that moved like fireflies trying to do jazz hands.

"Excuse me!" Lunibelle shouted. "Please return our bird!"

The octopus stopped blinking. All his lights froze. Then suddenly—ZING! They flared brighter, illuminating its entire jelly-like body.

Inside, Yellowy could be seen flapping her wings furiously and squawking. She tried pecking at the walls, but they bounced back like soft glass.

"She flew in herself," the octopus boomed, in the voice of a professor who had read far too many books. "Completely voluntary. I don't interfere with volunteers. It's all rather legal and binding."

"But she didn't mean to be swallowed!" Jack protested. "That's not consent, that's confusion!"

"Intentions," said the octopus, puffing up proudly, "are never facts. I deal in facts. I am an octopus of evidence. If something swims into my belly, I assume it wants to be there. Why else would anyone dive headfirst into a glow trap?"

Willy barked and charged forward in a blur of fur and bubbles, trying to nip an arm—but the octopus flicked a single limb and sent him spinning backward as though a waterlogged pinwheel.

"I meant no offense," Lunibelle said quickly, pulling Willy behind her. "We're just passing through. Could you please let her out?"

"Nothing has ever left my belly," the octopus huffed, curling his arms in the universal pose of resistance. "But I promise, if it wants to, I can let it out. I respect evidence, and evidence respects me."

B. A Glowing Friendship and a Gentle Release

A thoughtful quiet bloomed between them.

"Could you explain why evidence respects you?" Lunibelle asked carefully.

"Because I am also evidence, so evidence respects me," said the octopus matter-of-factly. "And they all adore me."

"Who adores you?" Jack asked.

"Who? Is that even a question? All the fish and shrimp in my belly adore me. I have eight arms—more than any of them—and each one has suckers. They don't have a single sucker," the octopus boasted. "Plus, I glow. A dazzling blue light, like stars falling into the sea. Glowing is the ocean's pride! Stars are the sky's pride!"

"I can glow too," Lunibelle said firmly.

"What! You can glow? That's nearly an impossible possibility—or perhaps a possible impossibility," the octopus declared. "How do you glow?"

"Because I'm your friend," Lunibelle said modestly. "So I can glow too."

"You know I value evidence. Without proof, I won't believe it," the octopus insisted. "I won't be like humans, luring fish with shiny things only to trap them in nets. That hurts the sea."

"Like you, I glow with my own light," Lunibelle said. A soft silver glow rose from her body, slowly shifting to green, then red.

Jack stared. He had never seen her glow in colors before, and for a dizzy second, he felt she was even further beyond him—more star than child.

"Oh... my..." the octopus murmured. "Stars and currents... is this real?" Its arms shimmered in awe. "You—you truly are my friend. And you glow... like the heart of the ocean itself." A pause, then a soft, uncertain sigh. "I value evidence, so I believe you—but your friend is in my belly. How do we prove it truly wants to come out?"

Before anyone could answer, the octopus mused, "Since you're my friend, I'll help you. I have an idea—if you're willing to try it."

"Please tell me. I'll do exactly as you say," Lunibelle nodded earnestly.

The octopus wiggled with delight. "Yes! Now you're speaking my language. But we must do it officially. By the glow of Arm Six, do you swear? You shall enter via Arm Six. Ask, 'Do you wish to leave?' and she must raise her right wing and declare, 'I solemnly swear I wish to leave.' That will be recorded by my Central Arm Verification System and transmitted to my Very Intelligent Digestive Committee (a.k.a. me). If approved, you will both be escorted out. Deal?"

Lunibelle nodded solemnly. "Deal."

"Nooo," Jack hissed. "Lunibelle, it's dangerous."

"I'm very small," Lunibelle replied. "I fit inside all sorts of trouble."

Arm Six, flashing like blue jelly, snaked gently toward her and curled around her waist. With a whoosh and a giggle (from the arm, oddly enough), she was delivered through a gleaming valve and into the belly of the beast.

Inside was not nearly as gooey as one might expect. It looked rather like a squishy ballroom lit by bioluminescent chandeliers. Yellowy hovered near the center, flapping indignantly beside a jelly-bean-shaped organ that blinked with the word *Occupied*. She was muttering, "I object! I object to everything!"

Yellowy was startled when she saw Lunibelle. "Are you captured here too?"

"I came to get you out," said Lunibelle calmly.

"You came for me!" Yellowy chirped. "But now we're both inside!"

"And we must do it by the book." Lunibelle straightened, cleared her throat, and announced with theatrical flair:

"Yellowy, do you wish to leave?"

Yellowy flapped dramatically. "I solemnly swear I wish to leave!"

A small beep echoed from the belly walls. The Central Arm Verification System (which looked suspiciously like a glowing sea cucumber) hummed to life.

Outside, the octopus paused mid-arm-twirl.

"Well! That's official!"

Arm Six promptly reversed course, delivering both passengers into the open sea with a polite pop.

"Thank you!" Lunibelle called, shaking mucus from her hair.

The octopus beamed. "You followed the rules! You provided evidence! Therefore, you are my friends."

"Friends?" Jack asked.

"Yes!" cried the octopus. "And what do friends do when they're reunited after one of them gets swallowed?"

No one could answer.

"They dance!"

"Oh boy," muttered Willy, shaking out his ears.

"I love dancing!" said Yellowy. "But we need music!"

"Ah," said the octopus. "I've got just the thing."

From deep inside its glowing belly, the octopus reached and pulled out... a music fish.

The music fish was shaped like a blimp with fins, covered in swirling rainbow scales. Its mouth looked like a trumpet, and its tiny eyes sparkled with mischief.

The fish took a deep breath, puffed up like a balloon, and let loose. Music flowed from its mouth—jazz, polka, lullabies, and something suspiciously close to disco. The octopus's arms began to flicker and wiggle in time.

"Everyone holds an arm!" the octopus instructed joyfully.

Jack grabbed one. Willy took another. Yellowy reached for a third. Lunibelle held the fourth.

And with that, they began to dance—drifting in circles, spinning, twirling, weaving through the water. The arms sparkled in sequence. Up and down, left and looping—they danced!

When the music paused, the octopus sighed. "Four arms danced. But I have eight. I must be fair to the others."

"Then let's have one more round!" Yellowy fluttered her wings.

The music began again—faster this time. The arms swooped and spun, tickling the sea and making jellyfish giggle.

At last, the music faded into a bubbly sigh.

The octopus looked positively thrilled. "That," he said, "was the happiest I've felt since I once swallowed a carnival!"

"Thank you for everything," said Lunibelle, bowing low.

"Please take these," said the octopus, offering four gleaming white pearls. "A gift for my friends."

They thanked the octopus.

"Do you know where the volcano is?" Lunibelle asked, her eyes twinkling with urgency.

The octopus's arms froze mid-motion before all simultaneously tapping its bulbous head in unison. "Volcano? Hmm..." he mused, his voice a deep, bubbling hum. "But if it's answers you're after, the Concert Hall is the place to be! Packed with geniuses, fools, and everything in between—someone's bound to blab something useful."

"How do we get to the Concert Hall?" Yellowy blurted, her feathers puffing up in excitement. Music was her favorite.

The octopus extended a single arm, its tip glowing faintly in the dim light. "That way," he said, pointing.

And just as the bubbles settled and the laughter faded, the sea ahead darkened once more.

Part IV: The Symphony of Silence

A. The Theater Where Stillness Sings

They said goodbye to the octopus after he pointed them in the direction.

As they went on—past coral towers and swaying seaweed canopies, past shy eels and sleepy sea cucumbers—the underwater twilight suddenly burst into a brilliance like theater light.

Before them stood a building made entirely of coral and shell, with oyster-shell chandeliers dangling from sponge balconies and clamshell steps leading up to grand mother-of-pearl doors. Across the front, spelled in swirly bubble-script, a glowing sign read:

TONIGHT: The Great Silent Symphony — One Night Only!

Jack squinted. "Silent symphony? Isn't that... a contradiction?"

"Music is supposed to make noise," Yellowy declared with a frown. "If it's silent, isn't it just... not music?"

"Let's find out," Lunibelle said, already walking toward the entrance with an eager twinkle in her eye. Her shimmer dimmed but didn't vanish; it hovered, as though silence itself were following her.

At the archway of coral stood a most dignified lobster, his tailcoat woven from sea silk and his spectacles glimmering with the faint transparency of jellyfish glass. In one claw he carried a little lantern—its flame swaying—and in the other, a ticket puncher that clicked with impeccable authority.

"Good evening," he said, in a tone so crisply polite it could have been pressed and ironed by the tide. "Tickets, if you please."

"Um..." Jack began, feeling about for pockets that had long since dissolved into seawater.

"We haven't got any," said Yellowy, fluffing her feathers.

The lobster sighed—small, dignified, like a bubble that had practiced being important. "Ah, I see. Well, as the sea often reminds us, we never quite know our treasures until the tide asks politely for them."

Something flickered in Jack's mind. He reached into his bag and drew out the four white pearls the kindly octopus had given them.

The lobster's face deepened to the proud pink of polished coral. "Pearls! Of course. The ocean's way of saying, 'You're expected.' Please, step through—and do mind the bubbles; they bruise easily."

He bowed and handed them a program printed on a leaf of seaweed. The ink was changing color with the currents, and the words danced playfully as though they knew they were being read.

They entered the opera house and held their breath.

The audience brimmed with extraordinary creatures: lionfish sequined in their own scales, clownfish with bow ties, jellyfish in top hats (some precariously tilted), sea slugs in sparkly shawls, and one grumpy crab gripping opera spectacles in both claws. An enormous old sea turtle—perhaps the same one who once sang of tides—sat dabbing his eyes with a sponge.

"Is that...?" Jack started.

"Hush," said Lunibelle, guiding him to their seats.

The house lights dimmed—slowly, like a long, thoughtful sigh. The coral chandeliers faded to a twinkle. A hush swept through the theater. Only the occasional bubble rose toward the ceiling, each one applauding in slow motion.

Then, the pearl curtain parted.

In the center of the stage stood a whale.

Not just any whale—this one wore a black tuxedo stitched from eel threads, coral cufflinks gleaming at his fins, and a baton gripped delicately in one. He turned slowly to face the audience and bowed.

His eyes twinkled.

Behind him was the orchestra.

It was unlike any orchestra Jack—or anyone—had ever seen. The sea snails, with their spiral conch shells, blew invisible melodies into the water, while crabs tapped rhythmic percussion on clam shells with military precision. Sea stars plucked coral harps, sending ripples through the water, while parrotfish sawed tiny violins with their fins, their brows furrowed in musical concentration.

And then... silence.

Total silence.

The conductor whale raised his baton. It sparkled.

He brought it down in a single, sweeping motion.

Nothing happened.

But everything happened.

Jack felt it in his chest—as if silence had found a way to sing.

B. A Melody Is Felt, Not Heard

The seaweed at the sides of the stage—two long, elegant strands—began to dance. Not just to sway, but to dance. They pirouetted, spun, and dipped like ballerinas. Their tips quivered in perfect time with an unheard rhythm.

Jack felt it in his chest. His heart skipped. He wasn't hearing music—he was feeling it.

As the seaweed performed its *pas de deux*, a group of seahorses pranced onstage from the left. Their flippers tapped in tight, crisp rhythms, sending invisible pulses through the water. The rhythm tickled Jack's toes and made Yellowy's feathers ruffle in delight.

"I can't hear it," she whispered, "but my tail is doing the cha-cha-cha!"

The whale conductor turned dramatically, spinning mid-air, and gestured toward the back of the stage.

Suddenly—WHOOSH!—eight dolphins zipped into view. They moved in formation, leaping and twisting in acrobatic spirals. Some spun like coins, while others flapped their tails to a beat only their bones seemed to understand. They dove in and out of coral hoops and left glittery trails in their wake.

One particularly bold dolphin performed an underwater somersault, landed in a bubble ring, and bowed. The audience—though silent—wiggled in their seats, eyes sparkling.

The parrotfish violinists sawed faster. The crabs drummed harder. The sea stars plucked strings with wild abandon. The water itself began to thrum.

The Silent Symphony reached its crescendo—and Jack felt it in every hair, every tooth, every fingernail.

The conductor pointed his baton at the ceiling.

From above, a beam of light burst down. Within it, millions of plankton lit up, forming glowing shapes—notes, treble clefs, even the outline of a waltzing jellyfish.

The seaweed dancers spun faster. The dolphins zipped wildly. The orchestra played on.

Then—suddenly—blackout. The lights disappeared. The music, the movement, the glowing plankton—all vanished in a blink.

And in that rich, velvety darkness, two glowing shrimp floated into view and spelled out a final message:

THANK YOU (in perfect cursive, of course).

The curtain closed.

The audience, still silent, rose in waves of gentle reverence. No clapping. No cheers. Just the quiet swish of water as everyone nodded to each other with wide, astonished eyes.

Jack stood slowly. "That was... the most beautiful music I never heard!"

"I think," said Lunibelle, "we were listening with our hearts."

"I could feel it in my wings," said Yellowy, still twirling in slow circles. "The sea danced with us."

They stepped outside into the coral-lit night. The sea was calmer now, as though it too had been swept away by the magic.

And there, just outside the theater entrance, stood the old sea turtle—blinking slowly and dabbing his eyes again.

"Mr. Grandpa Current!" Lunibelle called happily. "Grandpa Current!"

"Oh! You are also here!" he said in his gravelly voice. "I cry every time—especially at the shrimp finale. Exactly $N + 1$ tears, without fail."

He paused for a while. "By the way, where are you going?"

"We're looking for the volcano," Yellowy said, flapping her still-excited wings.

"Are you?" the old turtle blinked, as if hearing it for the first time. "Well, it's about time. Come—hop on. I'll take you there myself."

Part V: Where Time Turns Back

A. Before the Ash-Rain Falls

The old sea turtle, noble as a drifting castle, paddled slowly across the ancient seabed, as he had done for the past thousand Wednesdays. Jack, Lunibelle, Yellowy, and Willy sat comfortably on his wide, barnacled back—an underwater chariot gliding through forgotten currents.

They gazed at the beautiful scenery along the way.

"The volcano's ahead," rumbled the old turtle, squinting at a cluster of underwater hills in the distance. "Or maybe it's behind. No, no—definitely ahead. My memory tends to lag behind my shell."

Lunibelle sat cross-legged at the front of the shell, gazing at the looming mound. "When we arrive," she said gravely, "I must use... the Doo."

Jack blinked. "The what now?"

"The Doo," Lunibelle repeated. "The Doo that must never be done—except when it must."

"I was told never to interfere with life on Earth. But today, we're not doing it for ourselves. We're doing it to save the fish."

"We have arrived," the old turtle announced, gliding to a stop.

They reached the foot of the volcano—a monstrous mountain of jagged rock and smoldering ash. Its dark, gnarled stone loomed like the snarling head of a hungry lion. Foul steam hissed from its cracks, twisting like spectral tendrils. At any moment, its maw might yawn wide, devouring all who dared stand before it.

Jack stumbled back, his heart pounding. He swallowed hard. "So this is where the eruption happened? Where the little fossil fish got buried?"

Lunibelle nodded. "Two hundred million years ago."

Willy whined softly.

"Don't worry, boy," Jack soothed. "We're not climbing it. We're... going back in time."

"Everyone," Lunibelle instructed, "close your eyes. Breathe slowly. Relax your thoughts. I'll tell you when to open them."

Jack, Willy, and Yellowy obeyed. The water grew quiet. No fish stirred.

Then Lunibelle whispered, "Open." They did.

And the world had changed.

The volcano had vanished. Instead, they stood on a sun-drenched seabed where coral bloomed and fish darted between the reeds. Clam shells opened lazily. Tiny shrimp performed synchronized dances, their antennae flickering. Everything was... alive.

"We've gone back two hundred million years," said Lunibelle, "to the moment before the volcano erupted."

"It's beautiful," whispered Jack. "And peaceful."

Lunibelle turned to him. "Jack, bring out the fossil. Hurry!"

Jack hesitated. He touched the fossil through his pocket first, as though asking permission. *What if it didn't work? What if I erased her instead of saving her?*

Still, he reached in and pulled it out—but instead of stone, he held a squirming, blinking fish. The tiny creature wiggled free, flopped in the water, and blinked. "Where am I?"

"In your home," said Lunibelle. "The one before the eruption."

The fish looked around blankly. "I... seem... to remember!"

"You were playing hide-and-seek," said Lunibelle. "Your mamma was calling you."

"Yes! She shouted, 'Little fish! Run! Run!' And then I was buried!"

"Well, not yet," Jack said. "And hopefully, not ever."

"You must go," Lunibelle urged. "Warn your mother. Warn everyone. Get them out of here before it's too late!"

The fish, still blinking, nodded. "I... I'll try! Thank you!"

And she zipped away in a blur of fins and bubbles.

Jack exhaled, though his chest remained tight.

"Do you think she'll make it?" he asked—though what he really meant was: *Have we done enough?*

"I think she will," said Lunibelle. "She's got her whole future ahead of her."

Jack nodded slowly, yet part of him still clung to the little fossil in his pocket—as though some fragment of her might still need him.

But even as Lunibelle spoke, the water began to shift again.

B. Lunibelle's Bold Rebellion

Something was terribly wrong!

Lunibelle's head snapped around, her pupils narrowing to slits. The water thickened with the metallic tang of magma. The currents coiled around them.

Her voice was sharp and clear: "This place is unstable. The eruption's about to begin. We must go. Now."

No room for debate. No time to hesitate.

The seabed groaned beneath them—a sound like the world cracking its knuckles. Jack's hands flew to his ears. Willy's fur stood on end, his body coiling into a trembling sphere. Yellowy didn't even squeak—she jammed her head beneath her wings, as though sheer will could undo disaster.

Lunibelle's countdown cut through the chaos like a blade.

"Ten... nine... eight... seven and a half shrimp cocktails... seven... six..."

The first fissure split open—a jagged maw of molten orange, devouring coral towers in a single gulp. Bubbles of superheated gas exploded upward, scalding as they passed. The water itself shrieked.

"Five and three jellybeans... five... four..."

Jack's knees buckled. Willy's claws dug into the seabed, scarlet ribbons swirling from the gouges. Yellowy flailed, helpless against the current pulling her toward the chasm.

But Willy did not think of himself. With a guttural bark, he lunged forward through the boiling currents, planting his body between

Jack, Lunibelle, and the onrushing blast. His fur sizzled, his paws tore at the burning seabed, yet still he pressed forward—shielding them as if his own back were a wall against the volcano. It was the same fierce, selfless courage he had shown once before in the race against time, and it burned brighter than the lava itself.

Lunibelle didn't flinch. She couldn't. Her glow sharpened, the colors from earlier returning like banners of defiance.

"Three... two... one and a quarter... ONE! NOW!"

Her command was not a plea—it was law.

The world snapped into place. Cool sand beneath their feet. Night air in their lungs. The gentle crash of waves where seconds ago there had been annihilation.

The stars hung unchanged—utterly unconcerned.

Jack spat out a mouthful of saltwater.

Willy uncurled, his fur still smoking at the tips. "What in the nine seas was that?"

Yellowy opened her beak, closed it, and opened it again before sound came out. Finally she managed, squawking, "Next time, I'm staying in the lobby!"

Lunibelle wiped soot from her cheek. Her hands didn't shake.

"Proof," she whispered. "I did it!"

The volcano was gone. The sea was calm. And Jack still clutched the fossil.

Except... it was no longer a fossil.

It was just a smooth, ordinary stone.

"The little fish..." Jack breathed. "She's gone."

He looked up at Lunibelle. "Where do you think she went?"

Lunibelle smiled gently. "Home. Not in time—but in life."

Jack fell into a deep thought as they made their way home.

Willy nudged the front door open, and the house lay hushed as if in a deep, quiet slumber.

"Have a good night," Jack murmured to Lunibelle.

"Have beautiful sea dreams," Lunibelle trilled. Her hand flew to her mouth, her eyes suddenly alight with a mischievous, crackling sparkle that was her last glimpse before she slipped back into the refrigerator door like a flash of lightning.

Then, before the latch could even click, the silence was broken. The clock on the wall delivered a single, silvery chime—a sound both charming and strange.

Jack's head snapped up. One in the morning!

"We'd walked out at two, but now, somehow, we were standing here a whole, impossible hour earlier!" Jack squinted up at the clock. "Only one person to blame for this!" He smiled.

Two days later, in his bedroom, Jack was just beginning to drift off when his dad poked his head in.

"Hey, kiddo. This afternoon, I was looking at that little fish fossil of yours and—" His brow crinkled. "Where's the fish?"

Jack sat up slowly. "She went to find her mamma."

His dad raised an eyebrow. "She what?"

"She went home," Jack said simply.

His dad stared at the smooth stone, then shook his head and muttered, "What in Newton's apples...?"

Later, Jack reenacted the moment for Lunibelle, mimicking his father's confusion with wide eyes and wobbly hands.

They both burst out laughing.

Some things—even in the age of science—are better left unexplained.

Chapter VII
In Search of Two Identical Snowflakes

Part I: The Book That Tries to Be a Cartoon

Jack borrowed many books from the library for Lunibelle, because that was how she grew—her growth followed knowledge, not years. Lunibelle nearly turned into a bookworm herself, head nestled in a mountain of pages, occasionally glancing up with sparks of wisdom twinkling in her eyes.

"It's fascinating! Human knowledge is captured in words," Lunibelle mused. "And glasses were invented just for reading."

"You don't even have glasses!" Jack exclaimed.

"We don't need them," Lunibelle said with a grin at Jack's astonishment. "We can see very far—like this book says—hundreds of millions of light-years." She tapped *The Universe* with a gentle finger.

"But you don't use words. Where does your knowledge come from?" Jack leaned closer, eyes wide.

"Our knowledge flows in streams of information," Lunibelle said, wiggling her fingers in front of her eyes like shimmering threads.

"What's an information flow? What does—" Jack began, but Lunibelle raised her right index finger to her lips and smiled at him.

Jack paused—he understood. Her three rules meant this path of questions must end.

After a while,

"Have you ever seen a cartoon?" Jack asked suddenly, as if a breeze had blown the thought into his head.

Lunibelle blinked her eyes. "A what-now?"

"A cartoon!" Jack repeated, throwing up his arms as if performing a magic trick. "It's like a storybook that's learned to move—and dance—and blink! Like magic pages that flip themselves!"

Lunibelle, who adored the word *magic* almost as much as she loved asking questions, leaned in. "Do you have one? A magic dancing-book?"

Jack sprang up and darted to the bookshelf. Books packed every shelf—tall ones, thin ones, squat ones, stout ones—each with its own hue, waiting in line to spill their stories.

"Are all these yours?" Lunibelle whispered reverently. She loved books; they had taught her more than a thousand teachers could.

"Yeah." Jack grabbed one and flipped it open, his fingers moving fast.

"Did you buy every single one?" Her curiosity was endless.

"Only a few." He pulled out another. "Most were gifts."

"A new book is a new friend, huh?" Lunibelle murmured, her voice tinged with longing.

Jack pulled out a thick, colorful storybook. The cover flickered faintly, as if it still remembered loving hands holding it. "This one's from my grandma—when I turned three. It still smells like forest and mushrooms."

He stroked the cover gently, and for a moment, the room fell still. "Grandma," he whispered, "I miss you so much."

Lunibelle placed her silvery fingers on Jack's sleeve. "She must be kind. Like my grandma."

"She lives by the forest," Jack said, his gaze drifting far away to the house that had quietly melted into pine trees and birdsong. "A tiny wooden house with green windows. I used to think fairies lived in her pantry."

Lunibelle clapped her hands. "Let's visit her one day! Perhaps she'll tell us about a lot of magic."

Jack's eyes lit up. "Deal."

Then, with the dramatic flair of a magician, he placed the book upright on the coffee table. "Now—watch closely."

Lunibelle stood by Jack. Jack held the book like a proud little door and flicked his thumb across the pages—WHAP, WHAP, WHAP, WHAP, WHAP!

The pictures almost danced... but didn't.

Lunibelle's expression shifted from wide-eyed wonder to puzzled curiosity. "Hmm. That was... very windy. But I don't think I saw anyone blink."

"Yeah," Jack sighed. "It doesn't quite work like a cartoon. Just flipping pages isn't enough."

"But why not?" Lunibelle asked.

Jack scratched his head. "They're just giant flip-books. You take all these drawings that are almost the same, but not quite, and swap them out quick. Your eyes can't keep up, so all those still moments blur together into movement."

"Ohhhh," Lunibelle breathed. "So the magic isn't in the picture—it's in the difference?"

"Exactly!" Jack nodded.

"Then we must go see one! A real cartoon!" Lunibelle twirled on her toes, spinning.

Jack nodded and unfolded the newspaper. "Let's see what's playing... Aha! There's *The Cloudy Mailman, The Endless Road, Ant Kingdom...*"

Lunibelle's eyes sparkled. "Any others?"

"Hmm... *Toilet Paper Ninja and the Cereal Box Council, The Soggy Umbrella Society—*"

"Any other movies?" Lunibelle asked.

"Ah—here's one... *In Search of Two Identical Snowflakes.*"

The room went quiet.

"Say that again." Lunibelle placed both hands over her heart.

"In Search of Two Identical Snowflakes."

She repeated it. "That's the one. I love snow. I love how it turns the world pure white—like frosting on a giant cake. It reminds me of home."

"Then that's what we'll see," Jack declared. "It's showing tomorrow afternoon at three o'clock. We'll bring scarves and dreams."

"Perfect!" Lunibelle beamed. "I shall wear my boots."

As the afternoon faded into evening, they sat side by side among the books. The room felt like a story-nest.

"What do you think the movie will be like?" Jack asked.

"I hope the snowflakes sing," Lunibelle said. "Or whisper secrets as they fall. Or dance across rooftops like tiny ballerinas."

"Maybe," Jack said, arms outstretched, "there are millions—and billions—and trillions—of snowflakes, and I bet somewhere out there, two of them are exactly the same."

"Just like the stars in the sky," Lunibelle mused. "I've never asked my parents if any two stars were the same."

"There must be," Jack whispered.

That night, Lunibelle dreamed. The stars unpinned themselves from the sky and tumbled softly to earth, turning into snowflakes as they fell. They gleamed as they landed, covering the ground like a blanket woven from galaxies.

Lunibelle reached out her hand, and one graceful snowflake floated down and settled on her palm.

"Hello," she whispered.

"Greetings!" said the snowflake, its six crystal arms unfurling like petals. "I come from a galaxy far, far away—one where dreams drift through space and land wherever they're needed most."

"You know I'm searching," Lunibelle said. "I want to find two snowflakes that are the same."

The snowflake twinkled. "Yes, yes! Word travels fast on the solar wind. But I cannot stay long. Each of us makes a journey, brief and beautiful."

"Then before you go," Lunibelle asked, "can you tell me... how do I find the two?"

The snowflake shimmered, spun slowly, and whispered, "N—"

But before it finished, it melted in her hand and turned into a shining drop of water. The drop winked mischievously, as if to say, "Good luck!" Then, with a puff, it disappeared.

Lunibelle woke with a gasp. "N... What does that mean?"

And somewhere, far above, a snowflake rode a breeze toward the stars, its message unfinished but not forgotten.

Part II: The Silverscreen That Gulps Them Down Whole

The next afternoon arrived, dressed in its finest spring shawl. The streets smelled of newspaper ink, pastries, and warm brick walls—and even the car horns.

Jack led Lunibelle to the cinema, the explorer escorting his princess of stars. The cinema itself was a grand, slightly creaky building with velvet curtains and a popcorn machine that hissed and chuffed steam. To Lunibelle, it looked as if a royal palace had been carved from ice cubes and butter. Before entering, Jack bought a bag of popcorn—fluffy, golden, and ridiculously salty—and a can of soda so fizzy it seemed ready to hiccup.

Lunibelle stared at the popcorn. "What is this?"

"It's popcorn," Jack said, offering the bag. "It's part of the ceremony. You munch it during the movie."

She placed one in her mouth. Her eyes widened. "It's like eating a tiny, crispy star-ball!" She giggled and tossed another in.

They took their seats in the very first row, which Jack claimed was the best spot for "big eyes and big adventures."

The theater darkened. Lunibelle clutched the seat's arms. "Is this the beginning or the end?"

"Beginning."

The lights faded. The screen flickered to life. A town appeared—blanketed in snow, wrapped in white from roof to root. Children in mittens and mufflers darted on the street.

One little girl, with the brightest red mittens, stretched out her hand. Several snowflakes fell...

"Look!" she shrieked, her eyes wide as saucers. "Sky-stars! They're falling right out of the clouds!"

The other children came running and tumbling to look.

"Are they all the same?" one little boy, whose nose was dripping, squinted up at the sky.

"Nope!" the girl declared, shaking her head so her pigtails bounced. She poked at the tiny white shapes. "Look closer! They're not the same at all!"

"But they should be the same!" a grumpy voice piped up from the back. "They're all just snow!"

"Let's find out!" a third child yelled, jumping up and down. "Let's catch a million and see!"

And so, their great snowflake hunt began!

Inside the theater, Lunibelle tugged Jack's sleeve. "Shouldn't we help them?"

"Help them? We're just watchers."

"Then we should watch ourselves helping," Lunibelle said. "Close your eyes."

Jack obeyed. The moment his lashes met, he felt something strange—like falling and rising all at once. A smell of snow and hot chocolate brushed past.

"Now open!"

Jack blinked. He was standing—not in the theater—but in the snowy town itself. Snowflakes twirled past his ears. He wore a warm coat and boots. Lunibelle stood beside him in a pink velvet coat and orange mittens, her breath forming tiny clouds.

She stretched out her mitten. A snowflake drifted onto it.

"This is the most breathtaking ice flower I've ever seen!"

Jack stared. "Wow."

"Look!" Lunibelle pointed. "It's the girl with the red mittens!"

Jack walked over. "Hello there!"

"Hi!" the girl chirped.

"What are you doing?" Jack asked deliberately.

"Looking for two same snowflakes," she said proudly.

"Did you find any?" Jack asked.

She shook her head.

Lunibelle bent close, whispering the dream's riddle into the snowy air. "Did you find N?"

"N?" The girl frowned. "You mean... noodles?"

Lunibelle shook her head. The girl spun away, chasing the breeze.

Jack looked at his gloves. Snowflakes landed—soft and fragile.

"They're all six-pointed stars," Lunibelle murmured. "But each one is its own poem!"

"Look at this!" she pointed. "Six branches, tiny forks! Who carved such delicate beauty?"

"Nature's handwriting," Jack replied. "An invisible burin."

Snowflakes sparkled. Lunibelle whispered to one, "Would you like to be my friend?" It shimmered brighter—as if saying a yes.

"I want to bring them to my parents," she giggled. "Jack, do you think they'll stay frozen in my suitcase?"

"Only if your suitcase has a winter inside," Jack said with a smile.

"I haven't found two the same yet," Lunibelle sighed. "But surely, somewhere..."

Jack pointed. "Let's try the forest."

They trudged into the woods.

Suddenly—a squirrel! Soft fur, a green pointed hat with a white ball on top. He was digging.

"Excuse me!" Jack called.

The squirrel looked up guiltily. "Yes?"

"Do you know where two identical snowflakes are?" Jack asked.

The squirrel scratched his head with his tail. "Can't say I do."

"Do you know where N is?" Lunibelle asked.

"Nuts?" The squirrel puffed out his chest. "I've hidden thousands this fall! I know each one's location, even when covered by the snow. Not a single nut is alike—yet everyone belongs to me!"

Jack chuckled. "You're very talented!"

"This is not related to talent; it's know-how."

The squirrel bowed.

"Old Bear might know. Lives in that great tree." He pointed proudly with his nut.

Part III: The Bear Who Snores Through the Answer

The squirrel hopped ahead with surprising grace for a creature with snow-caked paws and a nut in his mouth. Jack and Lunibelle trudged behind, lifting their legs high.

The woods twisted around them in sleepy spirals. Each tree leaned slightly, as if whispering today's news to its neighbor. Frost curled on every branch. Somewhere far off, a fox sneezed. Somewhere closer, a snowdrop giggled—then toppled over.

"If there hadn't been a squirrel to lead the way," Lunibelle whispered gratefully, brushing snow off her cheeks, "we might've ended up walking in figure eights until spring."

"I'm good at figure eights," Jack said proudly. "Except when I trip and turn them into figure doughnuts."

The squirrel twitched his nose. "Less talking, more trudging. Mr. Old Bear doesn't like to be kept waiting—or waking—or anything that starts with a 'w,' really."

They reached a clearing where a great oak tree stood—the library of the forest—tall, quiet, and full of stories nobody could read without an invitation.

Jack knocked gently. No answer. He knocked again—slightly louder. Still nothing.

"He's definitely hibernating," Jack said, pressing his ear to the door. "I think I hear snoring—or possibly a bassoon solo."

"How do we wake a bear?" Lunibelle asked, inspecting the wood for magical runes or honey buttons.

"You don't," said the squirrel. "Unless you're foolish, fearless, or holding honey."

Before Jack could reply, the ground trembled beneath them. Snow fell from the branches in cautious drizzles.

"Is this an earthquake?!" Jack gasped.

"No," the squirrel said calmly. "That's just your story sneezing."

And suddenly—

WHUMP!

Jack landed flat on his back—in the middle of the movie theater seat. Popcorn flew like buttery fireflies. Lunibelle sat in the seat next to his and rubbed her eyes.

A robotic voice hummed, "The story will resume after it blows its nose. Please wait."

Lunibelle popped up beside him, brushing snow from her hair. "We must go buy some honey."

"Honey? Right now?"

"To wake the bear. Bears love honey. Some would risk a bee's sting just to taste it."

They dashed to the concession stand. On a little shelf beside the cotton candy sat a jar labeled: *Sun-Gold Blossom—Bear Approved!*

They grabbed it and, with a hiccup of film-reel magic, were back in the snowy forest. The squirrel was still there, tail twitching.

"Good to see you again!" Jack said.

The squirrel blinked. "See me again? I haven't moved an inch. Stories don't move. Hmm."

Jack frowned. "That's strange."

"Everything's strange," Lunibelle whispered. "We brought a gift."

Jack uncapped the honey jar and let the scent drift into the door's keyhole.

For a heartbeat—nothing. Then, from deep within:

"Is that... honey?"

The voice was slow, rumbling, and soft-worn, like an old quilt.

The door creaked open. A giant brown bear blinked at them. He wore blue striped pajamas and a sleep hat flopped sideways over one ear. He looked halfway between a bedtime story and a breakfast dream.

"What's all this white nonsense?" he mumbled. "Still winter?"

"Yes, sir," Jack said politely. "We brought you honey."

Old Bear's eyes widened. He sniffed and sighed. "Ah. Yes. The good kind—the kind with sunshine stuck inside."

He licked the honey thoughtfully. His eyes sparkled. "So... who are you?"

"Visitors!" Lunibelle beamed. "On a quest!"

"A quest, you say..." The bear yawned. "Do come in."

Inside, the treehouse glowed warmly. Pinecone volumes lined the shelves. A cuckoo clock ticked slowly.

Old Bear settled onto a cushion. "So. Why are you here?"

Jack cleared his throat. "We're searching for two identical snowflakes."

The bear blinked. "Ah. A noble quest. Also... extremely unlikely."

"But it's the movie title," Lunibelle said softly.

"What did you say?" the bear asked. "I only see the mountains..."

"You must know a lot about snow," Lunibelle encouraged.

"Everyone thinks I'm old enough to know everything," the bear said, gesturing to his impressive belly. "Because I've been through many seasons and eaten many berries."

"You must know something," Jack said. "Anything at all?"

"I know..." the bear mumbled, blinking slowly, "...that spring in the woods is lovely. The flowers bloom. The bees dance. The frogs debate philosophy on lily pads..."

His head drooped mid-sentence. A snore rumbled from his nose.

Jack and Lunibelle exchanged glances.

"What do we do?" Jack whispered.

"This happens," said the squirrel, completely unfazed. "Old Bear gets... drowsy in winter."

"But how long does he stay asleep?" Lunibelle asked.

"Until something worthy wakes him."

"Show him honey," Lunibelle reminded softly.

Jack held the honey jar beneath the bear's nose.

The bear twitched.

"I once danced with a parrot on a pond... I think," he muttered.

"Sir!" Jack tried again. "Do you know where we can find two snowflakes exactly the same?"

Old Bear stretched slowly. "I sleep through the whole winter; I never play with snow."

Jack's shoulders slumped.

"But," the bear added, his voice softer now, "I have a brother. Name's Nick. He lives in the North Pole. If anyone knows... he does."

"The North Pole!" Lunibelle's eyes widened. "That's far?"

"Depends," said Old Bear. "If you walk, far. If you fly, less so. The owl runs the flights at Ice-Sparkle Park—down the hill."

He handed Lunibelle a tiny icicle key. "For the owl's dictionary. He's picky about answers."

They thanked Old Bear, waved to the squirrel (who bowed dramatically), and stepped back into the snow. They hopped down the path as if joy had melted into their boots.

Part IV: The Shiny Stub That Asks a Riddle

The path to Ice-Sparkle Park was blanketed in snow. It crunched beneath their boots. Jack and Lunibelle followed it down the hill, laughing as their breath turned into foggy dragons.

A sign iced in frost appeared. Jack brushed it clean: → *Ice-Sparkle Park — For Snow, For Sky, For Wonder*

The entrance glowed with translucent blue ice bricks. Above the archway, words curled: *All who enter must remember: flying is a matter of belief, not balance.*

The park sparkled. There were igloos that hummed lullabies, snowmen roasting marshmallows, an automatic rink, and rabbits playing tag around an ice fountain.

Dozens of enormous snowflakes lay scattered across a wide clearing. Each was wagon-wheel-sized, a crystalline marvel glowing in blues, pinks, and greens. One even flashed many colors as though it had swallowed a rainbow. At the edge stood a solemn owl in spectacles, perched behind a ledger thicker than three dictionaries.

"Hoo goes there?" the owl asked.

"We're here to fly," Jack said, smiling.

"To the North Pole!" Lunibelle added.

"Tickets!" the owl barked, its voice sharp as a gavel.

"What tickets?" Jack blurted.

The owl swiveled its crystal eyes. "You mean to say... you don't know? A ticket is a puzzle. Answer wrongly, and you vanish like the rest."

Jack's hand found the icicle key. He held it up. "Old Bear gave us this—for your dictionary."

The owl trembled reverently. A side panel popped open, revealing a snow-leather book with a frosted lock. The key fit perfectly. Pages gleamed with hundreds of definitions.

"Now," the owl intoned, "define *ticket*."

Jack tried. "A guarantee of entry."

"Wrong!" The owl hooted like a game-show buzzer.

He tried again. "A permission slip?"

"Denied!" the owl shrieked. "Think not as a student—but as a seagull in a storm!"

Jack froze. Lunibelle stepped forward. "He's not asking what a ticket *is*. He's asking what it *means*—to him."

The owl's pupils narrowed. "One last guess."

Lunibelle planted her feet, lifted her chin, and then, with a glittering roar: "WHAT DO YOU LIKE TO EAT THE MOST?!"

The owl erupted into panic. "Sir, MOUSE, sir!" it squawked, saluting so hard that its feathers striped themselves.

"Then the answer is mouse," Lunibelle smiled. "Because a ticket is what gets you what you want most. Sometimes paper, sometimes an idea, sometimes a snack."

The owl blinked. Then burst out laughing—a cello plucked by mischief. "Correct! Or at least... correct enough!"

From nowhere, it produced two glittering tokens, each shaped like a snowflake. "Present these to the flake you choose. Snowflakes don't need wings to fly—only wishes."

Jack and Lunibelle walked to the largest flake—a pale blue crystal with silver veins. As they approached, it lifted gently into the air.

They climbed aboard. The snowflake tilted, then rose into the sky—as though it had always been meant to be there.

Part V: Into the Whirling Vortex of Forgotten Questions

"Please state your destination," asked Snowflake.

"The North Pole," Jack replied confidently.

Snowflake flashed. "Coordinates locked. Buckle your belief. Take-off in five... four... three..."

Jack and Lunibelle sat at its center as it lifted higher and higher, and the air grew thinner, colder, clearer. Soon, all of Ice-Sparkle Park was just a glowing dot below them.

"Look at that!" Lunibelle pointed. "Those aren't clouds... they're sky-whales!"

Enormous, slow-moving creatures drifted beneath them—whales made of mist and light, their translucent fins curving gently as they floated through the upper air. A flock of snowbirds soared past in perfect formation, spelling out *Dream Big* in trails of glittering frost.

"I didn't know the sky had so many thoughts," Jack whispered.

"It's full of them," Snowflake replied. "But most melt before they hit the ground."

Snowflake shifted course. The horizon filled with shimmering blues and silvers—the Arctic.

And then—suddenly—trouble.

A storm cloud loomed ahead—vast, swirling, and purple. It looked grumpier than a goat in the rain.

"Warning," Snowflake said, wobbling slightly. "Turbulence of thought detected."

"Turbulence of what?" Jack yelped.

"Unresolved questions and memory static."

Lunibelle leaned forward. "Let's go through it."

Jack gawked. "Go through the storm?"

"Yes! If it's made of confused thoughts... maybe it just needs sorting out."

Snowflake dipped its crystalline edges and flew straight into the cloud.

Instantly, voices filled the air—half-finished sentences, broken wishes, questions with no answers:

"Did I remember to say goodbye?" "What would've happened if I'd said yes?" "Do birds dream of falling... or flying?"

A memory brushed past Jack's ear—his fifth-birthday balloon floating into the sky. Lunibelle heard her mother humming a lullaby that didn't exist yet.

The clouds grew thick with confusion, and chaos spun into a massive vortex. Snowflake was sucked in, whirling faster and faster.

"Locked in the vortex! Locked in the vortex!" Snowflake repeated.

Lunibelle's curls danced wildly in the storm wind. "We're spiraling deeper!"

"What if we can't get out?" Jack shouted, clutching Snowflake's icy ridges.

Voices tugged at their coats, whispering: "Unfinished lullabies...

missing mittens... people you almost became..."

"We have to remind the storm who we are!" Lunibelle cried. "Or it'll rewrite us!"

Snowflake spun faster. The center of the vortex opened like a giant yawning mouth.

"ALARM OF MISMATCHED SOCKS!" Snowflake flashed yellow.

"ALARM OF FORGOTTEN BIRTHDAYS!" It flashed green.

"ALARM OF QUESTIONS THAT REFUSE TO WAIT!" It blazed purple.

"SUPREME ALARM OF FEAR ITSELF!" It shrieked red.

Jack looked at Lunibelle. Her cheeks were bright with windburn, but her eyes were steady.

"We need to say something real," she said.

"Like what?"

"Something truer than fear."

Jack remembered his sketchbook. He yanked it from his coat and flipped to a blank page—but it curled, flapped, and filled with other people's handwriting.

"I don't even recognize these thoughts," he muttered.

Lunibelle squeezed his hand. "Write anyway. Your truth matters."

Jack gritted his teeth, then took a deep breath. With trembling fingers, he wrote: *You were never lost. Just waiting to be heard.*

He held the sketchbook high.

The wind hushed. The storm paused. The questions whispered one last time... and then fell silent.

"Recovering control," Snowflake declared.

The vortex unraveled—purple to violet, to lilac, to soft snow blue. The spiral slowed, then stilled.

Snowflake burst through the top of the cloud and into a clear sky.

Lunibelle clutched Jack's waist, her eyes shining.

For a moment, they couldn't speak.

Jack wrote *We did it!* in the sketchbook and showed it to her. She nodded, tears bright in her eyes.

The stars felt close enough to touch.

"Emotional clarity restored," Snowflake reported cheerfully. "Approaching destination."

Below, the Earth glowed white. Icebergs stood like sculptures carved by wind and time. And in the distance—beyond a curve of glacier—was a village made entirely of snow.

Snowflake began to descend.

Jack reached for Lunibelle's hand. "We're really here."

She nodded. "Let's find the snow that never repeats."

Snowflake purred in delight, as if it had waited its whole life for this moment.

Part VI: The Snowflakes Who Dance in Their Own Shapes

Jack and Lunibelle stepped off Snowflake and onto a landscape that whispered many secrets.

The North Pole was not what Jack had imagined. There were no clumsy igloos or penguins with scarves. Instead, it was a kingdom spun from frost and imagination. The snowflakes here didn't fall;

they floated, wandered, and explored the air as if tiny paper poets looking for new thoughts. The wind sang songs rather than howling. Trees glowed faintly, trying not to wake sleeping north bears.

Tucked into this hush stood a teapot-shaped house—round and squat, steaming gently from its chimney spout.

Jack stared. "Is that a teapot?"

"That," said Lunibelle, eyes twinkling, "must be Nick's house."

The door creaked open before they knocked. A polar bear in a snowflake-patterned scarf and slippers stepped out. His face was soft and thoughtful—someone who made a living out of daydreams.

"Welcome," said Nick, "to the House of Steeped Questions. Come in, come in."

Inside, the walls curved inward as though stories were being told. A fire of fizzing, ice-blue flames crackled. The couch looked carved from a snowbank and covered in knitted dreams. A kettle whistled a winter song.

Nick poured peppermint-and-fish tea. "So," he said, adjusting his scarf, "you want to find two identical snowflakes."

"Yes!" Jack nearly bounced off the couch.

"A noble quest—also a very tricky one," Nick said.

"Why?" Lunibelle asked.

Nick tilted his head. "That depends on who's looking, and why. Improbable things are where miracles hide.

"The answers might be in the Snow Museum." He pointed toward a frosted window. "Come. I'll show you."

Outside, a sled awaited—bone white, glittering with jelly-bean-sized bells.

They walked out. Nick climbed in, followed by Lunibelle and Jack.

"Hold on. The museum dislikes loud entrances."

The sled zipped across snowy plains—past accordion-playing icicles and a school of narwhals rehearsing *The Snowflake Sonata*. The wind smelled of whipped vanilla and forgotten snow days.

The Snow Museum flashed—a gigantic snow globe at the end of a crystal bridge. Two penguins in tuxedos stood by the doors, offering scarves of woven icicle thread.

Inside, walls of frost sheets, etched with snowflakes, gleamed.

"Welcome to my life's collection," Nick said reverently.

They explored exhibits: *Symphonies in Six Points*, *The Flake That Thought It Was a Star*, and the *Hall of Unfinished Flakes*, where trembling snowflakes hovered in jars.

"They almost became identical," explained a voice.

An arctic fox in a too-long scarf padded forward.

"Professor Pufftail," Nick introduced. "Our flake philosopher."

"They changed at the last microsecond," Pufftail said. "Choice, fear, even a sneeze from a cloud—it doesn't take much. Snowflakes are whimsical."

"So it's always almost?" Lunibelle asked.

"Almost is the rule," Pufftail replied. "Sameness is the miracle."

Deeper inside, they found a silver staircase spiraling up and down at once.

"*Vault of Lost Possibilities*," Nick read the inscription on the wall. "*Walk it backward while dreaming forward, and it tells you who you could have been.*"

At the bottom sat a velvet-blue book: *The Two That Matched, Once.*

Jack opened it. The first page read, *They were found in a boy's pocket, after he forgot to be afraid.* The rest was blank.

Beside it stood a snow typewriter.

"Should we write the ending?" Lunibelle asked.

"Maybe we are the ending," Jack replied.

For a moment, snowflakes outside slowed their descent. One hovered at the window, pressing close.

They started flipping the pages of several books.

Nick asked, "Find anything?"

"Not two the same," Lunibelle said, "but many almosts."

"Then you've found most of the truth," Nick said.

They left the museum wrapped in thoughts heavier than coats. Outside, a flake landed on Lunibelle's mitten.

"Hello," she whispered.

It shimmered. Another landed beside it.

Jack leaned in. "You two look alike."

The flakes sparkled mischievously, but no—their forks differed.

"Almost," Jack said.

"Almost is beautiful too," Lunibelle whispered.

And somewhere above, a snowflake laughed.

Part VII: The Truth Isn't Hiding in the Finding

The next morning arrived with a hush so soft it could have been mistaken for silence. Jack and Lunibelle returned to the Snow Library, determination stitched into their scarves and tucked inside their mittens. Today, they would search with every piece of wonder they had.

They split up—Jack began with the books under A, while Lunibelle wandered off toward Z.

When Jack whispered "A," the entire A-section gleamed blue. Books floated from shelves and bowed like courteous butlers. Titles blinked open. Pages fluttered. Jack read carefully, noting crystalline diagrams and theories of symmetry.

Meanwhile, Lunibelle stood before the Z-shelves, where the books were zany and self-aware. Some laughed at their own titles. One tried to knit her a scarf while muttering spells. She held two books, one in each hand, reading them back and forth. Suddenly she heard a tiny book that sang its contents to the tune of a snowflake falling. Another whispered its title wrong on purpose, just to see if she noticed.

They met in the middle by midday, surrounded by a garden of open books that laughed when no one looked.

"Nothing," Jack said, sliding onto a stool shaped like an ice-cream scoop.

"Not yet," Lunibelle corrected. She tugged at her mitten, deep in thought.

By evening, they had only reviewed one and a half sections.

"There are too many books. We can't possibly read them all," Jack said, frowning.

"We need to change our approach." Lunibelle nodded.

The next day, they changed their method. Jack dove into science—physics of crystals, histories of storms, maps of snowfall. He borrowed a glowing magnifying glass from a pinecone-shaped librarian. The glass outlined each snowflake diagram in shimmering yellow, but every one revealed differences, never sameness.

Lunibelle took the other path—myths, magical patterns, and ancient whispers. She explored a section called *Secrets Not Even the Wind Knows*, where books were heavy as pillows. One whispered, "You already hold the answer," then closed with a sigh. Another offered a riddle written backward: *To match the flakes, do not seek them—become them.*

By the third day, Lunibelle slumped beside a mountain of encyclopedias. "Maybe... we should stop."

Jack looked up, startled. "Stop? But we haven't finished every book."

"It's not that," she said softly, resting her head on a floating book. "Maybe this isn't something we find in the pages."

She closed her eyes. Then—

A flash of memory!

"The snowflake in my dream," she gasped. "It said 'N'!"

"The N-section!" Jack jumped to his feet. "Of course!"

They raced through the aisles. The N-section glowed like a stage awaiting actors. Books stretched and yawned, covers opening like mouths.

They searched feverishly. But the answer seemed nowhere to be found.

Then Jack saw it—a tiny blue book wedged between atlases. Its cover was plain, its corners curled. The title read: *Why Nothing Matches.*

He opened it. The first page said: *Snowflakes shine because they are different. The world is beautiful because it is different.*

Jack read it aloud.

Lunibelle didn't speak. Her silence brimmed with joy, as though the words had always been hers.

"I thought I wanted to find two the same," Jack whispered. "To prove the impossible could be true."

Lunibelle nodded. "But maybe what's true... is already all around us."

They returned the book to its shelf, both quieter and fuller.

As they walked toward the exit, a snowflake fluttered through the skylight. Jack caught it gently on his glove.

"Hello again," he said.

Lunibelle touched her finger to it. Another flake landed beside it.

"They look close," she said.

"They do," Jack smiled, "but one has a curl in the middle, and the other a sparkle twist."

"They played about their shapes," Lunibelle giggled.

"Or maybe," Jack said, "they told the truth in their own way."

The Snow Library dimmed its lights. Outside, snowflakes danced in slow spirals.

Jack looked up. "We searched the library, but maybe we should have looked at the sky."

Lunibelle raised her head. "Each flake a note in a song. And none out of tune."

They walked through the hall, past candlelit windows and drifting stars. Jack hummed. Lunibelle twirled. They had not found two the same.

And that was perfect.

   *   Difference is not the opposite. It is the essence of beauty. *

Chapter VIII
The Secret Hoard of the Hidden Toys

Part I: The Mystery of the Vanishing Toys

It was an ordinary Tuesday morning. Or a Thursday. Or possibly the forgotten eighth day of the week—Splendiferday. The kittens never bothered with calendars, so who could say?

Parcel's four kittens woke to a catastrophe—the kind of catastrophe that rattles cupboards, ripples breakfast bowls, and makes shadows hold their breath.

Every single toy in the house was gone!

Jack's basketball? Vanished—not a single bounce left behind. Lunibelle's glittering snow globe, with its tiny orbiting planets? Slipped into the void like a stolen dream. Willy's chew bone? Not a tooth mark in sight. Yellowy's prized golden mirror? Had taken flight, lighter than a dandelion seed. Parcel's beloved yarn ball? Simply unraveled into the great unknown, leaving behind only a whisper of where it once lay.

And worse still—the kittens' own favorite toys were missing, too!

The kittens ricocheted through the house, tails tangled with panic. Meow1 scrambled to the top of the bookshelf, her tiny paws dancing across the dusty spines of forgotten fairy tales. She found a pair of opera glasses perched atop a snowman figurine and pressed them dramatically to her nose. "Missing!" she cried. "Gone! Vanished into the veil of uncertainty!"

Meow3 flung open the refrigerator and glared at the vegetables inside. "I am think... toys do not typically reside among such boring things." She poked a lettuce leaf suspiciously, as though it might transform into a rubber duck at any moment.

Meow4, in a stroke of questionable genius, wedged his entire head into a cereal box and charged across the kitchen. "Attack formation!" he shouted, kicking a teacup, a toaster, and an entire bowl of blue-berries.

Meanwhile, Meow2 plunged into the sink, convinced his rainbow marble had gone for a swim. He resurfaced proudly holding a soggy sponge, waving it. "I found it!" he squeaked. "Only it feels squishier than before."

Jack stumbled in, rubbing his eyes and tripping over Meow2. "What's all the noise?" he asked, blinking at the chaos.

"Vanished! Evaporated! Even my tail looks suspicious!" wailed Meow1.

"Even my purple squeaky eggplant," moaned Meow2.

Lunibelle floated in behind him, her eyes wide and searching. Parcel padded in with her usual solemn dignity. Willy barked once in confusion, tail wagging as though he might sniff the toys back into existence. Yellowy fluttered to the couch, feathers fluffed in agitation.

"This is serious," Jack declared, clapping his hands. "Emergency meeting."

The kittens nodded and donned napkins as capes. Lunibelle provided a cookie tin for a table. Willy sat proudly on a slipper as if it were a throne. Yellowy preened herself, declaring, "I shall preside from the couch."

Jack tapped a spoon against a juice box like a gavel. "Let's go over what we know."

"All the toys are gone," Meow1 announced gravely.

"No footprints," said Parcel, her ears twitching. "No broken windows."

"I am think... the wind might have stolen them," offered Meow3.

"Or a greedy rainbow who wanted all the glitter," suggested Meow2.

"Or... or a winged giant with invisible pockets!" Meow4 exclaimed, cereal dust still on his whiskers.

Yellowy fluttered indignantly. "It wasn't me—I only take shiny things with permission."

"Parcel," Jack said, "what do your motherly instincts say?"

Parcel flicked her tail and narrowed her eyes. "Something magical. Something sneaky. Possibly something with feathers."

Everyone turned to Yellowy.

"I said not me!" the canary squeaked, hopping up and down.

The room fell silent.

Lunibelle scribbled on a scrap of paper. "Suspects: Wind, rainbow, invisible giant, magical sneak."

Meow3 stood with great ceremony. "I am think... our toys may have left us a clue. We must look again."

Meow4 jumped up. "Then we search every sock drawer and under every bed! Adventure begins now!"

Just then, the rug gave a tiny hiccup, as if in agreement. A single dust bunny rolled by, dramatically.

Something was happening. Something absurd.

And this, dear reader, is how the grand nonsense adventure began—with four kittens, a baffled boy, a mysterious alien, a loyal German Shepherd, a sharp-eyed cat, a sparkly canary, precisely zero toys, and a question so outrageous it rattled the wallpaper:

Where did all the toys go?

Part II: The Envelope That Buzzes and Flies

No one knew where to find the toys—or even a single clue—until Meow4 spotted something glinting beneath the coffee table. He pounced and tugged out a dusty picture book.

The kittens crowded around, their whiskers twitching with excitement. Jack and Lunibelle leaned over their shoulders. Parcel and Willy pressed closer, while Yellowy hovered just above the book.

The pages were filled with drawings—castles, jungles, and floating clouds. But right there, nestled among the illustrations, were their missing toys. Jack's basketball bounced cheerfully beside a pirate ship. Lunibelle's snow globe spun atop a tiny mushroom house. Willy's chew bone floated lazily down a chocolate river, bobbing like a raft on a sweet adventure. Yellowy's mirror dangled from a fairy's necklace, gleaming with mischief. Parcel's yarn ball had twined itself around the antlers of a cartoon deer.

The kittens gasped. Meow1's pink jingle bell tinkled on a fairy's wrist. Meow2's marble rolled past a smiling cloud. Meow3's puzzle cube glowed with geometry. And Meow4's heroic action figure clung to a paper airplane soaring high into the illustrated sky.

Jack blinked in disbelief. "How—how did they—?"

Lunibelle pointed to the bottom of the page. There, written in curling letters that shimmered in and out of sight, was an address: *13 Wick Street, Magic State, 8th Continent. Post Number: 0000000.*

"We have to go there!" Meow4 declared, puffing out his chest.

"But how?" asked Meow1, whiskers trembling.

"Give me an envelope," Lunibelle told Jack.

Jack sprinted into Dad's office and returned with a crisp white envelope.

"Here you are," Jack said.

"Bigger!" Lunibelle sighed dreamily, holding it up. "Bigger, bigger!"

With a WHOOSH and a RUSTLE, the envelope began to grow, expanding and unfolding until it was big enough to hold all of them. Across its surface, glowing letters declared: *Payable by the Other Party.*

"We mail ourselves," Lunibelle smiled. "Come in, please."

"Can we be mailed?" The kittens exchanged stunned glances. Then, one by one, they leaped in. Meow1 went first, wiggling with delight. She flattened instantly into a purring pancake. Meow2 followed, less gracefully. He squeaked as his whiskers folded. Meow3 slid in with scholarly indignation, muttering, "I am think... this defies all known physics." Her voice came out muffled, as though trapped between pages. And then came Meow4, belly-flopping with

heroic abandon. He even tried licking himself flat, but he only suc-
ceeded in making his fur stick out.

Parcel curled protectively around her kittens, a vigilant shadow of
fur. Willy woofed once, as if to say, "Really?"—then leaped nobly
into the envelope. Yellowy tucked herself in like a golden feather. Jack
dove in with the grace of a basketball player. Finally, Lunibelle slid
inside like mist and sealed the flap with a kiss. The envelope hummed
with a soft, magical sound.

A shadow passed overhead. The
Eagle Postman descended, enormous
and official. His feathers were mot-
tled with stamps from distant lands.
His beak was sharp. His eyes were
hidden behind postman sunglasses. A
cap perched rakishly on his head bore
the insignia of the *Interdimensional Postal Service*—an envelope with
wings, grinning mischievously.

"Special delivery to Magic State?"
he asked.

"Indeed," Lunibelle replied from inside.

The eagle plucked the envelope gently in his talons and tucked
it into his mailbag, which was embroidered with tiny planets and
postcards. Because the envelope was too big, half of it poked out.
With a powerful flap of wings, the Eagle Postman soared into the
clouds, carrying the fattened, giggling, absurd little bundle of heroes

191

toward nonsense, missing toys, and unspeakable kitten mischief.

Part III: The Island That Swims

The envelope sailed through the sky, tucked beneath the Eagle Postman's wing. Inside, the kittens pressed their squashed faces to invisible peek holes, watching clouds drift by.

"I am think..." observed Meow3, her whiskers bent flat. "These clouds need to lose weight."

"Do you think the next place has snacks?" asked Meow2 nervously.

"I hope the next place has dragons!" shouted Meow4, kicking his little paws in excitement.

"Meow4! You stepped on me!" Meow1 yowled, flattening her fur.

Parcel sighed. "This is what happens when you let kittens interpret reality."

They had hardly finished arguing when the envelope wobbled, tilted, and then—PLOP!—landed with a gentle bounce atop a small island.

The Eagle Postman set them down, adjusted his cap, and rumbled, "Transfer station—Floating Island. Mind your verbs." And with that cryptic warning, he flapped away into the clouds.

The island itself swam through the sky, its sandy edges trailing ribbons of mist. Palm trees swayed lazily, as though pondering weighty decisions. Brightly colored fish swam in the air, weaving between the fronds and humming nonsense tunes like, "BLOOPITY-BLOOP, I lost my soup spoon." A breeze carried the unmistakable scent of tropics.

"That fish just blinked at me," said Jack.

"I am think..." replied Meow3, "reality has taken a holiday."

Paws patting the sandy cloud-ground, the kittens scampered ahead. Willy padded close behind, sniffing suspiciously, as Yellowy nervously fluttered through a swarm of flying fish.

At the edge of the island, an ancient turtle basked on a rock. His shell was popped open like a picnic basket. Inside were tiny chairs and a checkerboard waiting for visitors. He cracked one sleepy eye and smiled. "Greetings, backwards travelers," he said, his voice like rust. "Or... is it forwards? Hard to say around here."

They soon noticed it. Everything on the island ran in reverse. A wooden sign read: *emocle W.* The palm shadows spelled: *ecalper siht ni sdrow lla gniog era sdrawkcab.* Even the fish bore tattoos like: *uoy evol I* and *em ot esoporp uoy lliW nehW?*

"Oh no," groaned Jack. "This place speaks backwards."

"I am think... linguistic catastrophe is imminent," Meow3 muttered.

The kittens were already causing trouble. Meow4 shouted "Goodbye!" cheerily to a passing fish. The fish frowned and darted away. Meow1 called "Hello!" to a rock, and the rock turned a somersault, giggling. Meow2 politely requested a map, only to discover he had inadvertently proposed marriage to a pelican. The pelican blushed and offered him a fish. Meow2 squeaked and hid behind Parcel.

Parcel guided them firmly, preventing worse disasters. But misunderstandings spiraled anyway. The kittens nearly ordered seventeen left shoes and a singing lamp before Jack pulled them back. "Is it too late to crawl back into the envelope?" he groaned.

The group agreed quickly.

Before Lunibelle sealed the flap, she noticed a slip of blue paper resting nearby. It flashed and read: *Goodbye, keep going forward, and never look back.* She tucked it into her pocket and climbed in last.

Inside, though flat as pancakes, they discovered they could still move as if in a shadow-puppet world. The kittens quickly invented the CLAPPY Envelope Game to pass the time. They chanted full verses, their paws tapping in rhythm:

CLAP CLAP—paper hat, / Pat your paws and sit like that!

CLAP CLAP—upside down, / Spin around and wear a crown!

CLAP CLAP—FLAP goes ZOOM, / Jump three times across the room.

CLAP CLAP—stamp your tail, / Now MEOW and lick the mail!

The envelope trembled with laughter.

Part IV: The Whale Postman's Belly

Amid the kittens' play, Yellowy tilted her head and asked, "Where are we headed?"

"I am think..." Meow3's voice sounded lowered. "...we'll go where we should go."

Suddenly, a deep, booming WHOOOOMP echoed across the skies. The clouds parted, the air-fish scattered, and a massive shadow drifted overhead.

A whale!

A whale wearing a postman's sash embroidered with stamps from impossible places—such as the Moon's Inside and the Apple Orchard of Imaginary.

The whale's mouth cracked open, wide as a canyon. "Mail pickup, hooo!" bellowed the whale, his voice sloshing.

Before anyone could object, the whale slurped the envelope off the ground—and everyone with it.

Inside the whale's belly, everything was... surprisingly organized. Stacks of letters floated in bubbles. Packages were neatly arranged on shelves as if in miniature mailboxes. A warm lantern swung gently overhead, casting golden ripples as the whale swam through the skies.

The kittens gazed in awe. Meow4 poked his belly and declared, "I decide... this place is oddly perfect."

"I am think..." agreed Meow3. "Here is like a real world."

But the strangest thing of all was this: in the middle of the whale's belly, an old sailboat floated calmly. And in the boat sat an even older man.

He wore a red fez, smoked a long pipe, and blinked one eye very slowly.

"Welcome aboard," said the old man. "I'm Captain Popper. You're just in time for star stories."

"Star stories?" Meow2 whispered, wide-eyed.

The old man nodded and pointed upward. Above them—impossibly—stars glittered across the whale's inner sky. "Every one of those," Captain Popper puffed, "is sugar."

Meow4 gasped. "SUGAR?!"

"The North Star is spun sugar, like cotton candy. Orion's Belt—three perfect sugar cubes. Some nights fizz like soda; some nights drip molasses."

Lunibelle laughed softly, her eyes catching the lantern light. Parcel curled her tail around the kittens. Yellowy preened quietly on Jack's shoulder. Willy lay down, nose between paws, though his ears stayed perked.

The group sat, entranced, as Captain Popper puffed one last peppermint ring. "That's the sky's secret. Stars don't burn. They glow from joy."

Meow4 nearly exploded with excitement. "I want to lick the Big Dipper!"

Meow2 whispered, "Do the stars ever fall?"

"Only when they're tired," said Captain Popper. "Or when someone sings them a lullaby."

"Do you live in here?" Jack asked.

"I vacation here," Captain Popper said, adjusting his fez. "Where else can you nap in a bubble and send letters to Mars's third volcano?"

Just then, the whale's belly gave a polite rumble. The lantern swayed. "Time to go," said Captain Popper. "Destination approaching. Good luck!"

With a mighty PFFFSHHH, the whale tilted back, cheeks ballooning.

"Hold your noses!" shouted Jack.

With a deafening roar, the envelope shot out of the whale's blowhole in a glorious arc of glitter. They didn't even have time to say goodbye to Captain Popper.

They soared into the clouds, dripping glitter and whale breath but otherwise quite cheerful. As they tumbled downward, Lunibelle laughed. "Next stop: Mirage Desert," she announced, pointing to the flashing landscape below.

The kittens cheered. "I hope the sandcastles bite back!" Meow4 roared, tumbling in excitement.

"I don't want to become a sandcastle," muttered Meow2.

Captain Popper's voice echoed faintly: "Keep your eyes open and your sugar spoons ready!"

And down they drifted, toward more absurdity, riddles, and desert mirages—ready or not.

Part V: The Whispering Bones Beneath the Sand

The envelope fluttered down from the clouds. It twirled, twitched, and somersaulted, humming with postal magic before plopping belly-up on a warm bed of golden sand.

The flap creaked open. Out tumbled Jack, Lunibelle, Willy, Parcel, Yellowy, and the kittens, blinking against the blazing sun.

"Whoa," Jack whispered, shielding his eyes. "We landed in a golden field."

"Very dazzling!" Meow1 agreed.

The desert was unlike anything they'd seen. Dunes rolled like mountains. The sand shifted colors in pulses: peach, lavender, champagne, and silver.

Meow4 leaped into action. "So hot! So soft! So everywhere!" He galloped like a tumbleweed, somersaulted into a dune, and vanished headfirst.

"This sand sparkles!" Meow2 sniffed.

"I am think... maybe it's alive. Maybe this is no desert at all—it's a giant dragon napping beneath a sand blanket." Meow3 always thought a different way.

Boundless. The desert was a searing, golden void where the sun reigned supreme and unpitying. Not a tree, not a shadow, offered respite. The heat was immediate, suffocating. Thirst, a fierce, clawing hunger for water, took hold—quickly escalating to a burning, all-consuming need.

Yellowy flapped above, her sharp eyes scanning. "Oh! Water! Palm trees! Over there!"

Jack squinted. Indeed, not far off, a glistening lake beckoned with palms and parrots. "Water!" he cried, dashing forward.

Lunibelle's warning came too late. With every step, the lake drifted farther. It wobbled, giggled, then somersaulted away before reappearing just out of reach.

"A mirage!" Lunibelle said. "It's desert magic!"

Meow4 zoomed after it. "I WANT A BATH!" The lake rolled its eyes and scooted away. "You'll never catch me!" it chimed, dissolving into sparkly nonsense.

Willy gave chase too, sand spraying behind him. "Run, Willy!" Meow1 cried. But Willy collapsed panting, flopping like a pancake. Yellowy darted after the mirage, her wings slicing sunlight. Poof—the entire scene vanished in a puff of giggles.

The group gathered on a dune, thirsty and dusty. "I am think..." Meow3 said solemnly, "if we wish to reach an illusion, we must become an illusion."

"Or," Parcel suggested dryly, "we could simply walk that way instead."

So they trudged—down dunes, up dunes, past whispering beetles and a cactus humming a welcome. Then Meow4 yelped. "A bone! A... a head!"

They crowded around. A white skull grinned up at them, sun-bleached and half-buried. "Hello," it rasped.

Jack nearly jumped out of his sandals. "Did... it just talk?"

"I did," said the skull. "I'm Camelet. Camel extraordinaire. Former traveler of deserts, eater of prickly pears, and grandmaster of toe-wiggling."

"Where's the rest of you?" asked Yellowy.

"Scattered like puzzle pieces," Camelet sighed wistfully. "A storm tore me apart long ago. My bones lounge in the sand now, enjoying early retirement. But oh, I long to walk again."

"Mr. Camelet, we'll find them," said Lunibelle kindly. "We'll bring you back."

"You're sweet as sugared cacti," Camelet sniffled. "If I had tear ducts, I'd sob."

"All right! Assignments!" Lunibelle declared. "Jack east, Willy west, Parcel south, I'll go north. Kittens—pair up and help. Yellowy, you're our Flight Liaison Officer!"

Off they dashed, sweat on brows, tongues lolling. They found rib bones dancing with tumbleweeds, knobby knees hiding behind sand statues, and vertebrae tucked under beetles.

"My paws are soup—with sand in it!" moaned Meow4.

"I am think... this hip bone is," said Meow3, prodding gently.

One by one, bones came together until a grand camel skeleton rose on the dunes.

"He's HUGE!" Meow2 whispered.

Camelet's skull clicked into place. "I'm back, baby!" he boomed.

Cheers erupted. Camelet wobbled to his feet. "After centuries of sand naps, I can finally STRETCH!"

"We did!" the kittens cried proudly.

"What can I do for you, my de-sanders?" Camelet asked.

"Take us to the mirage!" the group chorused.

"The mirage? Tricky. No real creature may enter it. But since you helped me..." Camelet paced in sandy circles. "Aha! If you become part of me, then I can carry you in!"

"Wait, what?" Jack stammered.

"Into the belly! Come on in—spacious, ventilated, and guaranteed not to digest!"

The group scrambled inside. It smelled of sunlight and cactus-flavored gum. A tiny chandelier of sand grains swung above. The kittens lined up, each hugging the one in front.

"Buckle up!" Camelet crowed. He galloped toward the horizon, and just as the mirage shimmered, they passed through.

Part VI: The Land That Wobbles Like Jelly

DING-DONG, DING-DONG—the copper bell on Camelet's neck rang, singing the thousand-year-old song of wind and sand. With a BANG, he strode into the mirage.

Colors rippling. Air turned syrupy sweet. Trees waved slowly. The sand beneath their feet became soft. Jack stretched out a hand and passed it through the palm trees as through smoke.

"We're inside a dream," Lunibelle whispered, excitedly.

Camelet stopped beside a crystal-clear spring. They tumbled out of his belly as if sweets from a piñata.

"Waa-ter!" Meow4 shouted. He plunged in headfirst, emerged gurgling, and declared, "I've become a very wet balloon."

The others splashed and sipped. The water tasted of cucumber, lime, and watermelon, all melted into a glittering silver sip.

"This is the best water I never imagined," said Jack.

They wandered beneath banana-shaped palm trees. A floating sign twirled midair: *Mirage City—This Way, That Way, and Probably Somewhere Else Too.*

They entered a city that wobbled.

"Welcome to Mirage No. 1736. I'm Mayor Mr. Flutter." A gentleman stood at the entrance, a smile playing on his lips. "It's been a while since an alien has visited."

"We are not aliens!" Willy exclaimed. "We're from Earth."

"Oh, well, Earth isn't far away," Mr. Flutter noted casually. "Five years ago, five Martians dropped in. They were quite interested in our water, and we were happy to teach them how to make it."

"Excuse me, Mr. Flutter," Lunibelle asked, "but why does everything sway like ripples on water?"

"That's a very interesting question!" Mr. Flutter said with a deliberate shudder. "We're made of water and gas, and our shapes reflect the tiniest changes in temperature and wind speed."

"If winter comes," Yellowy chirped, "will you freeze solid?"

"Lucky for us, winter doesn't exist here," Mr. Flutter smiled. "Well then, allow me to introduce an excellent tour guide—Ms. Fennec Fox." He waved a hand, and a golden fox with unusually large ears appeared beside him. "She'll show you around." With that, Mr. Flutter simply vanished.

"Hello, everyone." Ms. Fennec Fox's large ears twitched. "I'm your guide. My code is QU856, and this is my 367th mission."

"Hello!" everyone said in unison.

"First thing to remember," Ms. Fennec Fox said, her voice a gentle warning. "Because the gravity here is so weak, don't use all your strength when you walk, and whatever you do, don't run." She glanced at them all. "If you use too much strength, you'll shoot right up and land a long way from where you started..."

Before she could finish, Meow4 leaped with all his might, rocketing off like a cannonball. Everyone was stunned.

"Oh my gosh!" Parcel covered her mouth, her eyes wide. "Will we still be able to find him?"

Ms. Fennec Fox giggled. "In my career, this has happened half the time. He's probably landed..." She looked in the direction Meow4 had flown, "...in Wandering Lake."

So they headed toward Wandering Lake.

There he was! Meow4 had landed in a flamingo's nest. The mother flamingo, who was incubating her eggs, happily mistook him for a chick and was bathing him in the lake with her long beak!

Meow4 floundered like a soggy tennis ball. When he saw Jack and the others, he was about to scream, but the flamingo plopped him back into the water.

Ms. Fennec Fox politely asked the flamingo to return Meow4.

Meow4 shook off the water, no longer daring to run, and quietly followed behind.

Every building here was wrong in the most delightful way. One stood upside down, its chimney puffing clouds from the basement. Another spiraled into itself like a soft-serve cone. One house bounced politely, as though it had excellent manners and a touch of the hiccups.

"This building used to be a giraffe. That one sleeps during the day and parties at night," Ms. Fennec Fox said, pointing to a particularly odd house.

"Can we visit it now?" Meow1 really wanted to go inside.

But just like that, Ms. Fennec Fox vanished! Everyone looked around, unable to see her anywhere.

"Don't worry!" Ms. Fennec Fox's voice came from nowhere at all. "I'm in the state of Mirage Breaking because of the temperature fluctuation. It happens often."

"Could you come back?" Yellowy chirped, a little afraid that she'd be gone forever.

"Oh, yes, I should be back soon. Just follow my voice. I'm still showing you the route."

Everyone perked up their ears.

"The house is closed during the day," the voice explained, "but I will show you a lot of interesting things around it."

They walked along the winding path, and the scenery around them kept changing, colors interlacing and alternating as if in a dream. They saw the sun and moon dancing, butterflies in sunglasses pulling a boat full of stars, and their own shadows reflected in the sky, chatting with each other. On the way, Ms. Fennec Fox vanished and reappeared several times.

"Look to the right. This is an old castle. Eight kings once lived here," the guide's voice announced. "Then, for some unknown reason, they abandoned it, leaving no trace."

"Like the Pyramids of the Sun and Moon in Mexico," Jack said. "Can we go inside?"

At that moment, Ms. Fennec Fox reappeared, calling out to the majestic gates, "Respected Castle, Code: QU856, may we enter?"

"Hello, Code: QU856," a hoarse voice echoed from the castle. "The temperature frequency is unstable. Mirage No. 1736 will soon disappear."

"Well, this tour ends here," Ms. Fennec Fox smiled. "Be prepared. You'll be back in the desert. Thank you for coming!"

They held tight. And POOF—they were back on the golden dunes.

"Was that real?" asked Jack.

"I can still taste the invisible pizza," Meow2 whispered.

Not far away, lounging on a floating postage-stamp-shaped rock, was a spotted leopard. His mailbag dangled lazily.

"Mailman!" Parcel announced.

"About time," Jack added.

The leopard stretched. "Mail moves fast when you move faster than wind."

"Can you take us to Stealing City?" Lunibelle asked.

"Special delivery?"

"Sideways kind," said Yellowy.

"Hop in."

The kittens dove in the envelope. Jack slid after them. Willy curled his tail. Parcel floated in like a queen. Yellowy twirled. Lunibelle winked and sealed the flap.

The leopard crouched. Then—ZING!

They flew past black mountains, hiccupping clouds, and tumbleweed philosophers. Camelet's voice echoed in the wind: "Remember—kindness, intelligence, and a little heat!"

They soared. They spun. They tumbled with the stars.

Ahead, rooftops peeked from mist. Signs flickered.

They were arriving—to a city where nothing stayed in place. To a kingdom of stolen treasures. A place called—Stealing City.

Part VII: The Crooked City of Catch and Keep

The envelope spiraled downward like a leaf, tumbling through the clouds until it landed with a gentle thud on a crooked cobblestone street.

They had arrived: Stealing City.

The moment they climbed out of the envelope, the group knew this place wasn't ordinary. The buildings leaned suspiciously—eavesdropping on passersby. The streets coiled like spaghetti left in the sun. Streetlamps stood in mismatched socks, as though they had dressed themselves half-asleep.

Alleyways whispered jargon, flickering in and out of existence.

And everywhere—toys.

Piles of teddy bears slumped in storefronts. Stacks of board games teetered like wobbly towers. Bicycles hung from lampposts; yo-yos dangled from doorknobs; skipping ropes twisted.

Jack exclaimed, "My basketball! It's bouncing without me—how dare it?" He pointed toward a crooked shop called the *Everything Missing Emporium*, where his orange ball bounced faintly in the window. Lunibelle's snow globe glistened beside it, swirling with miniature planets. Parcel's yarn ball sat tangled in socks. Yellowy's mirror glittered on a top shelf. Willy's chew bone dangled from the ceiling, spinning on a string.

The kittens stared, wide-eyed. "It's all here," breathed Meow1.

"I am think..." declared Meow3. "This city suffers from serious ethical problems."

A puppet zipped past on tiny wheels, pursued by a feather duster wearing sunglasses. A doll's pram trundled along by itself, giggling faintly.

"They steal toys," said Lunibelle firmly. "Not just ours. Everyone's."

Stealing City was famous—at least among nonsense creatures. A place where toys vanished from children's homes, snatched by invisible hands and sold for pennies on streets.

"We have to get them back," Jack declared.

"Agreed," nodded Lunibelle. "But we'll need to see the king."

The city swirled around them like a moving painting. Shopkeepers sold alarm clocks that shouted compliments, umbrellas that poured glitter, and dictionaries that chased you when mispronounced. A crocodile in a tuxedo bowed and offered Jack a balloon that smelled unmistakably of Tuesdays. Jack declined.

The kittens darted everywhere. Meow4 tried to trade a rubber band for a glow-in-the-dark kazoo. Meow1 attempted to liberate a plastic pony. Meow2 got tangled in yo-yos and had to be rescued by Parcel.

Everywhere, the city lived with mischief. Street signs rotated like weathervanes. Benches shuffled away when approached. A mailbox sneezed glitter and a coupon for invisible jam.

Meow3 paused at a mural of a weeping boy surrounded by toy shadows. "I am think... this city hides sorrow under silliness. Perhaps even its king."

They passed through Whimsy Way, Confusion Crossing, and Tangle Alley, where marbles refused to roll straight.

Finally, a sign appeared—painted backwards and upside down: *To the King, Try Not to Trip.*

A staircase unrolled like a tongue. Lanterns flickered sleepy eyes. A brass band of invisible instruments played a fanfare that kept changing tunes.

At last, they reached a towering gate. Beyond it rose the Palace of Pilfering—sagging from rusting toy chests and fairy tales that had misplaced their endings. Balloons clung to towers.

The kittens froze. Parcel narrowed her eyes. Lunibelle nodded knowingly.

"We've made it," she said. "Now comes the strange part."

The kittens exchanged glances. "And to think," Jack said, "this all started with a missing marble."

They stepped forward together—ready for whatever royal absurdity awaited them.

Part VIII: The Palace of Pilfering

Eventually, they arrived at the Palace of Pilfering.

"Welcome to the king's domain," the door whispered.

A red carpet unfurled with great ceremony—only to promptly trip Meow4 like a mischievous tongue. He yelped and tumbled into a heap.

At the top of the wobbly steps sat the King of Stealing City, lounging lazily on a throne built entirely of yo-yos. He was small and plump, with a beard trailing across the floor and a golden crown. His royal sash read: *Possession is Nine-Tenths of the Law (the Other Tenth is Nonsense).*

"Ahhh," drawled the king, peering lazily over a stack of stolen kites. "More disgruntled customers?"

"We're not customers," declared Lunibelle, stepping forward. "We've come to get our toys back."

Parcel sat regally beside Lunibelle, her gaze fixed on the lazy king.

The king yawned, tossing a yo-yo lazily. "Take them." He shrugged. "I couldn't care less about a chew bone or a snow globe."

"But what about everyone's toys?" asked Jack, gesturing to the towering piles of missing treasures.

"Why should I?" The king frowned, scratching his beard. "They're mine now."

Meow4 puffed up his chest, fur bristling. "Toys are important!" he declared. "If the toys are lost, we'll cry the saddest cries."

Willy whimpered in agreement, his tail between his legs.

The king snorted. "So? Tears make the desert greener. I like toys."

Jack stepped forward too. "You know why it matters? Because I couldn't sleep at night. I kept thinking—what if it's gone forever? What if I never feel the bounce in my hand again?"

The king blinked. "It's just a thing. But it's my thing."

Meow3 stepped forward, eyes narrowed thoughtfully. "I am think... integrity is the most important quality of a king."

The king's yo-yo wobbled in midair. "Integrity?" he repeated, as if tasting the word for the first time.

Lunibelle met his gaze, her eyes glowing. "Toys don't belong to you," she said gently. "They belong to the children who love them. And if you want your kingdom to be admired... well, honesty and courage go further than stolen toys."

The kittens nodded vigorously.

The king scratched his beard. His yo-yo sagged. A long, peculiar silence stretched across the hall.

At last, the king sighed—a sound like an old wind-up toy running out of springs. "You know..." His voice was quieter now, trembling at the edges. He plucked a yo-yo from his throne, turning it slowly in his hands. "When I was small... I never had toys."

The kittens froze. Even the streetlamps leaned in, their socks dangling in mismatched curiosity.

"No teddy bear. No marble. Not even a silly little jingle bell." The king's fingers fidgeted with the yo-yo, his eyes drifting somewhere far beyond the Palace. "Just shadows. And leftover dust. And a yo-yo with a string so tangled it only went down, never back up."

Even his golden crown sagged, as if it, too, remembered.

"So when I became king... I wanted all the toys." His voice trembled between regret and longing. "I wanted pyramids of toys, mountains of them! Enough to fill every shelf, every drawer... every aching emptiness."

The kittens' whiskers drooped in sympathy. Parcel's tail curled protectively around them.

Lunibelle stepped forward, her eyes glistening. "But filling shelves isn't the same as filling hearts."

The king chuckled faintly—a small, rusty laugh. "No. No, I suppose not."

Jack looked the king in the eye. "You said you didn't have toys when you were little. Then you know how it hurts. So don't pass that pain on. Be the king you needed when you were a kid."

The king looked down at Meow4, puffed up with righteous fury. At Meow3, wise beyond her fluff. At Meow2's wide, hopeful eyes. At Meow1's determined frown.

"I shouldn't have inflicted my childhood pain on you," the king admitted, his voice steadying. "Or on anyone."

He straightened his golden crown. "You're right. Toys belong to those who love them. Who laugh with them. Who... well, occasionally flatten themselves into envelopes for them."

The kittens burst into giggles.

The king clapped his hands. "All right then. You win."

The ground trembled. Windows rattled. Streetlamps danced. From every corner of Stealing City, toys tumbled free—rolling, bouncing, and giggling their way home.

Jack's basketball bounced into his arms. Lunibelle's snow globe hovered into her hands. Parcel's yarn ball tangled itself delightedly around her paws. Yellowy's golden mirror sparkled in the sunlight. Willy's chew bone plopped neatly at his feet. The kittens' entire collection wobbled after them like a parade of joyful nonsense.

The king smiled faintly. "I admire your honesty, your courage, and your surprisingly well-organized brigade of fluff and chaos."

Meow4 struck a proud pose, fluffing his fur.

"I can send the toys home with you," offered the king, his voice lighter now. "With... reliable postage, of course."

The kittens piled back into the magical envelope, giggling and squirming. Willy climbed in after them, chew bone clamped proudly in his mouth. Yellowy fluttered inside. Lunibelle sealed the envelope with a kiss.

"Royal Special Delivery!" the king announced, snapping his fingers.

A burst of wind whisked the envelope into the sky, spinning and twirling, carrying them—and every returned toy—home.

As the crooked city faded behind them, Jack grinned. "That," he declared, "was the strangest mail journey ever."

"I am think..." agreed Meow3. "We'll never beat it."

But Lunibelle just smiled mysteriously. "Oh, you never know with nonsense," she replied. "The mail delivers more nonsense than you ever expect."

And with that, they soared toward home, the envelope carrying laughter, toys, and the sweet, silly nonsense of a perfect adventure.

Chapter IX
The Secret Waiting Behind the "Please Top" Sign

Part I: Grandma's Ivy-Laced Cottage

One fine, slightly crinkly morning, Jack's dad called, "Ready? Hop in the car, crew! We're off to Grandma's!"

Jack jumped for joy. He adored Grandma. She smelled like raspberry jam and always laughed with her eyes. And she always said something odd, as though the forest had whispered secrets to her in her sleep.

But today wasn't just about hugs and cookies. Jack could hardly wait to introduce her to their whole household zoo: Willy the German Shepherd (always noble), Parcel the cat (very queenly), her four kittens—Meow1, Meow2, Meow3, and Meow4 (absolutely chaotic), Yellowy the canary (who could whistle in five keys), and—most importantly—Lunibelle, Jack's special guest.

They drove through a mountain that seemed to have forgotten how to be small. The trees leaned close, trading jokes in bark and silence. Then, just as the road curled, Dad pointed ahead and said, "There! Grandma's house!"

It wasn't just any house. It was *The House*—a wooden cottage tucked at the edge of an old forest, looking as though it had grown there on purpose. The wood had turned a wise silver-gray from years of moonlight, and ivy hugged the walls like an old friend.

A little stream giggled beside it. Mushrooms popped up like curious meerkats. Ferns stretched lazily in the shade, and the windows blinked sleepily in the sun.

As soon as the car stopped, Jack flew from the car and dashed to the half-open door. "Grandma! Grandma!" he shouted.

Inside, nestled in a velvet chair by the fireplace, Grandma rose and opened her arms wide—and Jack landed in them.

"I was just thinking about you!" she said, smoothing his hair. "Your dad sent word last week. And look at you—taller than the last cucumber I planted!"

"I missed you so much," Jack whispered, his voice a little wobbly.

"I made your favorite sugar-cakes," Grandma said, her eyes twinkling, "and I found mushrooms in the forest that hummed when I picked them. You must always listen before eating, because mushrooms tell you whether they're in the mood."

Jack grinned and snapped his fingers. Right on cue, Willy trotted in with something in his mouth—a picture frame.

Jack took it and handed it to Grandma. Inside was his drawing: little Jack walking hand in hand with Grandma through the forest, carrying a basket of mushrooms.

Grandma blinked once, then twice—and laughed so warmly she had to wipe her eyes with the corner of her apron.

Mom and Dad came in next. They hugged Grandma tight. Dad showed her a new automatic bread maker. "You just pour in flour and water," he said, "and it does the rest!"

Mom brought out a handmade winter coat. "For the coldest days," she said. "This one is stitched with warmth."

Grandma nodded and patted everyone's hands. "Machines bake, coats warm, but people love," she added softly—a phrase that seemed to belong to the cottage itself.

"Grandma, look!" Jack beamed, pointing toward the door. "This is Lunibelle!"

"Grandma!" Lunibelle called, stepping forward and wrapping her in a soft, sparkly hug.

"Well, hello there! Aren't you just delightful!" Grandma's face lit up.

She turned to Jack with mock sternness. "And you didn't even give me time to find a gift!"

"Jack told me all about your mushroom adventures," Lunibelle said. "Could we go too?"

"Of course! Of course!" Grandma clapped with joy. "Tomorrow morning! I've got the biggest basket waiting."

"And these," Jack said, motioning proudly, "are Parcel and her kittens."

"Meow!" Parcel offered politely.

Meow4 darted in, leaped onto Grandma's lap, and lifted his tail with theatrical flair. Grandma chuckled and gave him a loving stroke. "What a dashing little fellow!"

"And here's Yellowy," Jack added, looking around. "Wait... Yellowy?"

"Right here!" chirped a voice from above. Yellowy swooped down from the rafters and landed neatly on Jack's shoulder.

Grandma extended her hand, and Yellowy hopped over with a graceful bow.

Jack blinked, and Yellowy launched into a golden melody—clear and bright as sunshine.

"A canary who sings blessings!" Grandma's silver hair bounced with laughter.

She looked around the room, her eyes full of wonder. "With all of you here, Jack will never be lonely again. But be careful—the forest sometimes borrows children who don't keep their ears open."

And just like that, the cottage filled with laughter, warm hugs, pattering feet, and the sweet sound of love rustling through the old wooden floorboards.

Part II: The Wall of Woven Air

The next morning, Jack told Grandma, "We're going mushroom hunting in the woods!"

Grandma chuckled and replied with her favorite forest phrase: "Don't go too far and do come back before the trees start talking about stars."

"Don't worry, Grandma!" Jack echoed, as he had been saying since he was two years old.

Then he picked up a basket and gathered his entourage—Luni-belle, Willy, the cats, and Yellowy. Off they went.

Grandma stood at the door, watching them disappear into the forest. Sunlight blinked playfully from the branches of tree. The path felt squishy and smelled of moss and yesterday's rain.

Soon the basket was filling with mushrooms: round, stripy, curly, and squiggly ones.

But then Jack stopped. In front of them stood a wooden sign, planted firmly in the earth. On it, scrawled in twisty letters, were the words: **PLEASE STOP!**

"Please stop?" Lunibelle repeated, tilting her head.

"Huh?" Jack blinked.

They looked beyond the sign. The world tilted slightly to the left—as if the entire forest had been nudged politely by an invisible giant. The leaves of each tree wore different shapes and colors. The water in the stream flowed forward and backward, as if dancing. The mushrooms loomed larger and more colorful.

"Odd," Jack muttered. "I don't remember seeing this sign before."

"Maybe because you've never gone quite this far?" Lunibelle pointed ahead. "It seems there are more mushrooms there."

Willy sniffed the air suspiciously. The kittens sat in a row on a log, like black keys on a piano.

"We shouldn't go past the Please Stop Sign under any circumstance," Jack murmured.

"But if the mushrooms are bigger beyond this sign, then we must go—for Grandma. Besides, if a sign says 'Please,' perhaps it's just being polite." Lunibelle had no idea how important the Please Stop Sign was.

So Jack stepped over the sign, with Lunibelle beside him. Willy followed. Parcel, Meow1, Meow2, Meow3, and Meow4 scampered behind. Yellowy loop-de-looped overhead.

They walked. And walked. Nothing seemed to happen—or perhaps everything did, only very quietly.

Jack blinked hard. His mouth dropped open. "I can see... behind me, while still looking forward!"

His eyes looked the same—but the world had folded open like a pop-up book, front, back, sky, and stone all whispering hello... even a beetle on a branch, buttoning its finest leaves.

"Lunibelle," Jack asked, "what's happening? I can see in every direction—like 360 degrees!"

"So can I!" Lunibelle replied, curious. At the same time, her eyes scanned the surroundings in all directions, like a tiny radar.

"Then I'll gather a few of these 360-degree mushrooms for Grandma!" said Jack, and he began picking mushrooms from the grass.

"These mushrooms are huuuuge!" Meow4 shouted. "I need a hand to pick up this one!"

"I am think... I like this one the best!" said Meow3, watching in wonder as the mushroom in front of her kept changing color like a kaleidoscope.

"This one's like an umbrella!" chirped Yellowy, perching on its cap—which immediately began to spin.

It didn't take long before Jack's basket was full to the brim.

"I think we should head back now," Lunibelle suggested.

So they turned around cheerfully and made their way back—until they reached the wooden sign again. On the back, in the same curly script, it also read: **PLEASE STOP!**

They barely glanced at it, as if warnings lost their shape when reversed.

Jack stepped forward—BOING!—and was flung backward as if he'd hit an invisible trampoline.

Mushrooms spilled everywhere. Jack sat up, puzzled, brushed moss from his clothes, and tried again. BOING! Same result.

"Willy, charge!" Jack ordered. Willy charged—BOING! He bounced back like a rubber ball.

Parcel and the kittens tried too—a furry, bouncing blur.

It was no use. Something invisible—a wall? A spell? A politely firm air current?—was keeping them in. It even made a faint squeaky sound each time, as though the air itself were protesting.

"This is so strange," Jack frowned.

Everyone stood there, staring, trying to see what they couldn't see.

"I'll try to see how high this wall is," said Yellowy, spreading her wings and slowly flying upward. When she reached the invisible barrier, she clung to it and kept going.

"Yellowy's flown so high!" Meow1 craned her neck.

"She's become a tiny dot!" Meow4 squinted. "I can't see her anymore!"

After a long while, Yellowy fluttered back down, panting. "This wall seems to have no edge!" she gasped. "Even the clouds can't get through!"

"Mummy, what should we do?" Meow2 whimpered. "Can we go home?"

"We can go home," Parcel said gently, touching Meow2's head. "If we could come in, we can go out."

Jack turned to Lunibelle and asked in a low voice, "What should we do?"

"Well," said Lunibelle, glowing a thoughtful violet (which meant she was quite serious), "if we can't go back... perhaps we should go forward. After all, if the wall keeps us from leaving, it may only be because it wants to show you something ahead."

Though she didn't sound entirely certain.

Part III: Mr. Spittleton's Splendid Bubble World

They walked deeper into the forest, where everything seemed to grow larger and larger. The violets grew taller than Jack. A single drop of water fell from a leaf and struck the ground with the boom of a cannonball.

Suddenly, they spotted something gleaming on a wide leaf—a spittle-bug, its body swirling with minty green.

"Excuse me, Mr. Spittlebug," Jack called. "Can you tell us what this place is?"

But the bug didn't reply. It began blowing bubbles, more and more, until it was nearly encased—only its head peeked out.

"Oh, were you saying something?" murmured Mr. Spittlebug drowsily. "Wait a moment. I'm having my bath. You can bathe too, can't you?"

Bubbles swallowed him up. His shape bounced lightly in the foam as he hummed:

Bubble, bubble,
Clean and scrub,
More is less,
Less is more,
Small is big,
Big is small,
Swirly-whirly,
Time to snore.
Bubble, bubble,
Clean and bright,
Make us wiser with your light.
Big is small, and less is more,
Dreams are keys, and math's the door.

Moments later, everything went still.

"Mommy," Meow4 whispered, pointing, "he's falling asleep!"

"SHHH!" Parcel whispered, placing a paw on Meow4's mouth. So they waited. And waited.

Finally, the bubbles began to POP—POP, POP, POP—like a bubble waltz. Meow2 tried to chase one, but it squeaked away. Willy snapped at another, but it burst into glitter on his nose.

Mr. Spittlebug's sleepy face emerged. "Ah! Much better."

"Hello again," Jack said carefully. "Have you finished your bath?"

"Call me Mr. Spittleton," he replied, brushing away the last bubbles clinging to his body. "Indeed! Bathing is the most important thing in the world. The more bubbles you have, the wiser you become."

"Mr. Spittleton, I hope you don't mind me asking, but..." Jack began, "what is this place?"

"What is this place?" Mr. Spittleton repeated in surprise. "No one ever asks that! Even with all my bubbles, I've never heard such a silly question. Where did you come from?"

"From... from Grandma's house," Jack said, unsure.

"Never heard of it. Even with my brilliant bubbles. But I could ask them—"

"Mr. Spittleton, please don't!" Lunibelle interrupted quickly, afraid he'd vanish in foam again. She pointed behind them. "We came from the end of that path."

"Ooooh," said Mr. Spittleton, nodding his head and spinning a bubble above it. "You're from the other bubble world, aren't you?"

"You're absolutely right!" Lunibelle said brightly, trying to keep him engaged. "But we can't get back."

"You're in a different bubble world now," the spittlebug said proudly. "The universe is made of bubbles. You must've slipped through a bubble crack—very rare. Now you're inside a different one."

He paused, letting his audience of eight—give or take—digest this profound knowledge. (Of course, he wasn't showing off—just stating facts.)

"To leave, you have to wait for the bubble to burst before you can go back."

"How long does that take?" Yellowy asked quickly.

"About... billions of years!" He winked.

Jack had no idea what that meant, though he didn't dare interrupt.

"Mr. Spittleton," Lunibelle said in her softest voice, "you see, we have to go back. You have so many bubbles—surely one of them holds the answer."

"Of course!" Mr. Spittleton was delighted. "Your question is very peculiar—let me consult the bubbles!"

Before anyone could stop him, he began to blow. Lunibelle sighed. Jack patted Willy. Parcel kept a steady paw on the kittens, making sure they wouldn't do something unexpected.

They waited again. Bubbles swirled higher, shimmering with a thousand tiny ideas.

Finally—POP! POP! POP!—they vanished.

Mr. Spittleton reappeared. "Yes! I did find an answer." He paused, then said proudly: "This bubble has a few micro-holes—tiny drifting portals. Nearly invisible. Hard to find."

He tapped the bubble on his head. "Right?" The bubble jumped and landed neatly back in place.

Jack and the others stood still, eyes wide.

"Exactly! You can't even see it!" Mr. Spittleton's eyes sparkled—it seemed only he could.

"But... how do we get out?" Jack mustered the courage to ask.

Mr. Spittleton raised a finger. "You'll need four things to do the impossible." He stood tall (about one inch).

"For the quill—follow the path where porcupines write their prickly poems," he said, pointing.

"For the snake—seek the meadow where the grass will bind you." Another point.

"For the eyes—go to the place where you will find your courage." He pointed with his left hand.

"And behind you—for the wings, find the place where the clouds will sing." He made a circle with his arms. "Once you have them, bring them back. I'll stitch the impossible into a *Bubblecraft* and bind it with bubbles so slippery that only courage can climb it."

"Thank you, Mr. Spittleton!" they all said in unison, and turned toward their first quest.

"This way!" Parcel called, herding the kittens as they scampered ahead.

Part IV: The Silver Quill's Gift of Heartfelt Thanks

Their path wound through dandelion fields and between blades of grass. The sky above swirled with pastel clouds, and somewhere in the distance, a flute-playing breeze tiptoed across the meadow.

"Are porcupines friendly?" Lunibelle asked, squinting into the tall grass.

"Only if you don't sit on them," Jack grinned.

They wandered on until they heard a sound—soft, sniffly, and very tiny.

Following it, they found a mossy little nook.

There she was—a porcupine! She looked like a gentle ball of chubby toothpicks, with a twitchy nose and bright little eyes. Her quills stood tall, some striped like licorice, and when she trembled, they made a quiet tinkling.

She was a mother, holding an acorn in her paws, her eyes full of worry.

Meow4 run forward and nearly tumbled into her!

"Ah!" Parcel gasped. "Sweet whiskers! Be careful—those quills are nothing to joke about!"

"Hello, kitten," the porcupine mother said gently.

"May I touch your shiny quills?" Meow4 asked with bold curiosity.

"Certainly," she said with a smile, lowering her quills. "Just don't poke the pointy parts."

The other kittens rushed up, eager to try.

"Thank you," Jack said kindly. "Are you okay?"

"My baby…" she whispered, eyes brimming. "He was right beside me, and now—he's gone. He hasn't even grown his first quill."

"We'll help you find him," Jack said instantly.

They snapped into action. Lunibelle took command like a tiny general. "Yellowy, scout from the skies. Jack, check the hollow log. Parcel and kittens, search the grass."

Willy sniffed through fern patches. The kittens scattered like furry investigators. Meow1 unfolded a crinkly leaf map. Meow2 scrambled up a sapling. Meow3 interrogated a suspicious pinecone that stubbornly refused to answer.

A rustle came from a nearby hollow log carved with curious claw marks.

"Careful," Jack whispered. "Could be… anyone."

Inside lounged a red fox, curled around three napping fuzzballs.

"Hello, Ms Fox. We're looking for a baby porcupine," Jack said gently. "Have you seen one?"

"These are my babies," the fox replied, a little too quickly. "Lovely, aren't they?"

They leaned in. Three tiny critters... At first glance, they all looked alike—closed eyes, fuzzy bellies, gently snoring.

"Let's line them up," Lunibelle suggested. "Maybe something will reveal itself."

They did. Two snuggled together... and nudged the third one away.

"That's our baby," Jack whispered. "His invisible baby-quills must feel odd to them."

The fox's smile faltered. "Children shuffle and nudge—it doesn't always mean anything."

There was a silence.

Lunibelle's glow dimmed, her voice softening. "You're sure?"

The fox's gaze dropped for a heartbeat. "I... I'm sure," she muttered, too softly.

Doubt crept in. Maybe the porcupine wasn't here. Maybe they'd been wrong.

Jack sighed. "Let's keep looking elsewhere."

He turned to go. So did Lunibelle, the kittens, even Parcel—ears drooping.

But Willy stayed put. "Wait," he said softly. "Something isn't right."

The fox's tail twitched.

Willy stepped forward. "What's his name?"

The fox flinched. "I... I didn't name him yet."

A silence fell. Then Willy raised his snout. "Porcupines and foxes smell very different," he said gently. "Meow4, your paw still carries the porcupine mother's scent. Let's try."

Meow4 stepped forward and tapped the three tiny shapes. Two pulled back. The third—the nudged-away one—pressed close to his paw.

The fox closed her eyes. "I knew. I knew the whole time." Her voice was barely more than a whisper. "But he was crying. Alone. What was I supposed to do? Leave him? For a little while... he felt like mine."

"Would you like to say goodbye?" Jack asked softly.

The fox nodded, tears shining in her eyes. She gave the porcupette one last hug, nuzzling his soft head.

"Thank you for loving him," Lunibelle said.

Jack scooped the baby up. The porcupine squeaked and curled into his hand, tiny feet tickling.

When they returned him to his mother, she burst into joyful sobs, hugging him tight.

"Thank you!" she cried. "You are heroes!"

She pulled a pouch from beneath a mossy stone. "Please, take this."

Inside was a glimmering silver quill.

"It's magical," she said. "Sharp and true—and full of mystery."

"Thank you," Jack said, bowing.

Meow4 saluted—accidentally with his tail. Yellowy chirped a tiny fanfare. Parcel purred like thunder stitched with velvet.

The porcupine mother held her baby close and whispered, "Some creatures slither through hidden cracks. They always find a way."

Her words clung to Jack's heart like burrs—puzzling, yet important.

As they turned to go, the sky flickered—just a flicker—as if the world had hiccuped.

"Did you see that?" Lunibelle asked softly.

"Yeah," Jack said, gripping the quill. "Like something blinked."

Part V: The Grasses' Gift of Never Letting Go

Jack and his companions followed the direction Mr. Spittleton had pointed. The air grew damper, the trees less chatty, and the light took on a greenish hush. Ahead, a quiet pond shimmered like a mirror, rimmed with thick shrubs and suspiciously soft-looking grass.

"We're close," Jack whispered, eyes scanning the reeds. "Let's stay alert."

Lunibelle pushed aside stalks with a twig, like a polite explorer. Willy crept forward, nose twitching, sniffing the path as though it held a half-remembered secret. Parcel brought up the rear—silent but fierce—her eyes slicing through the overgrowth.

"Snakes love places like this," Parcel muttered. "Cool. Wet. Tricky."

"I remember my teacher said so too," Jack added. "We just have to find one."

"There!" Yellowy piped, diving like a comet. "I saw something slither!"

They rushed after her, the grass brushing their ankles. Then they saw it: a tiny snake, coiled like a shoelace in a patch of silvery-blue grass. At first, it looked harmless.

But Lunibelle's eyes narrowed. "Wait. Look—he's stuck. The

grass has him!"

The snake writhed gently. Grass tendrils clung to his body, like ivy with wicked intentions.

"Those aren't normal grasses," Yellowy whispered. "They're alive!"

"We can help him," said Lunibelle. "But be careful. One wrong move could..."

"I'll go," Jack offered. He stepped forward—and the grass moved. Other followed.

"Something's grabbing me!" Jack yelled.

Grassy strands curled like vines around his ankles, tightening with every move.

"My paws!" barked Willy. "They're stuck!"

The grass lunged for Lunibelle's twig, fooled by its movements, and missed her feet.

"Mama!" Meow1 shrieked. "I can't breathe!"

The grass was curling around her fast, climbing up like green fire. Her limbs twisted. Her voice broke.

Parcel lunged—and disappeared halfway into the grass's grip.

"Don't struggle!" Lunibelle cried. "It gets worse!"

Yellowy flapped into the air, narrowly escaping.

"It's Ugly Grass!" she shouted. "It's caught me by a feather!"

Everyone froze, like statues in a museum. No one could move without sinking deeper.

Meow1 whimpered. Her eyes fluttered. Her chest barely rose.

"Everyone, freeze!" Lunibelle ordered. "Even breathing too fast feeds it!"

The snake lifted its tiny head. "You helped me," he hissed weakly. "Now I'll help you... This grass is called Tangle-You."

"Is there a way out?" Jack asked, a sharp intake of breath catching in his throat. "Meow1 is not going to last!"

"There's a spring—called Unknot-Me," the snake said. "Just past the reeds. A drop of it unwinds anything."

"I'll go!" Lunibelle said calmly. First, she whipped the stick fiercely. The grass lunged for it, then she zipped past the edge, heart pounding.

Seconds ticked.

Jack's legs ached as though invisible vines were twisting his bones into knots. His logical brain raced: breathe less, struggle less, keep calm—anything to outwit the plant.

Meow1 let out a gasp—thin, fading, barely a sound.

Parcel's voice trembled with panic as she strained against the strangling grass, her claws useless. "Hold on, my darling... please, please hold on..."

Time snapped at their heels.

Then, far off through the reeds, they heard thrashing. A flash of silver darted between the cattails—Lunibelle, running like her glow depended on it. Branches scratched her arms, and thorns tore her dress, but she didn't stop. The gourd sloshed in her hand, one drop trembling dangerously near the rim. Her feet barely touched the earth as she raced back, eyes wild with fear and fire.

Lunibelle returned—mud-covered and panting—with a tiny gourd.

She splashed a single drop onto Meow1.

The grass snapped. It let go all at once, hissing and shriveling like burned paper.

Meow1 drew in a breath, meowed faintly, and curled up safe.

One by one, Lunibelle freed the others.

Last came the snake—SLIP! He wiggled free, amazed.

"You saved me," he said. "I'm Snakety. May I stay with you?"

"Of course," said Lunibelle.

"We were looking for you," Jack added, grinning.

"Snakety!" the kittens cheered.

Then, a rustle. A voice rose—low, leafy, ancient.

"Welcome... to the Great Grass Field."

It came from everywhere. Nowhere.

"No creature has ever escaped," it groaned. "You are the first."

"Thank you," Lunibelle said politely. "Would you consider... not tangling creatures anymore? Kindness makes the world grow better."

A long pause.

"We shall consider," said the Grass. "Perhaps twisting with kindness is another kind of strength."

The grass all around them sighed, long and low.

"Thanks for your kindness," said the voice, "take four strands. If danger finds you, toss one. It will do the rest."

Four long shining blades of grass drifted over.

Jack took them gently. "Thank you."

Lunibelle's light flickered, like a thought growing weary.

Jack looked up. "Didn't the sun just rise?"

The sky was darker.

"The bubble's twisting time," Lunibelle whispered. "We're running out."

Snakety lifted his head. "Wherever you go—I follow."

Part VI: The Buzzing-Sky's Gift of a Thousand Eyes

Jack and his companions had a new quest ahead: to find the Dragonfly's Eyes.

They arrived at a broad marsh, where the pond rippled like a dream, and tiny streams played tag among mossy stones. The green around them burst with light and motion. Dragonflies zipped overhead, wings flickering.

"We must find the Dragonfly King," Lunibelle said, peering upward. "Only he can give us the Eyes."

Just then, Yellowy swooped down, her feathers fluffed with alarm. "Jack!" she cried. "Something's wrong. The dragonflies—they're not flying right!"

Jack scanned the sky. Dragonflies fluttered frantically, not gliding but zigzagging.

Then he saw them.

Three enormous wasps ripped through the air. Their black-and-yellow stripes flared. Dragonflies fled in chaos.

"Wasps!" Jack cried. "They're hunting them!"

The kittens dived into the reeds. Snakety coiled in front of them, forming a shield. Yellowy darted overhead, wings flitting with fury.

"These aren't picnic wasps," she warned. "They're dragonfly eaters."

Jack's fists clenched. "Then let's stop them."

Without waiting, he charged forward. Willy barked and followed.

The wasps buzzed like electric saws—jagged, menacing, and hungry. They swerved with terrifying precision, stingers glinting, jaws snapping. One zipped straight through a dragonfly swarm and came out the other side with a shimmer of crushed wings. Another dove and slammed into the pond, then launched again as if water meant nothing. Dragonflies scattered like torn ribbons.

The heroes fought back as best they could. Willy barked, snapping at wings too fast to catch. Parcel launched herself skyward, swiping midair, but the wasps always dodged. Jack swung his arms, deflecting one—but a second clipped his ear. A third looped and struck his head.

For every move they made, the wasps made three. They circled, flanked, struck again. One slammed into Yellowy midair—she tumbled but caught herself just before hitting the water.

Jack's breaths came sharp and quick. His friends tired; the wasps did not.

"They're winning," he gasped, breath ragged. "They're winning!"

Then—

"We have to hold on!" Jack shouted.

Willy dashed through the meadow, barking loud to draw attention. Yellowy danced loops through the sky, a golden blur of confusion.

One wasp peeled off—aimed straight for Jack.

"Jack, down!" Lunibelle shouted.

He ducked, but not fast enough.

A burning sting pierced his arm.

"Gah!" Jack clenched his teeth as heat surged down his arm. His vision blurred. His skin ballooned.

"Jack!" Parcel cried.

"I'm fine!" Jack growled, even though tears rimmed his eyes. "We can't stop now!"

"Use the porcupine's quill!" Lunibelle called.

Jack grabbed the quill from his satchel. It gleamed in the sun, as though made for this very moment.

He stood tall, lifting the quill like a sword. The wasp paused mid-flight.

Jack lunged.

The quill glinted—just enough.

The wasp veered off with a furious buzz.

But two more closed in.

One zipped at Willy; he whirled and snapped. Parcel leaped, claws open.

"Tangle-You!" Lunibelle yelled.

Jack fished the enchanted grass from his pocket and flung a strand.

SNAP! It wrapped around one wasp midair—dragging it down.

Two more. Jack hurled the final strands—left, right—

WHIP! WHAP!

Both wasps dropped, tangled tight.

But they didn't stay down. One thrashed violently, the enchanted grass groaning as it strained to hold. The other buzzed furiously, dragging itself across the ground, stinger twitching like an angry needle.

"They're trying to break free!" Jack warned.

Lunibelle raised the quill beside him, eyes fierce. Yellowy swooped low, flapping her wings in warning arcs. Willy and Parcel stood guard, their breath ragged but steady.

Then something changed.

The wasps began to shiver—not from the grass, but from the silence. The sky above had filled with dragonflies.

Hundreds of them.

They hovered in formation, their wings humming in a rising, unbroken harmony—one single note of defiance.

The tangled wasps froze.

The dragonflies descended—not to attack, but to surround. They flew in elegant, spinning patterns that boxed the wasps in light and motion, confusing and dizzying them until the buzzing faltered... then ceased.

One by one, the wasps collapsed, fully bound by magic and fear.

A final flicker of their wings—and they were still.

The sky cleared.

Peace returned—first in a hush, then in a breath, then in a rush of grateful wings.

Silence fell.

Only Jack's breathing filled the field.

Lunibelle ran to him. She cleaned and wrapped the wound, hands trembling. Her glow dimmed to a worried lavender.

Then came the whisper of wings.

From every edge of the pond, dragonflies returned.

They circled Jack in radiant spirals, whispering thanks with their wingbeats.

One enormous blue dragonfly hovered before him. His wings gleamed with sunlight, his eyes vast and deep.

"You held the sky together with courage. We saw. We remember," he said, voice light and bright. "We will not forget."

Two red dragonflies approached, each carrying a plate bearing a golden eye.

"These are our treasures. Each eye contains a thousand little eyes," the Dragonfly King said. "With them, you will see what others miss—danger, shadow, secrets. But beware: seeing too much can be as blinding as seeing nothing at all."

Jack bowed—stiff, but proud. "We only did what was right."

He took the eyes. They buzzed softly in his palm, warm and strange.

"Thank you," Jack said.

"You have earned them," the King replied. "Now your journey sees further than your footsteps."

He rose with the others, a living ribbon of light.

Jack held the eyes to his chest.

"Let's keep going," he said.

His arm still hurt—but his courage soared.

Part VII: The Ballet's Gift of Wings and Wishes

With three magical ingredients safely in their care, Jack and his companions journeyed on. The forest thinned, and the trees began to sparkle faintly, as though each leaf had been dipped in morning dew—and a little kindness.

"Something's changing," Lunibelle observed, her soft glow pulsing with excitement.

The ground grew soft and petal-strewn. The air quivered like a harp string, vibrating with a gentle song. A distant music reached their ears—notes like crystal raindrops, delicate and bright, floating through the whispering leaves.

They stepped into a vast clearing—and gasped.

Hundreds of hummingbirds filled the sky, their wings painting ribbons of jewel-toned light. At the center rose a golden stage, woven from vines and dew-thread, glistening like spun starlight. Suspended just above it, on a swing of honeysuckle and spider silk, sat the Hummingbird Queen herself.

"Welcome to the Sky Ballet," she said, her voice bright and soft as sunlit wind chimes. "Applause is optional—gasps, however, are absolutely mandatory."

Jack and the others bowed without needing to be told.

"We seek your help," Jack said. "We need thirty pairs of hummingbird wings to build a *Bubblecraft* and return home."

"To earn our wings," the Queen replied, her eyes twinkling, "you must witness three dances. Name one correctly, and ten pairs shall be yours. Name all three, and thirty shall be your prize."

The first dancer, a lone hummingbird, soared and dipped, tracing graceful figure eights against the cerulean sky.

"Eight!" cried Meow4. "I call it the wiggle-jiggle!"

"It's not Eight!" Meow1 retorted, whiskers twitching. "It's dancing! A double round!"

A gentle smile played on the Queen's lips. "Nice try. Watch carefully and think deeply, for these dances are more than they appear."

Suddenly, the hummingbird darted straight toward the sun. Everyone squinted, shielding their eyes, as the bird vanished and a vibrant, multicolored halo blazed around the sun.

"The halo dance!" Yellowy exclaimed, her voice filled with awe.

"It's not the halo dance," Willy muttered, brow furrowed. "It's the hummingbird dancing within the sun's fiery embrace."

Then, the hummingbird reappeared, its rhythmic jiggle a miniature disco, its beat accelerating. A chorus of guesses erupted.

"I am think... it's a solo!" Meow3 declared.

"It's a solo," another voice echoed.

The Queen chuckled—a sound like tiny bells. "Wiggle-jiggle isn't incorrect, but 'solo' will suffice." Ten pairs of wings, iridescent and light as air, fluttered into a satchel like falling petals.

Next, two hummingbirds appeared, mirroring each other in tight, coordinated spirals.

"A-ha!" cried Willy. "It's a twin-twirl!"

"No, no," Meow2 squeaked shyly. "It's a... a twirly-two!"

"A harmonious flight," Meow1 suggested.

"It is a duet," Lunibelle said finally, her voice soft but sure.

"Indeed," said the Queen, her smile widening. The second set of ten pairs of wings drifted gracefully into the satchel.

Finally, the third dance began. A dozen hummingbirds flew as one, looping and weaving to form stars, fractals, and blooming ephemeral shapes.

"Oh, how beautiful, how complicated! It reminds me of my

home's sky!" Lunibelle gasped, her eyes wide with wonder. The others' eyes were wide as well—a silent confession that the dance seemed impossible to solve. It felt like a puzzle with no answer.

Then a sudden thought struck Lunibelle. "Dragonfly's Eyes!" she whispered to Jack.

Jack, ever prepared for whimsical magic, pulled two gleaming Dragonfly's Eyes from his satchel and held them to his own. Through them, the chaotic dance slowed, the world sharpened, and every wingbeat became a visible brushstroke in the sky. Every formation grew clear. And for one magical moment, a phrase appeared above them—woven from starlight and motion—*Harmony in Multiplicity.*

"A formation," Jack whispered, a knowing smile on his face. "It's called *Harmony in Multiplicity.*"

"Perfect," the Queen beamed, her face aglow with delight. "You have named them all."

With a graceful twirl, thirty pairs of wings, each one a miniature rainbow, rose in a soft swirl around them.

"These wings are gifted from joy, not taken in sorrow," the Queen explained. "They are faster than light, yet gentler than dew." She passed the glowing satchel to Jack. "Fly with purpose. And never forget: joy is the only fuel that never runs out."

"Thank you," Jack said, his heart swelling with awe and gratitude.

Yellowy flapped forward shyly.

"Our Yellowy would like to offer a dance in return," Lunibelle said.

The Queen clapped her wings. "Then let us behold a new star."

The hummingbirds fanned out like petals around the golden stage.

Yellowy flew up, her golden feathers glowing. At first, she wobbled, uncertain. She had always sung bravely but had never danced before an audience. But then the music began again—slower this time.

She twirled once, then twice. The hummingbirds responded, forming a whirling arch above her.

Yellowy looped through it, then dove and rose. The others followed in gentle patterns.

And then—just for one breathless second—they lifted Yellowy.

She hovered at the very top of the clearing, wings spread wide.

The sunlight touched her.

She glowed.

Then they lowered her gently, like a blessing.

The Queen's laughter rang like bells tossed into the breeze.

"A canary's joy belongs to the sky," she said warmly. "And now—it belongs to us all."

With gratitude, Jack and Lunibelle bowed deeply.

All four ingredients had been found. All roads now curled back toward the Bubble Prophet in his foamy kingdom.

Part VIII: The Flight That Bends Time

They returned to Mr. Spittleton's glade.

Mr. Spittleton stood on a mushroom podium, puffing triumphant melodies through a trumpet carved from birch bark.

"You have returned!" he cried. "And just in time—the next micro-hole opens in precisely... now-ish minus three and a half blinklings!"

Jack presented the four items like sacred pastries: the silver quill, Snakety the snake, the Dragonfly's Eyes (still glowing with truth), and the pouch of hummingbird wings.

Lunibelle clasped her hands. "Let's build the *Bubblecraft*!"

Mr. Spittleton executed a hop, a twirl, and a bow that made them applaud.

"First," he announced, "assemble the serpent!"

Snakety stretched long and proud.

"The quill!"

Jack handed it over. Mr. Spittleton glued it gently to Snakety's nose with a dollop of bubble paste. "Glue only works if applied while humming the alphabet backward," he explained solemnly.

"Eyes!"

Lunibelle floated the Dragonfly's Eyes into place. They glowed once, then clicked into position with a very official-sounding *PING*.

"Wings, please!"

Parcel, Yellowy, and all four kittens carried the wings in a parade of fluff and coordination. Meow3 dropped hers, declaring, "I am think... this wing is heavier than a philosophy." Meow4 strapped one on backward until Snakety sneezed bubbles in protest. They attached the wings to the sides of the snake's body until he resembled a glorious, feathery sky-dragon.

As the final wing was affixed, a hum filled the clearing—a harmonic buzz, part music box, part lightning storm.

The *Bubblecraft* glowed. The wind shifted. Time hiccupped.

"He's ready—or almost! Either way, he's fabulous. Aboard, my glittering champions!" Mr. Spittleton announced.

They climbed on. Jack first, Lunibelle was at his back, then Willy, Parcel and four kittens, with Yellowy perched high like a citrus-colored captain.

Mr. Spittleton tapped the *Bubblecraft* with a spatula-shaped wand.

"Eyes closed!" he cried. "No peeking, no blinking sideways, no doubting the fabric of physics!"

They shut their eyes.

Mr. Spittleton began his chant:

Bubble, bubble, swirl and spin,
Send this crew back home again!
Through the clouds, past the hole,
To where stories warm and memories hold!

FWWOOOSHHHH!

The wings exploded into motion. The air ribboned and shrieked. The *Bubblecraft* shot upward so fast it left time far behind.

The passengers closed their eyes. A soft whirring quickened into a furious hiss, then a pounding rumble, and finally a deafening BOOM in their ears. It felt as if they'd fallen into a drum the sky itself was beating. Then the sound thinned, dwindling into silence. Only a faint vibration hinted that the *Bubblecraft* was still flying...

Suddenly—

CRAAAACK!

A micro-hole ripped open. The *Bubblecraft* zipped through.

Silence.

Then... warmth.

Jack smelled pine needles. Pancake syrup. The particular scent that only home has.

He peeked.

They were back!

The same forest clearing. The wooden sign. The basket of mushrooms, waiting as though it had never blinked.

Willy barked.

Meow4 climbed a tree and announced, "WE HAVE LANDED!"

Yellowy chirped the last note of a song that had begun in another dimension.

"We returned," Lunibelle breathed, her glow flickering like the last firefly of a dream.

Jack looked around. Everything was the same. Grandma's warning—about forests borrowing children—echoed faintly in his mind. He felt taller inside, stronger, glowing in the quiet way only adventures can leave you glowing.

"Let's go home," he whispered.

Part IX: Grandma's Music Box That Hums a Bubble Melody

They followed the winding forest path. The sun slouched in the sky, pouring gold over the treetops.

When the cottage came into view—its chimney puffing gentle clouds—Jack's heart swelled so suddenly it felt an inflated balloon of joy inside his chest.

"Grandma!" he called, bounding up the steps three at a time.

The door opened before his hand reached the knob.

There she stood, holding a tray of sugar-cakes and wearing a smile that knew more than it ever said.

"Welcome home," she said, as if the words themselves were a hug. "Shoes muddy? Hearts shining? Perfect."

"You'll never believe what happened!" Jack blurted, tossing his satchel to the floor.

Grandma raised an eyebrow—a single, dramatic arc of curiosity. "Try me."

And so he did.

He told her everything: the sign, the secret path, Mr. Spittleton's frothy lecture, the grasses that wouldn't let go, the hummingbirds who danced like lightning wearing gowns, the snake who flew, the micro-hole...

Parcel added commentary, especially on the quill's glitter. Meow4 re-enacted the wasp scene with interpretive leaps—knocking over a stool in his enthusiasm. Yellowy hummed transitions. Snakety bowed politely whenever mentioned. Meow3 interrupted twice with, "I am think... Jack forgot the honey was so tasty."—though no one remembered such a part.

When the tale ended, Grandma placed a gentle hand on Jack's shoulder.

"My dear boy," she said, her voice soft as moss and twice as wise, "this forest holds more wonders than even the moon has secrets. And secrets multiply when told, so mind which ones you whisper aloud."

Willy curled up beside the fire.

The kittens climbed into their windowsill fortress. Yellowy perched atop the bookshelf and began to hum a tune that might have come from another sky entirely.

Jack leaned in, voice quiet. "Grandma... do you think the bubble world is still out there?"

Grandma's eyes twinkled. "Oh yes," she said. "It never goes away. It only waits—for a story brave enough to call it back. The bubble world never ends—it only pauses when no one is looking."

She reached into her apron pocket and pulled out a tiny music box. She wound it gently.

The tune that floated out was impossible. Not because it was loud, but because it felt like something remembered from a dream you hadn't had yet.

"I found this," she said, "in a bubble of my own."

Jack's mouth fell open. "You've been there too?"

Grandma only smiled the kind of smile that makes you wonder if you've been talking to a wizard this whole time—or perhaps a conspirator with the stars.

Later, they all gathered around the fireplace. Jack reached into his pocket and offered Grandma the quill.

"For when you're far away from home," he said.

She pressed it.

"Thank you, love. I shall keep it next to the treasure maps."

Dusk arrived and tucked itself around the cottage. The sugar-cakes vanished mysteriously, leaving behind only crumbs and satisfaction.

Laughter crackled like firewood.

The moon leaned in through the window.

And somewhere—just past the edge of the stars—a bubble popped. Not loudly, but softly, sweetly. And in the silence that followed, it sang a tiny tune only the brave could hear.

That night, no one needed to be told to close their eyes.

Because they were already dreaming.

And the bubble world... waited.

Chapter X
The Stories That Forget to End

Part I: It All Begins Beneath the Eavesdropping Clock's Hands

One day, everyone was in the living room.

Lunibelle and Jack were discussing dinosaurs and planning to visit the dinosaur museum. Willy, as usual, lay on the sofa, his eyes half-closed, his ears twitching, and his mind calculating the precise angle from which a snack might be flung.

Parcel wore glasses and mended the kittens' clothes with judicial precision. "This hole," she said, "was not caused by ordinary play. Someone tried to turn it into a sock puppet."

Yellowy stood on the chandelier, staring at the three hands of the wall clock, wondering once again whether time flowed backward when no one was watching.

The four kittens were in their usual whirlwind of mayhem—chasing, hugging, tumbling, and squabbling on the carpet.

"Mama! Meow4 bit my tail!" Meow1 yelled, pointing a trembling paw at Meow4, who was wrapped in a lampshade.

"She hit me with her tail first!" Meow4 protested. "It smacked my whiskers! They're very sensitive!"

"I am think..." Meow3 drawled, sprawled across the windowsill, "Meow2 wants me to be a football goalkeeper and not let me read books!"

"But I must have a goalkeeper," Meow2 whispered. He stood in front of a tiny paper football, already turning red. "It's the rules."

"Shall we tell a story?" Lunibelle suggested suddenly.

"YES!" Meow4 leaped from the sofa to the coffee table. "I love listening to stories the most! Especially ones without endings!"

"Stories without endings?" Meow1 wrinkled her nose. "That's like wearing socks with no toes. If there's no ending, it's not a story! If you don't have a tail, are you even Meow4?"

"I was born with a tail," Meow4 replied, now on the curtain rod. "Don't all stories have a tail—or is that just the same as an ending?"

"I am think..." Meow3 blinked slowly. "You should first clarify the concept. A story is a very round circle. So the beginning is also the end, and the end is also the beginning."

"I just want to jump out of this circle!" Meow4 shouted, leaping into the air like a ball of chaos before landing with a THUMP in Parcel's yarn basket.

Everyone laughed.

"If you stop telling the story," Willy declared, eyes narrowed, "that's the end."

"My grandma tells forest stories," Jack added. "She still hasn't finished. She's on chapter three hundred and something. I don't even think she remembers the beginning."

"Let's go to your grandma's house again!" Meow4 ran to Jack's feet. "Let's cross the Please Stop Sign again and meet the bubble bug! Last time I forgot to take a bubble home!"

"I am think..." Meow3's tail flicked. "If we go to that bubble world again, the chance of returning might be one in a million—a number that wears shoes far too big for any cat to walk in."

Meow4's eyes widened. He wasn't sure what a million was, but he suspected it was more than ten.

"Okay!" Lunibelle smiled. "Whoever has a story may begin. But it must be very interesting..."

"I'll be first! I'll be first!" Meow4 shouted. Since birth, his wish had always been to go first—at dinner, at games, and now, at storytelling.

"Your story must have an ending," Meow1 warned. "Otherwise we'll all be stuck inside your nonsense forever."

"But..." Meow4 hesitated. "Can I be in my own story?"

"You are already in your own head," Meow1 muttered, "so I suppose that's consistent."

"If you want," Parcel said, glancing over her spectacles, "you can weave yourself into your tale. That's how autobiographies begin."

"I won't be turned into two Meow4s, right?"

"From the beginning of the world until now," Jack grinned, "there has only been one Meow4, and I am sure it will stay that way."

"I am think..." Meow3 yawned. "The beginning of a story is the most important part—unless you start in the middle and then go backward, in which case, the middle is the beginning, and the end is maybe lunch."

Finally, the living room quieted.

Lunibelle and Jack sat side by side on the short sofa. Willy stretched beside them, noble and noblish. Yellowy fluttered to her favorite cabinet perch. Meow1 and Meow4 shared the long sofa. Meow3 nestled on the window ledge. Meow2 huddled beneath the coffee table, close enough to listen but hidden in case the story turned spooky.

Parcel sat on her small chair, needles flashing, patching a pair of socks.

The sunbeam quietly slipped through the window, found a cozy spot on the carpet, and sprawled out with its legs folded. "This is the most comfortable way to listen to a story," it thought, quite pleased.

The second hand on the wall clock watched the sunbeam with envy and slowed down, searching for the perfect position to pause. "The 3 and 9 positions are horizontal—far too tiring," it mused. "The 12 is too high up... Hmm, the 6 seems best, hanging upside down like a bat—effortless and close."

"Hey, hey!" the minute hand grumbled. "Second hand, if you stop right in front of me, how am I supposed to move?"

"How about we discuss this?" the hour hand said mysteriously. "All three of us want to hear stories, don't we? So let's just—temporarily, very temporarily—stop, leaving only the ticking sound. They," it pointed toward the living room, "are all listening. No one will notice us."

And so, all three hands came to a halt. The living room turned timeless.

The curtain rustled gently, reshaping itself into a very large ear.

The story was about to begin.

Part II: The Pear Who Wants to Be a Grape

Meow4 was still sitting on the sofa in a daze, blinking as though he'd forgotten how to begin.

"Are you frozen?" Meow1 poked him with a knitting needle Parcel had just dropped.

"I am think..." Meow3 offered. "The story needs the perfect beginning—not too crunchy, not too slippery."

"Let him talk," declared Yellowy, balancing on one claw atop a picture frame.

Meow4 jumped on the carpet from the sofa, he cleared his throat like an opera singer with hiccups. "Once upon a Tuesday afternoon... or maybe a Wednesday... possibly a Friday."

"What day is it?" interrupted Meow1.

"It doesn't matter," Meow4 insisted. "In my story, days wear masks. One day can pretend to be another. Even Sunday."

"I am think..." Meow3 suggested, "If Tuesday wants to be Friday, it should first attend a costume party."

"Right!" Meow4 beamed. "So on Costume-Friday, there were three pears growing on a pear tree. Obviously."

"Wait—pears?" Meow1 wondered, raising an eyebrow.

"Yes, but not just any pears," Meow4 announced with a twirl. "One was big, one was small, and one was neither big nor small."

"What color were they?" inquired the sunbeam.

The clock paused, just briefly—as if even Time was curious about the story to come.

"Yellow, blue, and green," Meow4 pronounced proudly.

"Blue?" Meow2 muttered from beneath the coffee table. "Are blue pears real?"

"They are in my story," Meow4 proclaimed. "The blue one tasted like cloudberries and bubblegum."

"Where is this pear tree?" Meow3 pressed. "I am think... location affects flavor."

"It grew in a garden that floated above the clouds and below a hot air balloon convention," Meow4 elaborated.

"I've never been to a floating garden," Jack murmured.

"Well, you're in luck!" Meow4 grinned. "Because the pears were tired of just hanging there, so they grew legs and ran away!"

"Pears don't have legs," Meow1 grumbled.

"They do if they borrow some," Meow4 stated confidently. "They borrowed them from the radishes."

Parcel dropped her sewing. "That's not how botany works."

"It's not botany—it's story-ny!" Meow4 cried, waving his arms.

"Anyway," he continued, "the blue pear wanted to be a purple grape, the yellow pear wanted to be a red apple, and the green pear wanted to be a watermelon. So they all visited the Fruit Salon—where fruits go to get haircuts and identity crises."

The kittens collectively gasped.

"The salon was run by a cantaloupe named Madame Rind," Meow4 continued. "She gave the blue pear grape-colored polka dots, painted the yellow one glossy red, and stuck black stickers on the green one."

"Did it work?" pleaded Meow2, ears peeking above the coffee

table.

"Sort of," Meow4 admitted. "They looked different, but they still smelled like pears."

"I am think..." Meow3 tapped his head. "The nature of 'pearness' cannot be erased with paint."

"Exactly!" Meow4 exclaimed triumphantly. "So they jumped into a fruit salad and swam back to the pear tree, which had grown wings and flown away in the meantime."

"They missed their home?" Lunibelle wondered.

"Terribly," lamented Meow4. "The tree was their umbrella, their trampoline, their bedtime story."

"Can't the tree come back?" Jack suggested.

"No," Meow4 announced dramatically, "because the tree had enrolled in Cloud School to become a thunderstorm."

There was a moment of stunned silence.

"And so," Meow4 concluded, "the pears built their own tree from popsicle sticks, shoelaces, and honeybee's laughter."

"Did it grow?" pressed Meow1.

"Not upward," Meow4 responded. "It grew inward. Into their dreams. And every time they dreamed of home, the tree gave them a hug."

Then Meow4 sat there, with no words coming out, his eyes simply looking around.

"Is that the end?" queried Willy.

"No," Meow4 corrected. "That's the middle. The end is when one of them turns into a banana."

"A banana?" everyone cried in unison.

"Yes. But I won't say which one," Meow4 explained, licking a paw mysteriously.

"Because?" Parcel prompted.

"Because endings should always have a tail... but sometimes the tail wags the tale."

And with that, Meow4 jumped back to the sofa, sat down and stole a marshmallow cube from Jack's tea saucer.

"I am think..." Meow3 whispered. "I give it three paws up."

"Wasn't bad," Meow1 conceded. "Though you need lessons on botany and narrative structure."

"I liked the shoelaces," Meow2 whispered.

"I liked that it didn't end properly," Yellowy mused.

Willy yawned. "I prefer stories with bones."

"Actually, Meow4's story was very good!" Lunibelle declared. "Who's next?"

"I am think..." Meow3 stated, standing up like a philosopher. "It is my turn."

Part III: Why the Puddle Refuses to Blink

The marshmallow cube lay stunned, the teacup upright again. Meow4 curled smugly into a ball.

The clock offered a cautious tick. The curtain fluttered as if it wanted to raise a paw.

"I am think..." Meow3 began, tail flicking with philosophical intent.

Everyone suddenly focused.

Meow3 stepped forward with deliberate grace, like a cat who had just solved a puzzle only he understood.

"I am think..." she mused, "that my story begins in a puddle."

"A puddle?" echoed Meow1.

"A philosophical puddle," Meow3 corrected. "One that reflects not just faces but questions."

"Like, 'Why do ducks waddle?'" Meow4 suggested.

"No," Meow3 denied. "More like, 'Why does a reflection never blink first?'"

Parcel adjusted her glasses. "Go on, dear."

"In this puddle," Meow3 continued, "lived a piglet who wanted to be a philosopher."

"I thought pigs liked mud, not meanings," observed Yellowy.

"This piglet," Meow3 explained, "liked both. He rolled in thoughts as deeply as in dirt. His name was Baconstein."

"That sounds delicious," whispered Meow2.

"Baconstein had friends," Meow3 went on, "a deer who liked running, a rabbit who played the flute, and a bird who spoke only in riddles."

"Sounds like our breakfast table," murmured Willy.

"One day," Meow3 resumed, "Baconstein announced, 'I am think... I shall become a philosopher.'"

"What did the others say?" inquired Jack, leaning forward.

"They replied, 'No.'"

"Why not?" pressed Meow1.

"Because," Meow3 elucidated, "they thought philosophers sat too still. The deer preferred motion, the rabbit wanted music, and the bird wanted riddles answered, not questioned."

"So Baconstein was sad," Meow3 confided. "He wandered into the forest in squeaky boots, mumbling about metaphysics."

"Did he find a mentor?" wondered Lunibelle.

"Yes," Meow3 declared, his eyes gleaming. "A fox. A sly fox. A fox with a monocle and a library stacked from walnuts."

"I am suspicious of foxes," Meow1 cautioned.

"So was Baconstein. But he was also curious. The fox taught him to twist words, to argue with shadows, and to win debates with squirrels."

"Is this philosophy or trickery?" challenged Parcel.

"That," Meow3 stated, "is the question."

The room went silent.

"Baconstein returned to the clearing," Meow3 resumed. "He wore a cape now and carried a book titled *Why Puddles Don't Blink*."

"Did his friends like the new him?" queried Meow2.

"No," Meow3 answered. "The deer complained he ran in loops. The rabbit noted his flute no longer sounded right. The bird posed a riddle: 'What is clever but stupid?'"

"That bird is too deep for breakfast," muttered Meow4.

"So Baconstein built a tower of bark and retreated to it," Meow3 narrated. "He scribbled notes such as: 'Am I a pig dreaming of bacon, or bacon dreaming of a pig?'"

"Whoa," breathed Jack.

"He debated himself," Meow3 added, "but the winning argument always came from his other self."

"But then," Meow3 continued slowly, "one day he heard laughter outside his tower."

"Was it the friends?" hoped Yellowy.

"No. It was squirrels arguing over an acorn's favorite color."

"Acorns don't have favorites," Meow1 grumbled.

"Exactly!" Meow3 smiled. "So Baconstein ran outside and cried, 'You are all wrong! Acorns love purple!'"

"Did the squirrels believe him?" prompted Meow2.

"No—but they invited him to join their game anyway."

"And?" Lunibelle urged.

"And Baconstein remembered how to play."

Silence again.

"That's it?" pressed Meow1.

"I am think... yes," Meow3 confirmed.

"But what happened to the deer, rabbit, and bird?" demanded Meow4.

"They're in the puddle," Meow3 revealed.

"The philosophical puddle?" Meow2 whispered.

"Yes," Meow3 nodded. "That's where all unanswered questions go—to reflect until someone dares to jump in."

"Would you jump in?" challenged Jack.

"I already did," Meow3 replied. "That's why my tail curls like a question mark."

Everyone turned to look.

Indeed, his tail curled just so.

"I give that four thoughts out of five," Meow4 declared.

"I'm not sure it even had a beginning," Meow1 questioned.

"I am think..." Meow3 whispered. "All puddles are beginnings."

"Well then," announced Lunibelle, clapping, "who wants to tell the next story?"

"I believe I shall," stated Yellowy, fluffing her feathers.

"Bird story!" cried Meow4.

"Does it involve muffins?" hoped Meow2.

"No," Yellowy replied. "But it involves altitude."

Part IV: Pickle's Backward Song That Never Quite Ends

The hour hand shifted forward by one blink. The second hand, relieved, sighed with a soft CLICK.

Yellowy shook out her feathers and stepped onto the coffee table with theatrical poise.

"My story," she announced, "takes place far away, in a rainforest so tangled that even the shadows get lost."

"Do shadows get lost?" Meow2 wondered meekly.

"They do if they follow parrots," Yellowy replied, eyes sparkling.

"I am think..." Meow3 mused. "Parrots are bright enough to confuse light itself."

"Correct!" cried Yellowy. "In the rainforest lived many birds—eagles, seagulls, sparrows, parrots—and one robin who insisted on being a windmill."

"Did it spin?" Meow4 inquired.

"It tried—but only when someone sang polka."

The sunbeam changed shape on the carpet. "A rainforest? I've always wanted to vacation there."

"You'd melt," muttered the hour hand.

"I'm a professional," the sunbeam proclaimed indignantly.

"Shhh," whispered the minute hand. "I think this story involves flight. Let's listen."

Yellowy fluffed her wings. "Now, all these birds decided to have a flying race. The prize? A crown woven from dew and a song sung backward."

"I've never heard a backward song," Meow1 observed.

"It sounds like a hiccup dancing," Yellowy assured her.

"So the eagles were confident, the seagulls smug, the sparrows nervous, and the parrots... late. As usual."

"The parrots wore roller skates," she added.

"Why?" Jack pushed.

"To confuse the rules," Yellowy explained. "They always did things sideways. One even flew backward."

"I like that parrot," Meow4 cheered.

Willy huffed. "Too many feathers. Not enough bones."

"Anyway," Yellowy continued, "they all lined up on a vine. But the vine wasn't ready—it was still brushing its teeth."

"The vine has teeth?" Meow2 squeaked.

"Only when it's nervous," Yellowy replied, nodding. "So the race started late. Very late. So late it circled back and became early."

"I am think..." Meow3 mused. "That is a temporal loop—as if toast that lands butter-side up in a dream."

Parcel squinted. "Does the story have a direction?"

"Yes!" Yellowy nodded. "Up!"

With a flap, she mimed each bird taking off.

"The eagle soared, slicing clouds. The seagulls screeched poetry. The sparrows got distracted by shiny things. But the parrots... they squabbled. One shrieked, 'I'm a pineapple!' and crashed into a balloon."

"Wait, where'd the balloon come from?" Meow1 pressed.

"It was carrying a wedding cake," Yellowy responded. "The bride was a flamingo."

Meow4 clapped. "This is the best story yet!"

"But," Yellowy continued, "as the race continued, something strange happened. All the fast birds grew tired. The eagle forgot which wing was left. The seagulls lost their rhythm. The parrots began reciting French opera."

"And the slowest bird of all—a green parrot named Pickle—just kept going."

"Pickle?" Jack grinned.

"Yes," Yellowy confirmed. "Pickle never rushed. He flapped gently, hummed lullabies, and carried the faint scent of guava. Birds laughed at him, but he didn't mind."

"That's like my dream," Meow2 whispered softly, surprising even himself. "Where I ran the slowest and still won the race—not by chasing butterflies, but by dancing with them."

Yellowy gave him a slow blink of approval. "Exactly," she affirmed. "Pickle didn't chase the wind. He flew with it."

"I am think... Pickle has peace of mind," Meow3 observed.

"At the end of the race," Yellowy continued, "there was no crowd, no camera—only a puddle of sky waiting to be stepped on. Pickle arrived last and found the crown lying in a dandelion."

"Where were the others?" Meow1 wondered.

"Exhausted. Lost. Singing about noodles."

"Pickle wore the crown and sang the song backward—

Snails wear mittens on Mondays twice,

Clouds open up umbrellas when it rains below,

The ant pushed the elephant into the river,

Left is right if you blink at night.

The Pacific Ocean sleeps in a teacup,

Cows graze on flying trees,

Moonlight sneezes when socks take flight.

"Which sounded like bees snoring!" Meow4 exclaimed.

"—And the sky applauded with soft thunder," Yellowy finished.

The room was quiet. Even the second hand blinked.

"Is that the end?" Meow2 queried.

"No," Yellowy countered. "It's altitude."

"What does that mean?" Meow1 puzzled.

"It means we all just flew a little—there is a long way to go," Yellowy concluded, and with that, she fluttered back to her cabinet.

Lunibelle nodded, smiling. "Who's next?"

"I hope it involves bones," Willy hoped, stretching.

Lunibelle nodded. "Then it's your turn, Willy."

Willy sat up. "Right. Get ready. Mine's a dream I had. But maybe it was real."

Part V: The Clattering Skeleton Who Loses Courage

A spoon clinked in an empty teacup, as if to announce, "Next."

Willy yawned once, deeply. Jack gently nudged the teapot toward him. "Willy, you always have the wildest dreams," he observed, grinning.

"All right. My turn," he rumbled. "But mine's a dream. Maybe."

"I like dreams!" Meow4 declared, closing his eyes. "Especially ones where I become number one."

"So," Meow1 scoffed, "in reality, you're always fourth!"

"BORF! ARF!" Willy cleared his throat. It sounded like someone about to bark. "This story," he explained, "happened in a dream. Or it happened in a place shaped like a dream. Or maybe I dreamed of a place shaped like me."

"That's confusing," Meow4 grumbled.

"I am think... that's the perfect start," Meow3 mused.

Willy settled into storyteller mode, his tail precisely curled, his brow solemn.

"I was walking in the woods," he began, "but the trees were upside down, and the sky was the ground. I had no leash, no collar, no responsibilities. Just me, my nose, and a feeling that something delicious was nearby."

"Was it chicken?" Meow2 wondered, barely peeking out.

"No," Willy replied. "It was a whisper. A whisper that smelled like ancient bones."

"'The smell of ancient bones,'" Meow4 guessed, "might smell like ugly old tree roots."

"I followed the smell," Willy continued, "until I came to a field of holes. Not rabbit holes. Not wormholes. Talking holes."

"Talking holes?" Meow1 asked.

"Yes. They argued about recipes. One insisted, 'All stew must begin with a carrot,' and another bellowed, 'But what if the carrot is sleeping?'"

"I like stew," Meow4 mumbled, already licking imaginary gravy from his paw.

"I ignored them," Willy admitted. "And I found the hill. The Bone Hill."

The kittens held their breath.

"It was made entirely of bones," Willy growled with a dramatic flair. "Tiny ones, huge ones, glowing ones, even dancing ones. They didn't lie still. They jiggled and jangled like wind chimes in a storm."

"Did they... talk?" Parcel inquired, pausing her stitching.

"Oh yes," Willy confirmed. "One greeted, 'Welcome, seeker of marrow.' Another challenged me to guess what animal it used to be. One even claimed it was a tree, not a femur."

"I am think... bones with mistaken identities are the saddest kind," Meow3 sighed.

"I climbed the hill," Willy went on, "and the bones made way for me, like I was their long-lost cousin. They rattled and hummed. A drumbeat rose. Suddenly, a throne of bone appeared, shaped like a wishbone wearing necklace."

"I like that chair!" Meow4 exclaimed.

"I sat on it," Willy continued, "and all the bones bellowed, 'Tell us a riddle!'"

"Did you?" Jack pushed.

"Yes," Willy replied. "I offered, 'Why don't skeletons fight each other?'"

"Why?" The Meows looked at each other.

Willy closed his eyes.

"Why?" Meows asked again.

"Because they don't have the guts." Willy opened his eyes.

The room groaned.

"But the bones loved it," Willy said. "They laughed until they clattered apart and back together. One bone—named Todd—did a somersault, saluted, and applauded with his kneecaps."

"I like Todd," Meow2 whispered.

"They invited me to their Bone Party," Willy recounted. "There was bone bowling, where femurs knocked over rib cages; bone limbo beneath a floating spine; and a guessing game called 'Whose Tooth Is It Anyway?'"

"Sounds wild," Meow1 commented.

"Best dream ever," Meow4 cheered.

Jack leaned forward, eyes wide. "Wait—did they really play bone limbo with a floating spine?"

Willy gave a solemn nod. "And I thought, if Jack had been there, he would have laughed too. That made me feel braver."

"That's amazing," Jack breathed. "If I ever dream that, I'm going to bring snacks."

Meow4 forgot to breathe. "Snacks for skeletons? Like... ghost chips?"

"No," Jack corrected. "Calcium chews."

"At midnight," Willy went on, "they gave me a medal of bone, forged from kindness and nostalgia. I wore it proudly. But then the dream shook."

"Shook?" Yellowy puzzled.

"Yes," Willy responded. "The sky collapsed like jelly. The trees turned into toothbrushes. And I heard a barking echo: 'Wake up! Wake up!'"

"Were you the one barking?" Parcel wondered.

"Yes," Willy confirmed, blinking slowly. "But it wasn't me waking myself up; it was the bones. They wanted me to go so that I could remember."

"What did they want you to remember?" Lunibelle asked.

"They wanted me to remember that all things—even dreams—are real if you treat them kindly, and that laughter is stronger than fear."

"Even without muscles?" Meow1 challenged.

"Especially without muscles," Willy asserted.

"We all look like bones!" the hour hand sighed. "Well, now I'm moving."

"Can we tick again?" the second hand requested.

"Let's tick just once," the minute hand suggested. "But slowly."

TICK.

The curtain rustled, as if clapping.

"I am think... these are the best bone stories that never end," Meow3 mused.

"Delicious, like blue pears," Meow1 added.

"Or like earthworms snoring," Yellowy chimed in.

"Or like bones that sing," Willy finished.

Because that's what good stories do: they don't end. They echo. They keep ticking.

Part VI: Boing, Bloop, and the Brave Little Bounce

Everyone was enthralled by the bone story.

The sunbeam found Meow2 hiding under the coffee table, rounded a few corners, and landed gently on his back—like a quiet cheerleader made of light.

"Thank you," Meow2 whispered, smiling into the glow.

Lunibelle noticed Meow2 kept raising his paws under the table, only to pull them back down—a jack-in-the-box too shy to spring. She clapped softly. "I think Meow2 has a wonderful story worth hearing. Shall we let him tell it?"

"Welcome! Welcome!" Meow4 bounced up, tail and paws waving like flags. "I'll love it before I even hear it!"

"Come out and share," offered Willy, stretching with a yawn. "Tell it from the good spot—right here by me."

Meow2 crept out from under the table. Each paw step, in his mind, thumped like drums in an invisible parade. The whole living room felt like a soft, waiting stage.

Willy's ears tilted forward. His eyes became like courtroom windows—serious, kind, protective. He leaned closer, guarding Meow2 as if nothing in the world would get past him.

"Are you ready?" Parcel inquired, her gaze warm with dignified care.

Meow2 nodded, eyes lowered. His whiskers trembled.

The curtain above reshaped itself—no longer an ear but a crescent moon.

"A new story deserves a new shape," it whispered.

The room stilled.

Meow2 pressed against Willy's side. Willy dipped his head and gave him one quiet lick between the ears.

"Many... many years later," Meow2 began in a hush.

"Many, many years later?" Yellowy fluttered down. "Shouldn't it be 'a long, long time ago'?"

But Meow2 froze. His tail puffed like a bottlebrush.

"I can prove it!" Meow4 leaped from the sofa. "It was many, many years later!"

"I am think... that 'many, many years later' is philosophical—backward fairy-tale time," Meow3 offered.

"You told me the story last night," Meow4 whispered loudly. "It was sooooo good! I didn't even fall asleep!"

"Are you blaming me?" Parcel countered, raising a brow, amused. "Okay, okay," she agreed with a chuckle. "I shall not interfere!"

Meow2 peeked up. Everyone was smiling. Jack nodded. "I'll definitely like it," he declared, "because stories grow best when they're shared."

"Many, many years later," Meow2 began again—this time louder, "a little Basketball rolled into the woods. The trees were tall, the grass was green, and a nearby stream sang to itself."

Meow2 sat taller. He took a steady breath.

"Basketball bounced and sang:
I am a little Basketball,
rolling into the forest to play hide-and-seek,
the squirrel jumped high to catch me,
and nearly knocked over a crow's nest!
Mushrooms are stools,
trees are baskets, vines are nets,
and woodpeckers are referees—DONG-DONG!
Timeout violation!"

Laughter bubbled everywhere.

"Timeout violation!" Meow4 echoed, swinging like a vine.

"Do woodpeckers really go 'dong-dong'?" Yellowy wondered.

"Only the referee ones," Meow2 confirmed solemnly.

"I am think... 'bloop' is the saddest bounce," Meow3 observed.

"But did Basketball have legs?" Meow1 asked suspiciously.

"No," Meow2 responded quickly, "but he wore purple shoes with lightning bolts."

"Whoa," exclaimed Meow4. "That Basketball has cooler shoes than mine."

Meow2 grinned.

"All the animals—rabbits, bears, turtles, and deer—ran when they saw him. They'd never seen anything so round. They thought he was a monster-meatball!"

"A MONSTER MEATBALL?!" Meow4 howled.

"Do turtles even run?" Meow1 challenged.

"In dreams they do," Meow2 insisted, growing braver.

"Basketball rolled to the river, feeling lonely. He sat on a rock and tried to bounce sadly—but sad bouncing sounded more like BLOOP than BOING."

The curtain sagged in sympathy.

"Who am I?" Basketball wondered, leaning on a tree. "No one likes me. I'm round, fat, and alone."

The tree's leaves brushed him gently.

"Leaves," whispered Basketball, "do you understand loneliness? Where do I belong?"

The room grew quiet.

"Then, SPLASH!" continued Meow2, "a little rabbit slipped into the river. Though he was scared of water, Basketball jumped in. He rolled under her and bounced her safely to shore."

"Hero ball!" Jack shouted.

"And from that day," Meow2 resumed, his voice louder, "the forest animals came out. They weren't afraid anymore.

The rabbit brought carrot cake.

The bear opened one lazy eye and muttered, 'Nap...?'

The turtle taught him to float.

And the deer cried, 'Let's play basketball!'"

"Did the deer win?" Meow1 probed.

"No," Meow2 replied. "Basketball always wins when the basket is made of clouds."

"I am think..." Meow3 mused. "Sometimes, winning means losing, and losing means winning."

"Basketball was happy," Meow2 finished. "He sang again:
I am a little Basketball,
now I bounce with all my friends,

trees cheer, mushrooms drum,
squirrels kick me with their hind ends!
Vines are nets, clouds are hoops,
birds swoop down and shout 'Hooray!
Every bounce is joy-filled,
and woodpeckers keep the score today."

Parcel sniffed.

"Are you crying, Mommy?" Meow4 demanded.

"No, just dust in my sewing basket," Parcel mumbled, dabbing her glasses.

"I am think... joy is contagious," Meow3 commented softly.

Meow2 looked up. Everyone was smiling. A few blinked slowly, like cats pretending not to cry.

"Is that the end?" Yellowy fretted.

"No," Meow2 announced, surprising himself. "Basketball is still rolling. He never really stops."

"Just like story time," Lunibelle observed, her eyes sparkling.

"Until next time," added Jack.

Applause burst from paws, wings, tails, tongues, whiskers, and from one very proud sunbeam.

The clock's second hand offered a small wag. "Well done."

Meow2's eyes widened. "I forgot to be shy!"

"You remembered to be brave," Willy encouraged. "That's the part of your story."

And that was better.

"Jack's turn!" Meow4 shouted.

Everyone turned.

"What about your story?" Meow1 sat straight.

"Maybe next time," Lunibelle suggested, glancing at the clock, which was now ticking dutifully.

"Maybe," the curtain whispered, curling into a wink. "Maybe story time will return."

The sunlight tiptoed out, it took with it one of Yellowy's feathers that had fallen onto the carpet.

Chapter XI
A Christmas Stolen from December

Part I: The Blossoms That Borrow Snow's Coat

"The flowers on those trees look like piled-up clouds of stardust," Lunibelle murmured, her damp, silvery nose smudging a perfect tiny moon on the windowpane.

She pointed out the window.

"They're a brilliant, happy white, as though the tree borrowed the very last coat of fresh snow and is now wearing it like a triumphant, fluffy cape. What are they called?"

Jack squinted at the petal-drenched trees. "Pear trees," he said. "They bloom every spring."

"Spring?" Lunibelle blinked slowly. "And what, dear terrestrial companion, is... spring?"

Jack leaped from the couch. He loved showing Lunibelle new Earth things. "Earth has four seasons—spring, summer, autumn, winter." He waved his hands as if inviting the four seasons onto a stage.

Lunibelle tried the names out. "Spring... summer... autumn... winter." She tilted her head. "Can we juggle them? Go winter, summer, autumn, spring? I like a surprise."

Jack laughed. "Sorry. They always follow each other like ducks in a row."

Lunibelle closed her eyes. "On my planet, we only have Bright and Dim. They trade places when the Moon Minister spins the Celestial Coin. Sometimes he folds weeks into weekends or borrows a holiday from another month—a magician pulling too many scarves from his sleeve."

Jack blinked. "Moon Minister. Right. Makes sense."

Lunibelle nodded. "He also runs the Bubble Orchestra and the Floating Library. He's very busy but easily distracted."

Jack sat down slowly. In that moment, he felt protective—Lunibelle's world was beautiful nonsense, but he wanted her to know Earth carried beauty too. "Your whole planet sounds as if it were invented by someone who kept losing their shoes."

Lunibelle beamed. "We never wear shoes! They were invented by Earth. We just float politely."

"We don't need calendars either," she continued. "But if we did, I could nudge them like puzzle pieces. It's easy to slip December into April—if you blink at the stars just right."

Outside, the wind stirred. Petals flew past the glass like pink confetti. Lunibelle traced a finger along the window.

"Do the petals fall because they're sad, or are they just practicing flying?"

Jack said, a little vaguely, "Maybe both. Maybe they're sad and brave at the same time."

Lunibelle thought about it for a while. "That's very Earth. On my planet, bravery is measured by smile level."

Jack scrambled to the bookshelf and pulled down a book full of painted pages—*What Are the Four Seasons?* He opened it, and Lunibelle curled beside him, her eyes glowing.

They turned the pages. Spring blushed in pinks and reds. Summer shouted in green. Autumn glowed gold. Winter whispered in white.

"If winter is white," Lunibelle said, twirling one silver arm, "then I must surely belong to winter."

"But winter is more than color," said Jack. He leaned in as if about to whisper a spell. "Winter has Christmas!"

Lunibelle's mouth curled into a surprised spiral. "Christmas?"

Jack gesticulated wildly. "It's a holiday! There are lights and trees and cookies and Santa Claus—"

"Who is Claus, and why is he sandy?"

"Santa Claus," Jack giggled. "He brings presents to kids. He lives at the North Pole and rides a flying sleigh pulled by reindeer."

"Reindeer?"

"Flying reindeer. Very official."

"Who gets his presents?" Lunibelle leaned forward, clearly hoping she might be included.

"Good kids," Jack said, puffing up as though he knew everything. "The ones who brush their teeth every day and remember their pleases and thank-yous."

"I think I did!" Lunibelle said with utmost seriousness. She nudged Willy beside her. "Right, Willy?"

Willy gave two sharp barks—WOOF! WOOF!—leaving no doubt.

"So... am I good?" Lunibelle peered up at Jack, eyes wide and hopeful.

Jack felt his chest grow warm. Protecting her joy felt like his truest duty. "You are very good!" he declared. If it made Lunibelle smile, he'd call her the Queen of Goodness, the Champion of Nice, or whatever she wished.

Lunibelle grinned—then her face scrunched with worry. "But... I'm not from Earth. Santa might not know me."

"Listen," Jack said, stomping his foot for emphasis. "If you stand here, you count—and that means presents!"

She clutched her chest as though guarding a treasure. "Then maybe I'll get a present! When is Christmas? Tomorrow? After Tomorrow?"

"December twenty-fifth."

She counted on her fingers, each tap glowing faintly. "But it's only April. That's at least eight forevers away!"

Just then, a chickadee landed on the pear tree, chirping, "Fee-bee! Fee-bee!"

"See?" Lunibelle pointed triumphantly. "Even the bird agrees—forever!"

Jack laughed. "Time zooms when you're not watching."

But Lunibelle's smile dimmed. "What if I'm not here when it comes? What if my parents come to take me back home?"

Jack froze. The thought hit like a snowball in his stomach. "Then... I'll hide you—in the coat closet, or under my bed."

Lunibelle giggled. "You couldn't. Even if they were staring right at you, you'd only see the wallpaper behind them. They're masters of sneak."

Jack swallowed hard. He didn't doubt her.

Silence tiptoed into the room. Outside, petals drifted down like wandering souls from the sky.

"I wonder," said Lunibelle softly, "if the blossoms on my planet ever feel lonely."

Jack pressed his chin to his knees. "Maybe. But I bet the wind tells them bedtime stories."

Lunibelle looked at him. "You always say the softest things."

Jack blushed.

Lunibelle drew a circle on the windowpane. "Spring feels like a do-over—like someone pressed the restart button on Earth."

Jack nodded. "It is. It's Earth saying, 'Let's try again—with more color this time.'"

They sat side by side. Outside, the petals tumbled like dancers who had forgotten their steps but decided to twirl anyway.

Part II: Can Sleigh Bells Ring in a Field of Tulips?

For two whole days, Jack's thoughts somersaulted in his head. "How do I give someone from another planet the most magical Earth gift ever?" he whispered to the ceiling. "And how do I do it in April?"

He stared at his math book as if it might have answers, then gave up and patted Willy's head. "You're no help either," he said fondly. "You're fluent in tails but silent in miracles."

Willy wagged it—as usual.

That afternoon, Jack and Lunibelle sat on the living-room floor, surrounded by cushions and books.

"I wish we could just celebrate Christmas right now," Jack sighed. "But that feels impossible."

Lunibelle's eyes lit up. "Why not?" she whispered. "Why not grab Christmas by its candy cane and tug it into April?"

Jack blinked. "Grab... Christmas?"

"Yes!" Lunibelle leaped up, her whole body glowing with excitement. "We'll lasso the holiday, dress April in snowflakes and cinnamon, and confuse the calendars!"

"But... there's no snow," Jack said. "And Santa doesn't take detours in spring."

Lunibelle planted both hands on her hips. "We'll summon December. I'll try. Noon tomorrow. You bring cocoa. I'll bring the blizzard."

Jack launched off the couch like a spring-loaded Pop-Up Pal. "You can actually do that? You can bring snow?"

"Snow, mittens, wonder, and one very confused groundhog," Lunibelle said with a grin. "I've been practicing with time folding—just a smidge."

Jack furrowed his brow. "Do you need permission—from, like, the sky? Or do you just ask nicely and hope they're in a good mood?"

Lunibelle only smiled and shook her head.

He stared at her in awe. "Okay—but... why noon?"

"Because twelve is a curious number," Lunibelle declared. "It carries breakfast inside and bedtime ahead. Perfect for miracles."

That night, Jack couldn't sleep. His dreams hiccuped and looped. Every time he closed his eyes, Santa winked from a pear tree. He worried too: what if it didn't work? What if Lunibelle felt forgotten all over again?

At dawn, he jumped out of bed, threw on his favorite penguin-in-a-hat shirt, and tiptoed downstairs, his heart thumping.

"Willy," he whispered, shaking his dog gently. "Today is the day April forgets itself."

Willy blinked, stretched, and rolled off his bed with a snort. It was as if he said, "You are full of peppermint today."

Outside, spring was doing her morning exercises—she cared about her figure. Tulips smiled, grass laughed beneath their feet, and dandelions exploded like tiny golden parachutes. Jack and Willy galloped through the dew, soaking up the last sensible moment of April.

When they came back, breakfast was ready. Eggs puffed like yellow clouds, toast glistened with jam, and even the bananas sat like smug princes on their yellow thrones.

"Mom," Jack smiled, spinning into the kitchen, "your breakfasts are better than Santa's elves'."

"You're extra bubbly today," she said, flipping a pancake with flair. "Did you win the joy lottery?"

Jack shrugged. "Maybe. Can I borrow your snow boots—for Lunibelle's fashion experiment?"

His mom paused. "Jack. It's fifty degrees outside. Are you planning a sledding party in the oven?"

"It's a fashion experiment," Jack said smoothly. "Also, can you lend me your winter coat for the fashion show?"

She narrowed her eyes but smiled. "As long as you're not surprising me again like on your birthday."

His dad wandered in, lured by the scent of sizzling potatoes. "Did I hear something about snow?"

Jack leaped up. "Yes! Can you take your winter jacket with you to work?"

"Did I miss a blizzard advisory?" Dad blinked behind his glasses.

The radio crackled: "Today's forecast—sunshine and sanity. High of fifty-seven. Zero chance of snowballs."

Jack sipped his orange juice. "Forecasts are useless when surprises are wrapped in snowflakes."

His parents exchanged a glance.

Jack stood, grabbed his backpack, kissed them both, and dashed out the door.

"Jack's been acting a little... extraordinary lately," his mom murmured.

"Last week he tried to train the fridge to say 'please come in.'" Dad added.

His mom shook her head with a smile. "What on Earth is that child up to now?"

If only she knew—time was about to be politely rearranged like building blocks.

Part III: The Calendar Plays Hopscotch

At exactly noon, the radio in every kitchen, café, school, and store let out a curious crackle. Then came the news: "Breaking news—The town of Somerville is experiencing an unexpected snowstorm. It may be April, but outside, it feels like December. Heavy snowfall. Stay warm, and—yes, you heard that right—Christmas is coming!"

Spoons froze in midair, and coffee dribbled onto saucers. All over town, people stood like dazzled penguins.

And then—

The sky threw open its stage curtains.

First came the clouds—not the polite kind that tiptoe in with whispers, but big, booming, woolly giants galloping across the heavens. They jostled, somersaulted, and stacked themselves into wobbly mountains of fluff, blocking out the sun. Not shy. Not subtle. Instead, a blizzard arrived, snowflakes plummeting down in clusters and choruses. They danced, dazzled, and practically sang with headlight-bright energy.

A man stepped out and shouted, "What in the butterscotch biscuit—?!" His coffee steamed with delight.

A woman clutched her strawberries. "Wow! Now it's Christmas again!"

"Did winter come back to surprise us with presents?" laughed a grandfather in corduroy, just as a flake landed merrily on his nose.

A wave of delighted surprise swept over the town—Christmas was almost here again! With sparkling eyes and boundless cheer!

Flip-flops were flung aside. Mittens were found and cheerfully pulled on. Wool socks, still in aestivation, were summoned from drawers with laughter and song.

Children didn't ask questions—they simply leaped into wonder. They laughed. They became tornadoes of boots and squeals and open mouths turned to the sky.

Sidewalks, dusted with chalk just hours ago, now wore soft carpets of snow. Lawns that had been green that morning yawned beneath glittering blankets.

In classrooms, the lessons happily vanished into thin air; students jumped, teachers smiled. At the zoo, the penguins danced while the flamingos joined in with flapping delight.

And on one street, in one very ordinary house suddenly turned extraordinary, Jack and Lunibelle pressed their noses to the window.

Jack whispered, "Snow really came!"

Lunibelle nodded, her eyes wide with wonder. Her fingers covered her mouth. She whispered, half astonished, half excited: "Did I break the month?"

"It's like you tucked April inside a snow globe," said Jack. His voice carried pure amazement and a flicker of happiness. "The sky... the sky forgot the calendar!"

Outside, the snow kept falling. The sky seemed to twinkle and wink, delighted by its own trick.

The calendar, once proud and stern, played hopscotch as if it had forgotten its job—and didn't feel the least bit sorry. Time tiptoed past it on new snow boots, giggling.

Meanwhile, a grand fashion show, scheduled for sundresses and watermelon heels, unfolded like a dream inside a glittering, frosted jewelry box. Under bright chandeliers, models walked the runway in gowns of silk, laughing as snowflakes kissed the glass outside. Cameras clicked. High heels tiptoed across the marble. The crowd clapped, enchanted and overjoyed.

Near a tall, frost-rimmed window, Jack's mom stood still. Her summer dress sparkled under artificial lights, but the shimmer on her face came from astonishment and quiet joy.

She watched the snowfall with wide-eyed wonder, her heart fluttering.

"How... did Jack know?" she said softly to herself. Her hands were still, but her thoughts twirled with bright delight. She remembered the way he'd stared out the window that morning, as if listening to a secret timepiece ticking backward into magic. And for the first time, she wondered if her son carried a piece of the impossible with him.

Across town, a wave of sheer, sparkly joy was erupting! With gleeful effort, people were hauling out their glorious Christmas trees, untangling their holiday lights, and carefully unboxing their favorite, dazzling ornaments.

The whole scene felt like Lunibelle herself—out of season, out of place, yet dazzling all the same.

And though no one—not even the calendar—could predict the exact magic the coming holidays would bring, everyone was bursting with happy anticipation.

Part IV: Frostington, Who Patiently Waits for Winter

The next morning, Somerville was blanketed in more than snow—it lay under a cover of astonishment.

Jack's home yard had turned into a sparkling, frosted carnival. Everything wore a white coat: the swings, the rosebushes, and the mailbox that usually grumbled about junk letters. Now it looked positively jolly.

Jack burst out the back door wearing one blue mitten (only one—why? who knows), a gray wool hat knitted by his mom, and Dad's snow boots—his own were nowhere to be found. "It's working! It's really snowing!"

Lunibelle followed. She wore an orange down jacket, light-blue pants, purple snow boots, and a cream-colored pom-pom beanie. She walked lightly, snowflakes dancing around her.

"Look!" she cried. "They're catching on my sleeves like tiny stars!"

The kittens tumbled out next, scrambling like buttons spilled from an overstuffed drawer.

"There's one in my whisker!" yelped Meow4.

"Mine tastes like icecream!" declared Meow2, licking a snowflake and promptly sneezing it away.

"Follow me!" commanded Meow1, leaping headlong into a snowdrift taller than she was. She vanished.

Parcel waddled out after them, wrapped in a shawl, muttering, "No discipline. No boots. No sledding license."

Willy charged into the snow as if it had personally offended him. "To the fence and back!" he barked, launching snow into the air like powdered confetti.

Yellowy fluttered overhead and landed on Jack's hat. "Winter! Winter! It's the middle of a midspring miracle!"

Jack spun in circles. Lunibelle spun upside down. The kittens spun vertically and diagonally until Meow3 announced, "I am think... dizzy comes in white flavor."

Then came the idea. "Let's build a snowman!" Jack shouted.

"A what-man?" asked Lunibelle.

"A stack-of-snow surprise guest," Jack said with a grin. "We'll need three balls, one nose, two eyes, and an outrageous hat."

They rolled snowballs. Meow4 was flattened accidentally. Meow1 was rolled into the middle one and emerged, laughing. Meow2 shouted, "Watch out! Not a twig! That's my tail!"

Willy helped push the bottom snowball, but ended up rolling down the hill.

Lunibelle giggled and raised her arms. "Let me try, Doo!"

With a swirl of her silver fingers, the snowballs began to roll on their own. They grew and levitated. They stacked gently with a FWOMP!

"Quick! Buttons, sticks, arms!" yelled Yellowy.

Jack added a carrot nose and coal eyes. Lunibelle added a checkered scarf. Yellowy added glasses made from two gumdrops.

"Behold!" cried Jack. "Frostington the Fabulous!"

The snowman winked.

Everyone froze.

"Did... did he just—"

Frostington lifted one stick arm and waved.

"I am think... I'm not hallucinating," Meow3 murmured. "He just waved at me."

"Good morning," said Frostington.

The kittens screamed and hugged him. Parcel promptly swooned—just slightly.

Jack looked at Lunibelle. Lunibelle looked at Jack.

"Did you do that?"

"I didn't mean to," she whispered. "But I cannot be sorry."

Frostington bowed deeply. "I've been waiting since last December to be assembled. Sometimes I wondered if I belonged at all—for snow out of season melts into nothing. But now, here I am. Thank you kindly."

Then he sneezed. Snowflakes flew everywhere.

And that's how winter, in the middle of April, got even sillier.

Part V: The Stocking That Bears Her Name

That night, the fireplace hummed gently.

Lunibelle stood quietly by the hearth, her wide eyes reflecting the soft glow of the flickering lights. Her gaze fixed on something that hadn't been there yesterday—a small red stocking stitched with golden thread, gleaming like ripples of sunlight across a lake at sunset.

Her name gleamed across the fabric, each letter curling like a star beam—**LUNIBELLE.**

She reached out with trembling fingers, tracing the golden letters as though they might float away if she wasn't careful. The stocking was real, the letters were real. But the feeling blossoming quietly inside her felt entirely new.

Jack tiptoed in, holding two steaming mugs of cocoa. "It's yours," he said.

"Can I get a gift—even though I don't belong here?"

The question slipped from her lips like a whispered wish—one she had asked many times in her heart. Yet in her eyes, galaxies still swirled, glowing with hope.

"Especially because you're not from here," Jack said softly. "You're visiting Earth, and Earth is trying its very best to love you back."

Lunibelle blinked very slowly. "I think... I loved it first."

"My mom made it," he whispered. "I asked for it. She didn't even ask why."

Lunibelle nodded and traced the gold letters again. "Your mom is... like a piece of sunshine."

Jack nodded.

They sipped cocoa. Hers sparkled with moonlight—somehow. Jack's tasted simply like home.

"Will Santa come?" she asked suddenly. "Even though I glowed too bright?"

Jack grinned. "Santa loves glow. He used to ride a comet, remember?"

Lunibelle mused. "Did he only ever come on Christmas?"

Jack wiggled his eyebrows. "Only on Thursdays."

She settled beside him. "If he comes, I mustn't peek, right?"

"You really, really mustn't," Jack agreed. "He'll vanish in a sneeze of glitter."

"Then I shall sleep in the fridge," she declared. "There's no peeking in there."

Jack nearly snorted cocoa. "It is a holiday! Lunibelle! You can't sleep in the fridge!"

"I already have done it," she said matter-of-factly. "It's cool, dark, quiet—like floating on an iceberg."

He stared. "That's not a real iceberg."

"I mean emotional iceberg," she clarified. "It's like sleeping on my

289

own planet."

The clock ticked. The lights twinkled. The cocoa steamed gently, as though exhaling contentment.

"Do you have stockings on your planet?" Jack asked curiously.

"We have star-pockets," she said. "They hang upside down from the sky."

"Do they get presents?"

"Sometimes meteor sprinkles—once, even a tiny black hole."

Jack blinked. "Wow! May I have one?"

Lunibelle laughed. "We'll trade. You can have a star-pocket. I'll keep the stocking."

They sat side by side, gazing at the mantel.

That night, snow whispered against the windows. The house breathed slowly, wrapped in its own hush.

The kittens lay curled on pillows. Parcel snored gently, her tail tucked over her nose. Willy stirred only once, chasing a bone in his dreams.

Lunibelle looked at Jack. "Thank you."

"For what?"

"For letting me feel like I belong in a world with stockings—even if I can only borrow one for a little while."

He smiled. "You always did."

"Good night, Jack."

"Good night, Lunibelle." Jack went to his room upstairs

"Good night, stocking." Lunibelle stood in the living room, her eye sparking.

"Good night, whole Earth," she whispered, as though sensing that her time here was running out.

In the frost-kissed quiet of the refrigerator, Lunibelle lay curled—a milky-white pearl nestled in the heart of a glistening ice shell, dreaming dreams spun of sugar, frost, and starlight.

Sleighs flew across constellations, their bells ringing with the music of winter winds. And oh! The Santa—wild-haired and bright-eyed—undoubtedly sits on a sleigh every Thursday, his cloak streaming behind him, his laughter scattering cosmic dust like powdered sugar across the Earth.

The cold around her hummed not with chill but with the magic of a thousand waiting holidays, wrapped in frost and glowing with warmth.

Lunibelle smiled in her dream.

Part VI: The Tiny Planet That Embraces Lunibelle

Christmas morning hatched in the sky—bright and friendly. The house was silent, still wearing its dreams. Light slipped through the windows.

In the living room, the Christmas tree sparkled quietly. The stockings puffed out their bellies in pride.

Lunibelle, barefoot, walked softly into the living room. She wore her favorite pink dress (Jack's mom made for her as Jack's birthday gift). She went to the fireplace and gazed at the stocking that bore her name.

It was full.

She reached in slowly, her heart pounding as though afraid the dream might collapse. Out came something small and glowing—a tennis-sized globe of Earth. It pulsed gently in her palm, as though it had its own heartbeat. The oceans twinkled. The continents gleamed.

Her breath caught. "It's alive," she whispered. "It's a whispering pebble of a home."

Nestled in the toe of the stocking was a pink envelope stamped with a star and sealed with a snowflake.

She opened it.

Dear Lunibelle,
Welcome to Earth.
Merry Christmas!
—Santa

Lunibelle stood quietly, her eyes filling with crystal tears—then spilling with joy.

Footsteps came thumping softly.

Jack appeared in the hallway, still wearing his reindeer pajamas, his bedhead shaped like a snowdrift. He smiled. "You found it."

Lunibelle nodded. "He came."

Jack sat beside her. "He always does."

"I didn't even peek," she said. "Not even a single eyeball."

Jack laughed. "Good. That's why it worked."

They looked down at the Earth in her hand.

"It's perfect," she whispered.

For a long while, they didn't speak. They sat still while snow spun slow spirals outside, ribboning the world in hush and in white.

Lunibelle held the Earth close to her heart. "On my planet," she said, "they told us Earthlings would be scared of us."

Jack tilted his head. "That's... not entirely wrong, but also not entirely true."

"They said, 'Hide. Never touch. Never blend in. Never ask for stockings.'"

Jack frowned. "Well, that's silly. You asked, and you got a gift. That's how Earth works. You show up, and eventually someone hands you a cookie."

Lunibelle smiled faintly. "They warned that Earthlings only like what looks like them."

Jack plucked at his pajama sleeve. "Do I look like you?"

Lunibelle giggled. "Not even a teaspoon."

"Exactly," Jack said. "But here we are."

She looked at him with something new in her eyes—something like sunrise.

"Where I'm from, family is defined by physical traits and shared features. But you've shown me that family can mean something different."

Jack looked thoughtful. "Family is the people who know you're a little bit strange, maybe even a little bit glitchy, and they look at you and think, 'Yep, I still want to sit here.'"

Lunibelle reached out and squeezed his hand. "You're my family now. I picked you. On purpose."

He grinned. "Even if I eat all the cinnamon rolls?"

"Especially then," she nodded.

They sat a little closer. The fire crackled as if it were politely leaning nearer, cupping its flame to hear better.

The kittens tumbled into the living room in a flurry of ribbons and meows. Meow1 had a bow on her tail. Meow2 was wrapped inside an empty gift bag. Meow4 chased a Tin Soldier as though it owed him a joke. Meow3 rolled her eyes and wrote a letter to Santa (even though it was too late to ask for a toy).

Yellowy danced across the curtain rod, singing a carol with the lyrics completely wrong but the tune perfectly right.

Willy sleep-barked, his tail wagging like it remembered the dream before he did.

Lunibelle looked around at the chaos—this joyful, ridiculous avalanche of warmth, belonging, and togetherness.

"It's funny," she said. "When I arrived, I thought Earth was a bit broken. Loud. Uneven. Confused."

Jack nodded. "It is—but it's also brilliant, and soft in places."

"Like your socks."

"Exactly."

They leaned back and watched the snow.

"Tomorrow," Lunibelle whispered, "should we go back to April?"

Jack smiled. "Yeah. But we'll bring Christmas with us. Even if it's invisible."

"Even if it's folded into my pocket?"

Jack nodded. "Especially then."

Lunibelle held the glowing Earth tightly.

"Maybe I'll show this to my parents—let them know Earth isn't so scary."

"Will they believe you?"

"Only if I let them taste your mom's potato pancakes."

Jack laughed, then grew quiet. "You'll go home someday, won't you?"

Lunibelle didn't answer right away.

"Yes," she said, her voice barely a whisper. "But I think a piece of me already lives here."

Jack nodded, eyes misty.

"I'll miss you when you leave."

"I'll miss me, too," she whispered and looked at her human clothes. "But you'll still have your stocking, your weird questions, and your warm house that smells of nutmeg."

And the snow kept falling, and Christmas stayed a little longer.

Two Little Creatures

One small Earth boy—woven from giggles and daydreams,

One silver girl—stitched from moonlight and whispered mysteries,

Sat side by side,

Knees almost touching,

Hearts quietly humming in time.

They share a now—a glimmering blink beneath the story-spilled stars,

where no one asks where they have come from,

only where the moment might go.

Chapter XII
Where Footprints Turn Into Stars

Part I: The Cobbles Where Memory Hums

Today felt just like yesterday—yet somehow, subtly, undeniably different.

"Shall we take a stroll by the seaside?" Lunibelle asked, her voice light and lacy. She smiled at Jack, who was perched comfortably on the living room sofa, his eyes half lost in thought—and half lost in her.

"Shall we bring Willy too?" he asked, already knowing full well the answer. Lunibelle nodded.

"Wait right here for me," she said, smiling.

Willy, the ever-faithful German Shepherd with ears sharp as radar, was always on alert. He bounded over to Jack's side with a soft bark, as if to say, "Something unexpected is afoot, my good sir."

Moments later, Lunibelle returned, wearing a snow-white dress that whispered around her knees.

"Wow!" Jack breathed. "That once two-inch-tall, chocolate-thieving, shy little ice girl has become someone I can hardly believe—mature, steady, gracious... she's changed so much."

"Shall we?" Lunibelle asked gently.

They walked along the street. The world blurred and bled around them, as if the sky had forgotten how to hold its colors still. People paused mid-step, mid-sentence, mid-thought. Someone on a bench, holding a newspaper, forgot both the bench and the news. A bird on a branch forgot its own song. Even the scent of fresh bread drifting from the bakery seemed to halt mid-air.

Willy marched ahead, tail high with cheerful purpose. Jack walked at Lunibelle's side.

"Do you remember the first time we walked to the seaside?" Jack asked, his voice laced with the memory of tides.

Lunibelle nodded slowly. Her eyes drifted over cobblestones, tree trunks, and lampposts—each humming with old, half-whispered memories.

Willy glanced back every few steps.

"Let's slow down a bit," Lunibelle said, her steps drifting into half-measures. Maybe she wanted to slow time itself. "I want to see everything clearly... It all feels like it happened just yesterday."

Back then, Jack remembered, they had to race against time. Every second was precious.

"You were only allowed outside for thirty minutes," Jack said with emotion.

"Yes, thirty minutes," Lunibelle repeated, her voice wrapped in a wistful sigh. "You always had to run just to make more time for me."

Jack chuckled. "Now you can stay as long as you like. No time limits. No hurrying."

"Yes... I was so curious back then. I knew nothing and wanted to know everything," Lunibelle mused, her eyes sparkling as she looked around at the familiar streets.

"Your questions fell like raindrops," Jack said warmly. "You soaked up the world so quickly, I wondered if your mind was made of sponge."

At the crosswalk, the traffic light blushed crimson—bashful as a tomato caught daydreaming at the market.

Willy, being a creature of rules and rituals, plopped down like a furry sentinel, awaiting the proper invitation to proceed. Jack and Lunibelle stood behind him.

Back then, the traffic lights were like strict judges, and red was their sternest verdict. Now, it looked kind and courteous—a polite little pause that seemed to say, *Take your time, dear traveler.*

Lunibelle tilted her head. "Has the light softened," she wondered aloud, "or have I been the one to change?"

Jack recalled the moment. "Remember when Willy ran across the street that first time? That poor policeman nearly swallowed his whistle."

Lunibelle giggled. "His eyes went wide as saucers, and his mouth was so round that he looked like he'd accidentally turned into the letter O."

They laughed together.

Lunibelle patted Willy and felt the world move gently around her, as it too was murmuring unforgettable pasts. Every street corner seemed to tell a memory. Every flowerpot on a windowsill gave a tiny bow, offering a silent farewell. The clouds dawdled overhead, reluctant to leave this moment behind. Even the wind was slowing down, its fingers feather-light, as if afraid to disturb the day's delicate hush.

"I used to think I had to do something to belong," Lunibelle said, her voice half a thought aloud. "Learn everything, be useful, be clever. But maybe... maybe just being here was enough."

Jack looked at her and nodded—not just with his head, but with something inside that had known her from the very beginning. He bumped her hand gently. "You always belonged," he said. "You brought magic into the ordinary, Lunibelle. That's something not everyone knows how to do."

She was quiet for a moment, then smiled.

And they kept walking.

"Look!" Lunibelle exclaimed, pointing ahead, her voice full of joy. "The sea!" She took a deep breath of its irreplaceable scent.

Just ahead, the scent of salt and sea was beginning to mingle with the afternoon. The gulls—that raucous choir of the coast—were just starting to warm up.

The end of the road was near—but only in the way stories have endings, while their meanings ripple on forever.

Part II: Two Journeys Weave Into Starlight

The sand gleamed with gold as they arrived at the edge of the sea. Willy, ever the enthusiastic beach explorer, leaped into action—bounding across the dunes. His paws kicked up clouds of sand that glittered in the sunlight.

Lunibelle gave a delighted gasp, then promptly slipped off her shoes and dangled them from her fingers. She stepped barefoot onto the soft sand, and the sensation sent a ticklish shiver from her toes straight into her smile.

"Oh!" she laughed. "It's like the sand is whispering to my feet!"

Each step was a giggle wrapped in sand, a tickle scrawled across the shore, a memory scribbled awake.

"I wish I could walk on the beach forever," she said playfully. "Do you think that's allowed?"

"Absolutely!" Jack declared. "The first time we came, you begged me to let you just touch the sand. Now you can wander as long as your heart desires!"

Willy dashed and danced with happy paws around Jack and Lunibelle, barking with all his might.

"He's so excited!" Lunibelle laughed, giving him a pat on the head.

Willy stared at her, then zoomed away, came back, barked, and zoomed off again.

"He wants us to follow him," Jack explained.

Lunibelle giggled and chased after Willy. Willy ran a little bit, then stood perfectly still, waiting for his friends.

When they got there, Willy sniffed the sandy ground, then lifted his nose to the sky.

"Something was here!" Jack knelt down and began digging.

"Mr. Conch!" Lunibelle cried, her eyes wide with delight. "Hello, Mr. Conch! How are you?"

Lunibelle remembered the first time she had held the conch, when it whispered about chasing time. Now she understood—time had been the chase all along.

"I'm fine, I'm fine," a whispery voice sang on the salty breeze. "Just came from the deep blue sea. Almost missed you!"

"What made you hurry so much?" Jack asked, gently wiping sand from the conch shell.

"Because a little fishy wanted me to tell you," Mr. Conch said happily. "She and her mother are safe, and they wanted to thank you!"

Lunibelle and Jack's eyes filled with happy tears. Willy wagged his tail so hard that sand flew into the air like celebrating fireworks.

"It was a very long trip," Mr. Conch puffed. "A two-hundred-million-year journey—and they said... oh, what did they say? I can't remember something from millions of years ago... They said... you're welcome to visit again!"

"Thank you, thank you, thank you!" Lunibelle whispered, touching the conch ever so gently.

"You will be home soon. Say hi to your parents," Mr. Conch's voice grew sleepy. "I need a rest now."

"I will pass on your greetings," Lunibelle murmured. "You're welcome to stay in our home."

The conch lay still, shining in the sunlight. Jack tucked it gently into a hollow in the sand, and Lunibelle carefully covered it, a tender secret for the sea.

They continued walking on the beach.

"How wonderful!" Lunibelle turned around and pointed to the trail behind them. "Look! Our footprints—what do they look like to you?"

Jack squinted at them. "Hmm... like long, wiggly lines."

"I think they're our story," she said dreamily. "Twisting, curving, going on and on... like the path of a feeling still searching for its ending."

Willy trotted around them in cheerful loops, circling as if a joyful, orbiting merry-go-round.

Then Lunibelle's eyes lit up with a sudden thought. "Let's walk together," she said. "Let's make our two sets of footprints into one. Wouldn't that be lovely?"

"Two into one?" Jack raised an eyebrow. "How would we do that?"

"Think about it," Lunibelle winked playfully.

"Oh, that's easy," Jack grinned. "I'll carry you on my back! Then it'll look like just one person walking. Climb on!"

"Really?" Lunibelle burst into laughter. "How far do you think you can carry me?"

"As far as you want to go!" Jack half-knelt and made preparations. "Truly! Why are you laughing?"

"Because," Lunibelle said, the corners of her mouth curving upward, "I have another way to do it. One where you don't have to carry me at all."

"No carrying? Then what—should I pull you in a sand-sled? Or maybe you'll ride on Willy's back?"

Lunibelle shook her head mysteriously. "Nope! I just need you to walk in front of me. Don't look back. Walk in a perfectly straight line. I'll tell you when to stop. Okay?"

"Sounds easy!" Jack said, rising to the challenge. "My mom taught me how to walk like a fashion model—heels and toes on the same invisible tightrope. Watch this." He stepped forward, shoulders bouncing dramatically as if he were strutting along the world's tiniest runway.

Lunibelle giggled. "You're taking this very seriously."

"I am!" Jack declared, concentrating. "Straight as a ruler!"

Jack kept walking...

"Stop!" Lunibelle called from behind. "No moving! No peeking!"

Jack froze like a statue in a game of Freeze Tag. He regretted not learning the art of eavesdropping from Willy, and so he listened carefully.

It seemed that Lunibelle was coming over... then there was no sound.

Jack closed his eyes and focused all his attention on his ears.

A soft shuffling behind him—sand whispering, perhaps something brushing the ground.

Is Lunibelle going to use her Doo? Jack didn't dare to move an inch. Will she wipe her footprints?

Willy, ever vigilant, stopped too and gave Jack a solemn stare.

"Don't move!" Jack whispered to Willy. "She's up to something."

Minutes stretched into years, and Jack wasn't sure what to do.

But then—TAP TAP!—Lunibelle gently patted his shoulder.

"You can look now!" she said, her voice full of gleeful triumph.

Jack turned, and his eyes widened.

Behind him, on the golden sand, lay a single file of footsteps—just one set, as if only one soul had walked there. Next to the last footprint, written carefully with a twig, were the words—*Thank you!*

Jack blinked. "You stepped in my footprints!"

Lunibelle nodded. "Perfectly," she said. "Step for step."

"The writing's beautiful!"

Hearing Jack's praise, the words on the beach rippled slightly.

"But... why thank me?" Jack was a little confused.

Lunibelle's face glowed, even brighter than the late afternoon sun.

"Because you were the first person I met here—the first voice that made me feel safe, the first smile that made me feel like home. You were my guide, my protector. You were hurt because of me, but you never turned away. You taught me the names of flowers, the shapes of clouds. You walked beside me, wherever I wanted to go. You told me to be patient. You asked your mother to make me clothes, so I could stay outside longer. You showed me how to wonder, how to listen. You taught me how to love—and how to be myself. When I fall, you're there. When I laugh, you share it. You've given me more than all the stars in the sky could hold."

Lunibelle's words spilled out, quick and clear, like scattered pearls—not because she wished to rush, but because if she paused, her voice might falter. It trembled, just slightly. It wasn't sorrow clutching her throat—only gratitude, pressed gently into her voice like a rainbow.

Jack looked at Lunibelle, who looked even more radiant in the sunlight.

"I followed your footprints," she added. "That's how I learned to walk here."

Jack swallowed hard—a knot of something, maybe emotion, maybe the salty fog curling between his words.

"But you gave me more," he said. "You made my world bigger,

brighter... stranger, in the best way. I should be thanking you."

For a moment, they simply looked at each other—the kind of look that knows a goodbye is peeking out from the next page, but doesn't want to turn it just yet.

"Let's sit on that big rock," Lunibelle said, pointing to a great stone that jutted from the sand.

Jack nodded.

And together, they walked toward it. Not quickly. Not slowly. Just... together.

Willy followed, of course. Tail wagging, as if to say, *This is how every story should walk.*

Part III: The Rock Who Prefers to Wait Rather Than Leave

They climbed up onto the great black rock where they had once sat before—when the world had felt a little newer, and the waves a little more mysterious.

The sea was still impossibly blue. The sky itself seemed endless—today, it felt even more expansive. Waves rolled in steady lines, growling gently as they crashed, then sighing as they retreated, as if the ocean murmured its deepest thoughts, laying them on the sand—truths too heavy to keep.

Overhead, gulls wheeled and called, their cries sharp and bright.

Lunibelle let the wind tousle her hair without trying to tame it. She simply stared out at the horizon, eyes distant, as though she were trying to see past the line where the sky met the sea—wondering, perhaps, what lay beyond that invisible edge.

Jack sat beside her, and for a moment, the memory of their first visit played in his mind. Everything looked exactly the same, yet... everything was different. But how? He couldn't quite put it into words.

So they sat, wordless, listening to the sea.

Until finally, Lunibelle broke the silence.

"I'm sorry," she said quietly.

Jack turned. "Sorry? For what?"

"For eating your chocolate buttons without asking."

Jack blinked, then laughed. "That tiny thing? It's not even worth mentioning. Honestly, I should have just put the whole jar in the fridge from the start."

"Really?" Lunibelle chuckled. "Well, then your dad would have said you exceeded your daily limit. What would you have told him?"

Jack grinned slyly. "I'd say... maybe a mouse snuck in and ate them."

"Would he believe that?"

"Well, my parents always believe me."

Jack extended a crust of bread toward Lunibelle. Her face lit up as she stretched her arms high, clutching the bread like a prized treasure. But before she could celebrate, a flash of white streaked down—a seagull snatched the bread right from her fingers.

Lunibelle's eyes blazed. "Hey! I know you!" she cried.

The bread vanished into the sky, seized quickly by the pirate-like seagulls.

"Goodbye!" Lunibelle waved to them.

She clapped her hands, then grew thoughtful. "Back then, I was so timid. If I'd been braver, I would've tugged your ear while you were sleeping and demanded chocolate."

Jack laughed. "Oh, Lunibelle, you were brave. Braver than I'll ever be. I mean, if I were dropped on some strange star, I'd just sit down and cry. But you? You explored, asked questions, made friends, and—don't forget—you went inside the octopus's stomach to save Yellowy!"

"I still remember the look on your face," he continued, his voice warm. "You didn't even hesitate. I was terrified, but you—you were ready to face anything. That octopus could have swallowed us all, but it respected your courage. And thanks to you, we even got four glowing pearls!"

Lunibelle looked out to sea again. "The ocean is so strange," she murmured. "It always feels like it's hiding more than it shows. I wish I could go back in one more time."

"We totally can!" Jack stood up. "Let's plan another sea adventure! Tomorrow? Next week? Anytime!"

Lunibelle didn't answer right away. Her silence lingered, stretched as thin as the horizon itself.

Part IV: The Dolphins' Mysterious Dance

Watching the seagulls fly away, Lunibelle raised her head, about to say something.

The distant *DONG... DONG... DONG* of the church bell drifted through the air; each note a silken thread tugging at the corners of old memories. It reminded them of a different ticking clock—the kind that counted moments, not minutes.

"Jack," Lunibelle said softly, "I have a question."

Jack turned to her, the look on his face saying, *ask whatever you want.*

"Before that day... had you ever ridden Willy?"

"Ride him?" Jack blinked. "Never even thought of it!"

Her legs swung gently. "Then what made you do that?"

Jack shrugged. "It wasn't really me. Willy knelt down."

"Weren't you afraid of falling?"

"In that moment?" Jack shook his head. "There was no room left for fear. I just climbed on and held tight."

Willy, sitting loyally beside them, swayed his tail in agreement.

"I truly was too reckless." Lunibelle's legs stilled. "I was only... and you ended up injured."

Jack rolled his eyes. "Lunibelle! Your life compared to my legs? That's no contest."

She turned to him, eyes bright. "Jack. Without you, I wouldn't even exist here. You... you gave me a place."

Jack swallowed, suddenly overwhelmed. He rubbed his eyes, pretending a stray splash of sea salt had blown into them.

"I'll blow it out for you!" Lunibelle rushed toward him.

"There's no more!" Jack instinctively dodged. "Oh, by the way, my grandma once told me a story about the Salt Girl of the Sea."

"The Salt Girl of the Sea," Lunibelle echoed softly. "How beautiful that sounds."

"She was made of longing and foam. Every time she cried, the tide rose," Jack began. "And people said she belonged to both the sea and the shore—never fully one or the other."

Lunibelle tilted her head, enchanted. But before he could say more, a pod of dolphins leaped from the ocean, arcing through the air in perfect harmony. They curved like commas, as if the sea itself wanted to keep their story's sentence alive. For a moment, it felt like their story might stretch on and on, curling across the waves without an ending. But every sentence, even the loveliest one, must find its full stop.

"Look!" Lunibelle stood and waved. "Dolphins!"

"Hello, dolphins!" Jack called out. "You're beautiful!"

"I think," Lunibelle whispered, half to the sea, "I've grown up."

Jack repeated the words quietly. "Yes. You've grown up."

"I understand things now," she said. "I think... that was the reason my parents sent me here."

Then she turned and looked Jack in the eyes. "But more than that—the most important thing—I met you. I became your friend. And for the first time, I learned what you Earth people mean when you say friendship."

Jack blinked quickly. "Being your friend has been the best thing in my life," he said. "Honestly, I feel like this is your home now—because you made it ours."

"I've felt that for a long time," Lunibelle nodded. "Ever since your mom made me that little dress. That was the moment. I knew then... this was my home, too."

"And I've told my parents," She added. "Earth is also my home now."

Jack's heart leaped. "Then stay! Please! You can live here! I'll even invite your parents to my next birthday party."

But Lunibelle looked away, her hair blowing gently across her face.

"Jack... my dad is coming to take me home."

Jack froze. The noise around him suddenly seemed to still.

"What?"

"I have to go back," Lunibelle said gently. "I promised."

"But... but this is your home, too," Jack whispered.

"I know," Lunibelle said. Her eyes shone—not from tears, but with something brighter. "But my dad said the time has come. It's all been decided."

Jack's words caught in his throat. His chest felt tight. A part of him wanted to beg, another to protest, and yet another knew he couldn't stop what was already set in motion.

"You... you're really leaving?"

Lunibelle pressed her lips together and didn't answer.

Out on the sea, a grand white cruise ship glided past, its bright flags fluttering from the rigging like a rainbow's farewell. The dolphins had shown joy's continuation; the ship showed parting's inevitability.

Jack summoned all his courage. "When?" he asked.

"Maybe... in a day or two," she said quietly.

Instead, they watched the ship.

The ocean once again displayed its profound depth and boundless expanse.

Part V: The Whisper That Changes Everything

On the afternoon of the second day after they returned from the seaside, the living room felt unusually full. Lunibelle sat surrounded by the entire crew: Jack, Willy, Yellowy, Parcel, and the four ever-wriggling kittens. The room was full of light and color, yet it held a hush.

"Thank you, everyone," Lunibelle said with a bright but slightly tremulous voice. "I've had such fun with you. We shared so many happy moments."

"No need to thank us!" piped Yellowy, ever the one to speak before anyone else. "There are still plenty of fun things to do! We haven't even started our *Make-a-Volcano-in-the-Bathroom* game!"

But Willy, ever the gentleman, took a step forward. He cleared his throat in that very particular way he did when he was about to say something important.

"I must interrupt," he said in a voice as proper as a waistcoat. "Lunibelle... is going home."

The room froze.

The world didn't merely grow quiet; it held its breath. The sunlight, once dancing on the windows, froze into a sheet of solid gold. The curtains, too, were motionless, as if caught mid-billow, and the wall clock's rhythmic ticking stretched into an agonizingly slow, single beat.

"Home?" asked Meow4, confused. "But isn't this Lunibelle's home?"

"I am think..." Meow3 said. "This is Lunibelle's home. We can prove it."

Meow2 blushed. He opened his mouth—out of shyness, or excitement—but no words came.

"Oh..." Willy said softly. "You see, when you first opened your eyes and saw Lunibelle here, it made sense to believe this has always been her home. But the truth is..." Willy paused to control his feelings. "She came from a very distant star, and now she must return to it."

"No! We won't let her leave. We need Lunibelle!" insisted Meow4, already climbing onto the back of the sofa.

Jack's chest clenched so tightly it hurt. He wanted to shout *No!* as loudly as Meow4—but the words tangled inside his throat, a knot of fear and longing.

"But we haven't even been to the underwater world yet! Please, Lunibelle, don't go!"

The kittens chorused their protest in a flurry of paws and pleas, their tiny tails trembling with emotion.

Parcel, whose own whiskers were twitching with the effort of staying composed, gently stepped forward. "Her parents must be missing her very much," she said kindly. "Just like you would miss me if I went somewhere."

"But Lunibelle is our family!" cried Meow4. He was the boldest kitten in the world, always ready to challenge anything —especially now.

"I am think..." Meow3 declared, determined to draw the correct conclusion from theory. "Because Lunibelle lives here now, she belongs here with us!"

Jack, who would normally calm everyone down, stayed frozen. He wasn't only silent—he was listening to his own heart break.

Part VI: The Gifts That Fill the World with Happiness

The news of Lunibelle leaving struck as though a boulder crashing into still water—shattering the silence and sending shockwaves through everyone's hearts.

Jack had never struggled so much just to speak. Yet he fought to regain his strength. At first, he failed. But slowly, a tiny ember of courage stirred within him—the knowledge that if he stayed quiet forever, he might lose her twice.

"But who will be our hockey scorekeeper?" Meow2 finally asked.

Willy, sensing Jack's silence, picked up the thread. His tail brushed thoughtfully back and forth. "We can still play under-the-table ice hockey," he said. "Lunibelle... she's the best scorekeeper we've ever had. I mean, without her there wouldn't even be an ice hockey league."

He sniffed. "Of course, without the puck, there could be no Lunibelle."

Everyone looked at each other, confused.

Willy immediately added, "Sorry, I mean, without Lunibelle, there is no puck. But Jack can also be the scorekeeper. He is very qualified. So... so yes, the game can continue..."

Meow2 looked at Meow3. "Our tails got tangled during the last game. I was afraid I'd turn into you!"

"I am think..." Meow3 said. "My mind refuses to let me become

Meow2."

"It was Lunibelle who untangled us," they both said together.

"But what if our tails get tangled again?"

Parcel pulled them both close and tapped their tiny heads. "I'll always know who is who," she said firmly. "And I promise—Meow2 will always be Meow2. Meow3 will always be Meow3."

"But what happens," Meow4 jumped up, "if all four of us tangle together—will we be a BIG MONSTER?"

Everyone laughed.

Even Jack laughed—a laugh that felt shaky at first but steadier with each breath, as though he was relearning how to hope.

Jack smiled again, his expression bright and serene—finally free from the whirlpool of emotions—and said, "I'll try to be a good scorekeeper like Lunibelle, so future games will be even more exciting!" He looked at the kittens. "Don't worry, if there are any more tangled tails, I'll find a way to fix it. A one-hundred-percent guarantee!"

"Hooray!" the kittens cheered.

Lunibelle smiled, trying to help. But her eyes flickered—just for a heartbeat—with something Jack had never seen before: hesitate. "I'm lucky to have two homes now," she said softly. "Sometimes I'll live here, and sometimes I'll live there."

"Mama, can I have two homes?" Meow1 asked.

"Well, anyone can have two homes," Willy said, now thinking more clearly. "You can make a new home when you grow up."

"But when are you coming back?" Meow4 looked at Lunibelle with hope. "How long will we have to wait?"

"Very soon," said Yellowy, finally steadying herself. "Yes—very, very soon. In the blink of a star's eye. Just like that."

It wasn't Yellowy's smoothest line, but the kittens, ever hopeful, took her at her word.

"I have something for each of you," Lunibelle said, beaming. She opened a box and began to give out her farewell gifts.

The kittens didn't cheer like they usually did. They simply stared at her wide-eyed, afraid that blinking might make her vanish—because everyone knew how quick magic Doo could be.

"Jack," she smiled, "thank you for taking care of me." She placed a snow-white diary in his hand, the cover gleaming with a faint frost. "This is my diary—covering everything from the moment I arrived on Earth until now." She looked at him, her eyes shy and meaningful. "Except the part where I turned into water and slept for a while. But everything else is here."

"This is the most precious gift I've ever received," Jack said, staring at the diary in his hand. "Whenever I read it, it'll feel like you're standing right in front of me," he said with a smile, "just like the first time you sat on the fridge watching me."

"So nice..." Meow4 murmured, wistfully. "If I had a diary..."

"You don't even know more than ten words," Parcel cut in.

Applause rippled through the room.

"This is for... Willy," Lunibelle said, turning to her brave four-legged friend. She handed him a painting—Jack riding on Willy's back, all four paws lifted midair, with a very startled policeman gaping in the background.

Willy's eyes grew moist. "Thank you," he said simply. "Thank you for every strange and wonderful place we visited. We'll miss you so very much."

Everyone clapped and cheered.

"Yellowy, my bird friend," she said, placing a whistle gently around her neck. "You're the best referee. This whistle will carry your voice farther than ever before."

"I've wanted one for ages!" Yellowy cried. "You read my mind! Maybe you'll even hear me blow it, from your star!"

The applause mixed with the kittens' shrill whistles.

"Parcel," Lunibelle said with a warm smile, "I noticed you squint when you thread a needle. Your old spectacles didn't work well." She opened a case. Inside sat a dazzling pair of golden spectacles.

Parcel stood suddenly, holding the golden spectacles aloft in awe. "They're perfect!" she cried. "You truly thought of everything!"

There was a beat. The kittens leaned in. Anticipation crackled in the air.

"Mommy, can I see?" Meow4—always bold, always quicker than permission—snatched the glasses from Parcel's paws.

A split-second pause.

"BWAH—WHY IS THE WORLD TILTING?!" Meow4 screeched. His legs flailed. He staggered left, spun right, then toppled spectacularly into a mountain of cushions with a magnificent *THOOMPH!*

The room froze for half a heartbeat—then erupted into howls of laughter.

Even Lunibelle bent double, laughter spilling out. But when she straightened, her eyes shimmered faintly, as though the laughter had hidden something else.

Part VII: The Crystal Snowball That Remembers Tomorrow

Lunibelle waited until the laughter died down a little.

"And for the loveliest kittens," she announced, "this mirror is for Meow1."

She drew out an oval mirror with a handle. "If your whiskers aren't straight, your fur is messy, or your clothes aren't neat, it will tell you."

"Thank you!" Meow1 couldn't wait to look at herself. The mirror frowned, saying "mmm... Your face is not clean."

Meow1 quickly washed her face with her paws.

The other kittens hurriedly cleaned their faces, too.

"Meow2, this is your gift." Lunibelle took out a brown basketball that flashed slightly. "I hope you become an excellent athlete!"

"Thank you!" Meow2, with a mischievous grin, grabbed the ball and hurled it toward the unsuspecting wall clock. The minute hand, in a frenzy, lunged to intercept, but the sprightly second hand leaped into its path like a defiant player. From the sidelines, a gleaming whistle pierced the air as Yellowy, proudly holding a brand-new whistle, cried out, "Fault!"

Everyone held their breath. "Excellent!" they screamed.

"For Meow3, this encyclopedia is yours." Lunibelle drew out a thick book wrapped in blue leather. "It will help you think more comprehensively."

"I am think..." Meow3 took the book respectfully. "It must contain the knowledge I mostly need. Thank you!"

Before Lunibelle announced the next gift, Meow4 was already standing in front. (He hated being ranked fourth most of all, and had already told Mommy he must be first to be born next time.)

Lunibelle took out a black ball the size of a walnut. "Meow4, every time before you speak, pinch this ball. The numbers from one to ten will appear in sequence. When it reaches ten, you start talking. It gives you time to think."

Meow4 squeezed the ball, waited patiently until ten flashed, then declared, "Excellent! Now I'm ready to speak in a scholar's way." He then added with a nod, "That's a most helpful invention, indeed. Thank you!"

"Jack," Lunibelle added gently, "I have two more gifts that I need you to deliver."

She opened a small wooden box, carved with swirling stars. Inside, nestled in satin, were needles that glowed with silvery light. "These are for your mom. Please thank her for the lovely clothes she made me."

Then she held up a round, ticking treasure—a silver pocket watch with a lid that clicked shut. "And this is for your dad. It keeps perfect time. Every second. Always."

Jack took both gifts. "My mother will use these needles to make more beautiful clothes," he said excitedly. "This watch is perfect for my father's scientific mind!"

That night, moonlight drifted into the living room like falling feathers. It touched everything gently—so gently it seemed afraid to interrupt.

The living room was quiet. Jack and Lunibelle sat side by side on the sofa.

"The moon is so bright," Lunibelle murmured, gazing out the window. "Just like the night I arrived."

"So many days..." Jack's voice was a bare whisper.

"So many days," Lunibelle echoed softly.

"In the blink of an eye," Jack said.

Willy sat silently beside Lunibelle. She reached down and stroked his fur, slow and thoughtful.

Lunibelle looked at Jack.

And in that glance—just a glance—was everything. All the words that didn't need to be spoken.

"Do you remember this?" Jack held out a crystal ball, its surface flashing.

"Of course," Lunibelle nodded, her voice warm with nostalgia. "The North Pole bear, Nick, gave this to you."

Jack passed the crystal ball to her. Cradling it carefully in her hands, she brought it close, her eyes sparkling. "This is the very first snowflake Nick ever caught at the North Pole. Look how breathtaking it is!"

"You once said," Jack smiled softly, gazing at her, "that you wished you could take a snowflake home. So... I'm giving it to you."

It was the first time Jack had given her a gift—not just any gift, but one born of his own courage, his own heart.

"Oh! This is wonderful!" Lunibelle pressed a delighted kiss to the crystal, her joy radiant. "It's the most beautiful gift ever! I'll show it to Mom and Dad! Thank you!"

"Please tell them," Jack added warmly, "that Earth is a beautiful place—and they're always welcome here."

"You're so kind!" Lunibelle's cheeks flushed with happiness. "All of you..."

Then Jack found the courage.

"Will you come back?"

Lunibelle's eyes shone brighter than ever, deep and dark and sparkling with the same light she brought from the stars. A soft blue glow blossomed from her skin—the quiet luminescence of emotions too deep for words.

She gave Jack a big hug.

And the moon—soft and silver—slipped behind a cloud, lingering as if it, too, waited for her answer.

Epilogue

The Promise That Stayed Awake

After Lunibelle departed, Jack and Willy often walked to the shore.Willy, ever faithful, ran straight to the very spot where Mr. Conch had first been found.Jack knelt and dug with his hands, but the sand remained empty.The great sea sighed and poured its foam into the hollow once more.

Several under-table hockey games were held. Yellowy blew the whistle Lunibelle had given her with great ceremony, and the players' skills improved rapidly. Jack became an excellent scorekeeper. The tails of Meow3 and Meow4 no longer tangled, and no one swallowed the puck anymore.

One day, Meow4 picked up the little ball Lunibelle had given him and gave it a pinch.The ball began to flash: 1, 2, 3…When it reached 10, he shouted, "I miss Lunibelle!"

Meow1 did not argue, as he usually did. He only nodded. "I miss her too."

"Mummy," Meow2 asked, "when will Lunibelle come back?"
Parcel removed Lunibelle's gift-glasses and said gently, "She will

come back."

"You *always* say 'she will come back,'" Meow4 protested, springing onto the sofa's back. "But when?"

"I am think..." murmured Meow3, staring at the wall clock. "She should be on her way."

"Too far," Willy said. "It'll take a lot of time."

"Yes, yes," Yellowy chirped, fluffing her feathers.

When Jack's birthday dawned, the house glittered with laughter .Yet Jack's gaze kept returning to the door.

"Do you suppose Lunibelle will come?" his mother asked quietly.

Jack's father consulted the little watch Lunibelle had given him. "She might," Jack whispered.

"Last time she said, '*I just knew I had to come,*'" his mother murmured.

But that night, Lunibelle did not come.The small chair by the window waited in gentle silence.

Jack lay in bed with Willy curled beside him. He said nothing, only shifted to make room.Sleep gathered him in.

"Jack! Happy birthday!"

He opened his eyes *within the dream.*

"Lunibelle! Why didn't you come?"

"I shall come," she said.

"When shall that be?"

"C—"

Willy nudged him awake.Morning light, pale and tender, filled the room.

"Lunibelle," Jack whispered.

No one answered.

He looked toward the ceiling.

Something shimmered there — soft, silver — and vanished like a sigh. Jack gave a quiet smile.

The promise, he knew, had stayed awake.

Jack's Super-Top-Secret Whisper!

(Psst... ready to hold your breath and wiggle your toes?)

Guess what—oh, guess what?! Jack just leaned close and breathed the twinkliest, most tingle-your-ears secret he has **ever whispered**. He said:

You can write a magical, rainbow-bright invitation to Lunibelle—the cloud-hopping, star-catching wonder girl herself!

Yes, yes, yes! You can call out: "Lunibelle, come quick! Let's be best-forever friends!"

Tell her your giggles, your worries, your sniffly-sniffle moments. She keeps all of them safe inside her sparkly heart.

And you can whisper a giant wish, like this:

"I want to visit you SO MUCH! Let's dive into the deep-down ocean to tickle a tiny, sleepy fossil fish... or zoom to the moon in a fizzy, glitter-popping rocket! And, um... if you happen to throw my headache-y math homework out the window— like you did for Jack—well... I won't complain!"

Jack says you absolutely MUST ask Lunibelle to use her Wish-Whirl Magic-Doo and whisk you away to the World Without Any Boring Numbers! It's the wildest, silliest, upside-down place on Earth... (and maybe Mars).

But wait—hug your teddy tight and listen very, very carefully. Jack also whispered a super-crucial mission:

Tell Lunibelle your secret home address— and most important of all— tell her exactly where your big, cold, yummy-food box (the refrigerator!) is hiding.

It is a Top-Priority, Tummy-Rumble Operation.

Hugs and happy thoughts— and may you meet your shining, starlight Lunibelle very, very soon.

Glossary of Curious Things and Emarkable Beings

Alphabetical Edition

The Ball That Counts to Ten

A small shimmering sphere given by Lunibelle to Meow4. It flash- es numbers whenever pinched, though no one is certain what hap- pens after ten — the ball refuses to say.

The Bubblecraft

Assembled by a snake, a porcupine quill, two big dragonfly eyes, and thirty pairs of hummingbird wings. It flies faster than light and carries Jack and his friends back to Earth.

Mr. Camelet

A camel whose scattered bones, parted for hundreds of years, are finally gathered and reassembled by Jack and his friends. Once restored, he carries them into the Mirage.

The Corn That Sang

Melodic corns who prefer singing in the field with a scarecrow whose head sways along with the rhythm. Their best-known song is *WHISH-A-WHOOSH*.

The Crystal Snowball

A gift Jave gives to Lunibelle; it contains the first snowflake in the North Pole. Lunibelle will bring it home and show her parents.

Eagle Postman

A proud sky-courier bearing the insignia of the Interdimensional Postal Service. He carries the great envelope that delivers Jack and his friends to their first stop: the Island That Swims.

The Floating Swimming Pool

The Floating Swimming Pool. Lunibelle's birthday gift to Jack, it slowly descended from the sky into the backyard. Later, Jack asked Lunibelle to return it to its owner

Fossil Fish

A tiny, ancient creature more than two hundred million years old. She forever misses her mother and the deep ocean, Lunibelle and Jack finally guide her home.

Footprints That Turn into Stars

Rare traces left by travelers from Lunibelle's world. The first step is ordinary; the next begins to sparkle; the third no longer belongs to Earth.

The Gift-Glasses

These are the glasses that Lunabelle gave to Parsel. Wearing these glasses allows her to see more clearly, making it easier to mend clothes for those mischievous little kittens.

Hoofy Brothers

Three builders who keep constructing houses that fall thirty times because they use no math. Jack and his friends help them at last raise a home that stands.

Jack

A twelve-year-old who does everything he can to make Lunibelle happier. He tries to answer every question she asks and helps her feel at home on Earth. Together they walk the thin silver line between the ordinary world and the one that begins to shimmer.

Jack Riding Willy

A heroic moment when Jack leaps onto Willy's back and gallops through wind, streets, and **flies** to save Lunibelle. Willy considers it one of his finest achievements.

Jack's Father

He is a strict science teacher who gives Jack a math problem each day. The father never understands why the small fish on the fossil disappeared.

Jack's Grandmother

She lives on the edge of the forest and often takes Jack mushroom hunting; her heart brims with love and wisdom. She once enters the world of bubbles.

Jack's Mother

She is a loving mother and a fashion designer who stitches color into the world. She made Lunibelle's first beautiful clothes, and while wearing them, Lunibelle can stay outside the fridge as long as she needs to.

Lunibelle

A tiny, silver-shimmering alien with curiosity crackling beneath her odd, wonderful surface. She leads Jack and his friends through imagical, dream-spun worlds. In the warmth of their friendship, she discovers that the people of Earth possess hearts as vast and kind as the cosmos. Now she knows this bright blue planet is her forever home, too.

Lunibelle's First Christmas Gift

A small shining globe and a greeting card from Santa. Lunibelle is astonished — and touched all the way to her shimmer.

Lunibelle's Shimmer

A brief silver glint that appears when Lunibelle thinks of someone far away. It stays only a moment — just long enough to be believed.

Meow1

Parcel's most formal kitten. She sits straight, speaks precisely, and corrects others with respectful firmness. Her whiskers never bend unless she is very, very surprised.

Meow2

A shy, athletic kitten who tries to hide behind anything smaller than himself. He runs faster than his courage usually allows, often surprising everyone — including himself.

Meow3

A thoughtful philosopher in a soft fur coat. Every idea begins with "I am think..." and often ends in delightful confusion for everyone except herself.

Meow4

The boldest kitten in the world — the first to leap, speak, tumble, nibble, or accidentally knock something over. His confidence shines brighter than his caution. Hating to be listed fourth, he asks his mother to birth him first next time.

Mr. Conch

an ancient seaside storyteller, first gives Lunibelle courage, and later he travels two hundred million years to meet the little Fossil Fish and delivers the Fossil Fish's warm message of thanks to Lunibelle.

Mr. Grandpa Current

An N+1-year-old sea turtle who travels on the current. Brilliant yet forgetful, he carries Lunibelle and her friends to the place where a volcano once erupted.

Mr. Old Bear

A sleepy forest sage who wakes only for honey. He cannot answer where two identical snowflakes are, but he does tell Jack where his brother, North Pole Nick, lives.

Mr. Spittleton

A spittlebug living in a bubble world beyond Earth. He believes every bubble holds wisdom and that bubble baths make one smarter. He builds a *Bubblecraft* to send Jack, Lunibelle, and their friends back to Earth.

North Pole Bear Nick

The younger brother of Mr. Old Bear — a North Pole Bear who gathers the first snowflake of the North Pole and builds the Snowflake Museum. He later helps Lunibelle and Jack uncover the truth about the two identical snowflakes.

Octopus

A shimmering, eight-armed marvel who believes himself to embody a law of nature — that every creature he eats has volunteered. Lunibelle bravely enters his belly and rescues Yellowy. Later, the Octopus becomes her friend.

Parcel

A patient mother cat with fur soft as twilight. She raises four extraordinary kittens, manages chaos with elegance, and believes politely in miracles.

Qoofy Brothers

Three corn farmers whose harvest is stolen by the Old Gray Wolf. Because they keep no records, the court first declares the wolf innocent. With Lunibelle's help, they create evidence at last, and the wolf is found guilty.

The "Please Stop" Sign

A curious gateway into the bubble world. Jack and his friends pass through it and discover they cannot return. After many magical trials, Jack gathers the four essential parts needed to build the *Bubblecraft* and fly back to Earth.

Symphony of Silence

Heard only with the ear of the heart and felt through the body, this Aqueous Aria travels as deep, powerful vibrations through seawater. Its performance lifts the spirit to a silent, sublime climax — a wordless understanding of the deep blue world.

Two Identical Snowflakes

A mystery Jack and Lunibelle explore across forests, mountains, museums, and libraries. Whether such twins exist, or merely pretend not to be found, remains politely unanswered.

The Wobbly House of Hoofys

The home built by the Hoofy Brothers — it falls thirty times, but who finally helps it stand?

Whale Postman

A deep-sea courier who opens his mouth to swallow letters. Upon reaching their destination, he ejects them through his blowhole.

Willy

Jack's loyal German Shepherd, courageous enough to chase time and tender enough to guard sleeping kittens. His bark is bold, his heart, boundless. He also becomes Lunibelle's close friend.

Yellowy

A bright canary whose singing is a little off-key yet full of confidence. She referees chaos with cheerful chirping authority.